A winter storm blows through Salem, Massachusetts, setting young witch Alexander MacBeth on a perilous path to adulthood as his dying mother gifts him an heirloom and pleads for him to use it to survive.

To do so, he will need to perfect his inherited witchcraft to protect himself from those who want him dead. In his journey to adulthood, he falls in love with dashing nobleman Crispin Nottingham. Abandoned by Crispin and pursued by the Puritans, he finds he must harness the wind to assist his escape and flee his homeland aboard a pirate ship led by the handsome captain, Henri the Twisted.

Struggling against distrustful pirates, an evil witch, and his continued longing for Crispin, Alexander sharpens his magical skills and falls into a romance with Henri. Chaos and danger confront him at every turn, even as he searches for love and belonging. A new sail on the horizon may signal hope or more danger than ever before—if Alexander can survive to meet his future.

WITCH IN THE

WIND

Damian Serbu

A NineStar Press Publication

www.ninestarpress.com

Witch in the Wind

First Edition, June 2024

ISBN: 978-1-64890-769-2

Also available in eBook, ISBN: 978-1-64890-768-5

CONTENT WARNING:

This book contains sexually explicit content, which may only be suitable for mature readers. Depictions of murder, graphic violence, and suicide.

To Bill Oliver: mentor, editor, cherished friend. Always fancy the sea!

I: Youthful Revelations

Chapter One

Survival

December 1692

Salem, Massachusetts

ALEXANDER HID IN the loft of the old barn despite the bitter cold blowing between the boards and swirling around him. He had traipsed through the snow from the nearby house to his secret hiding place in the hay to spend a few moments alone.

His body was undergoing major changes. Other boys went through transformations at this age too. Alexander learned as much from the gossip and stories he heard of expanding muscles, hair growing in new places, and voices deepening. Except those alterations hardly worried him.

He jumped when the violent wind slammed a door shut beneath him. He reached over and grabbed the small doll his mother had made him long ago, which he played with until his father announced him too old for such things. After that, he'd hid his toy up here.

No, nothing going on physically alarmed him, not even his emerging sexual excitement. The pastor's warning against sinful thoughts seemed out of touch. Though he'd never say it aloud, Alexander thought that a bunch of rot.

He came to his hideaway today because of the memory of his mother's lesson from last summer when he'd turned thirteen. Alexander curled up in a blanket, clutching his doll, warding off the freezing temperature as the blizzard covered the landscape outside the barn.

One hot summer evening after dusk, his mom had taken him out to a darkened field and spoken in a whisper.

"Your body is changing," she had said. He blushed at the memory, embarrassed that his mother noticed such things in him. "But that's not all. Listen closely, Alexander. It's a dangerous time. Not everyone understands your family. They'll come for us if we're not careful. There's a legacy in you that will blossom in the next year or so. I'll teach you about it. You must promise to keep it a secret. Come only to me as the changes stir and when you have questions."

He had nodded and said nothing else, too humiliated by the thought of talking to his mother about his body's transition.

Since then, he had asked a number of times about this mysterious new power in him, only for her to admonish that he was not ready to learn more. If his father ever overheard, he scowled and told them to keep quiet.

There came an alarm, as if a wisp on the tail of a storm, blowing a chill into his very brain. He reached for his mother's crystal, one she allowed him to examine from time to time if he promised to keep it hidden and never speak of its magic. The glass orb fit in the palm of his hand, smooth and clear. Peering into the crystal, he saw a vision of men: the pastor, the sheriff, and others, riding their horses hard through the storm and coming toward the farm. In the last month, images of the present had flashed into the crystal, a power he understood to come along with the other alterations to his being. No doubt his mother referenced these forces during that warm night in the field on his thirteenth birthday.

Minutes later, Alexander heard horse hooves pounding outside, and a horse whinnied as the posse came to a halt. The fact they ventured out on such a horrid night caused Alexander's heart to race.

Alexander peeked out a crack in the barn to see the men gather together after tying their horses to a post. The family's old dog bellowed a warning as the men approached the house.

"Goody Macbeth? Come out."

Instead of his mother, his father came to the door and held his musket.

Alexander shivered at the cold and then ducked under a pile of hay when he heard someone climbing up the ladder toward him.

"Alexander?" his mother whispered. "Show yourself. I know you're up here. We haven't much time."

Alexander sensed the urgency in her voice, so different from the gentle way she always spoke to him, even after a transgression. He saw her crawling toward him.

"Hush yourself and listen, child." She took him in her arms as if again a babe. He thought better of resisting, despite the adult in him protesting this infantile turn of events. "You remember what I told you about the changes you'll experience? I wanted to teach you about them at the appropriate time. I wanted to do it as my mother did for me. But they're going to take me away."

"I won't let them." Alexander reached for his own musket, but his mother held him tightly.

"Listen to me. You can't do anything."

Alexander frowned at the thought of cowardice. Except, he loved his mother too much to disobey. He relaxed again in her arms.

"Good. That's a good boy. If you lash out, they'll get you too. I need you to survive." She leaned over and glanced out the crack in the barn for herself. He glanced over her shoulder and saw his father in a heated discussion with the men.

Only when his mother pulled him back into the hay did he notice the tear trickling down her cheek.

"These are evil times in which we live, son. Not the evil they'll speak of, with Satan coming into their midst. No." She shook her head. "It's the innocent they kill. The complete misunderstanding of the power. This is what you must learn, and I've but a few minutes to teach you. You have power in your blood. To see the present, no matter where it may take place. To heal. To control the wind. Alexander, believe me, it's not from a demon. It's from your grandmother, and your great grandfather before her. Use it to protect yourself. Use it for good, no matter what you may hear otherwise."

"Where is your wife?" They both jumped at the sheriff's screaming voice.

"Are you a witch?" Alexander whispered to his mother. "Am I a witch?"

"Give me your hand." Alexander held his hand out to his mother, who took it and then pressed their index fingers together. A warmth cut through the biting cold that had taken hold of every other part of his body and then seemed to course through his veins. He felt dizzy for a moment, but then a new powerful control overcame him.

His mother spoke the truth of his ability. He could sense a capacity to stop the wind, then start it again; to see from a distance what people did at the moment in a different town, as when he'd spotted the men riding toward his home through the storm; to heal the scratch on his arm from when he scraped it on a nail on his way up to the loft.

"Do you understand now?" his mother asked.

Alexander nodded, though he only half understood. He learned of his power from her touch. He realized she thought it a force for good, and thus so did he. But she never answered about being a witch.

"'Tis not evil, son. No devil is involved. Survive."

She pressed her forehead to his and held the small crystal between them. In the glass, Alexander saw a vision materialize before them. Of their father, just below them in the yard. The dog barked again. They saw the other men approach him, demanding Goody MacBeth's imprisonment.

Then his father clutched at his arm, his eyes wide open as he slumped to his knees and fell into the snow at the feet of these intruders. Despite their earlier antagonism, they rushed to him. Only then did Alexander realize the doctor was among them. He bent over his father, then looked up to the other men and shook his head.

Alexander's mother pulled out of their embrace, tears streaming down her face. She grabbed the musket and headed for the ladder. Alexander moved to follow but she turned and stared deeply into his eyes. "No. *Survive*. Sneak to the house and go to bed. Don't let them know what you can do. Do you understand me? Survive."

He nodded slightly and watched her descend. Alexander followed closely behind, going to the opposite end of the barn. He instinctively patted their horse on the head and then went out the door. He knew without looking his mother watched him leave.

He ran quickly around the barn and snuck into the house, hidden the entire time by the thick and swirling snow, hoping the bitter wind carried away any sound he made or swept away his footprints.

Alexander crept to the window and opened the shutter, disobeying his mother's order to go to his bed. He could barely see the barn but the men stood close by. Again, they shouted for Goody MacBeth to come out, seemingly oblivious to his father now lying dead at their feet of their own doing.

What happened next came so quickly Alexander had no time to react, no doubt as his mother intended. The barn door swung open, and she fired the musket. It missed the men, hitting high into a tree above them. His mother was the best shot in the family. She had meant to miss.

Yet these men in their black clothing and moral purity rushed at her. Alexander felt the change in the air as she called forth the elements to come to her defense. No, not to defend herself, but to reveal her power and send them into a complete frenzy of fear and panic.

They set upon her, the brute cowards choking the life out of her. Alexander never moved from his post. Every part of his being despised these men. He wanted to attack them. He wished to kill them. He even sent forth some of this new ability and crashed a branch down at their feet.

His mother's words, though, stopped him. *Survive.* She had wanted him to survive, even as she planned her own death to protect him. Though it went against every instinct in his body, Alexander left the window and crawled into his bed and feigned sleep. He had no time for mourning if he was to obey his mother's wish.

A few moments later, the sheriff roused him. He spoke softly but with command. "Come. I'm taking you to your uncle."

"Where are my parents?" Alexander asked this question without so much as a quiver in his voice. He knew the answer but wanted the fiend to admit it.

"No time for that. Your uncle will explain."

Alexander attempted a few more questions of the sheriff and other men once outside, but they ignored him as they mounted their horses and propped him up behind the pastor. They soon headed through the blizzard at the same brisk pace with which they arrived, this time with Alexander as their prisoner.

As he reluctantly held tightly to the pastor, Alexander squeezed his eyes shut and saw the barn from above. His father's body lay already half buried in the snow, his mother's partially in the barn, the fabric of her dress fluttering in the wind. Otherwise, nothing moved. They not only killed his parents but left them unceremoniously to freeze under the heavy snow. How he despised these self-righteous men.

A rush of wind so powerful it almost knocked the pastor and him off the horse frightened Alexander, until he realized his own anger had called forth the energy. He calmed himself, again reminded that lashing out with his power would only expose him to danger.

Yet he hated even more the man who stood sneering in front of him when the pastor and sheriff rapped at the gristmill door. The other men had taken leave to go to their families. The scarred face, the husky arms and large stomach sent Alexander's stomach into knots. He smelled too.

"What's he doing here?" Uncle Bartholomew spat at them.

"He's your charge now." The pastor clutched nervously at his hat when the wind threatened to take it away. "His folks died."

Bartholomew frowned; then his eyes lit with recognition. "You proved she's a witch."

The sheriff shook his head. "Not definitively. She attacked us and died in the struggle. His father died before. His heart gave out." He pointed to Alexander. "He's yours."

The sheriff stalked off and told the pastor to get home, too, before he got buried in the wilderness. But the pastor lingered behind until the sheriff left. The three remained outside in the icy cold.

"You were right, of course. Goody MacBeth had the devil in her. Pay no attention to the sheriff. He deals with absolutes and the law. I deal with God. She called forth the elements just as you warned. Tis better for everyone she died."

"I knew before all you had the courage to examine her. What about the boy?" Bartholomew twitched his head toward Alexander.

"No. I feel no sign of the devil in him."

Bartholomew nodded and then escorted the pastor back to his horse. When he rode out of sight, his uncle shoved Alexander as hard as he could into the mill. Uncle Bartholomew lived and slept in a loft above. Alexander had visited but a few times with his mother, both of them always disgusted at the state of the place.

Alexander stumbled over the threshold but righted himself, standing rigidly as his uncle stared down at him. Bartholomew spit at his feet.

"I don't need a ward. Especially the son of a witch. Mind you, I've no choice. So you're an apprentice from this time on. Really more my slave. You got a problem with our arrangement?"

Alexander stared daggers at him. This man fought with his mother and father at every turn, demanding title to their land and accusing his sister of witchcraft. "I'm no one's apprentice."

Alexander stayed on his feet even after the violent backhand across his face. He tasted the blood in his mouth. Bartholomew pointed to a drafty corner in the side of the mill, where a blanket lay thrown aside. "Go sleep in the mouse shit over there. We'll start in the morning."

Chapter Two

Crispin

February 1693

Salem, Massachusetts

ALEXANDER CLEANED OUT the millstone for what seemed like the millionth time. The last two and a half months of living with his uncle felt like a lifetime already. Bartholomew had no idea how to run a mill. Alexander had heard his father say this to his mother all the time, to which she usually had giggled and nodded agreement but refused to disparage her brother. Yet Alexander's two months with this man proved his father's point. First of all, whoever heard of trying to operate a mill in the middle of the winter with a frozen creek and thus no running water to power the thing?

Alexander rolled his eyes. "This won't work. The stream's frozen."

"We've got wheat." Bartholomew slapped him upside the head. "You opposed to making a profit?"

Over and over they damaged the stone and thus had to repair a part of the operation. Alexander contributed to the problem when his uncle's shouting and anger got too intense. He learned to call forth the wind to damage the building, thus deflecting Bartholomew's ire from his nephew to the structure.

In fact, Alexander determined from the first to resist his uncle. He despised the man, as had his father. He was violent and hit Alexander regularly. Alexander never returned the favor, lest his uncle fly into a rage and beat him to death. That would defile his mother's last wish for survival. He knew instinctively to keep his magic hidden.

But neither did Alexander become a meek little mouse at the behest of a cat's torture. He ran from his uncle, did only as much around the mill as he thought necessary, and silently plotted for his escape when old enough. He contemplated an eventual return to his family's farm until his uncle vowed they would sell the farm in the spring for a handsome profit.

In some ways, they slipped into a routine of living together despite the hatred, of working together despite his uncle's ferocity, of mistrusting each other even as circumstances gave them no choice but to coexist.

Alexander particularly hated how his uncle trotted him off to church as he did this morning. His parents defied community pressure and never attended because they thought the lessons too harsh. His mother and father had Christian beliefs and they read the Bible as a family, but taking part in the Puritan rituals went against their philosophy, despite putting them at great risk. Only now did Alexander understand how much risk.

Bartholomew roused him early and threw him into the freezing ice water he stored in the corner. Alexander cleaned himself quickly, despite the cold, and then hurried to dress.

"Get going, boy." Bartholomew shoved him out the door, then tied a rope around his neck as he hopped on his horse and headed toward town and the brutally boring sermon and service. Alexander braced himself to sit in the church on a hard bench until sundown.

Alexander's face turned bright red as they rounded the corner and the other parishioners came into view and saw Bartholomew lead him like a dog.

The pastor greeted them at the door. He poked at Alexander's black eye when they stood in front of him. "Still disobedient, is he?"

"Too much of his mother in him."

They even spoke to each other as if standing in front of a dog, not a human who understood every word.

The pastor raised an eyebrow and glanced quickly at Alexander.

Uncle Bartholomew shook his head. "I don't think he knows. Or has it in him."

But Alexander did have *it* in him. He used visions of the present from the crystal to steer clear of Bartholomew's worst fits of temper. He controlled the wind to protect himself and slow down the impossible rate of work. He could heal himself after a brutal attack, but leave a bruise or two to satisfy his uncle.

They returned after a day of church and went to sleep, only for Bartholomew to kick him in the stomach early the next morning. "Clean this pigsty. Ever since you came to live with me, it reeks of rot and devil's piss."

Alexander jumped away from the second kick. "Your place smelled this way before I got here."

"I should beat you to a pulp. The Lord commands you to obey your parents. That's me now. I need you to work and get this place ready. We got an aristocrat coming to visit on some fool mission from Boston to check on us out here. He claims his coming here involves you. But his ma may invest in this here mill. You better not screw up the opportunity."

They worked silently at straightening up the place for a long time until Alexander, heavy with fatigue and worry about this new person coming to monitor him, stumbled and dumped a bucket of clean water over the floor. Alexander fell to the ground.

Bartholomew charged across the room and reared back to hit him in the face with a fist, when a voice coughed and a loud knock sounded at the open door. The man had already stepped into the premises, so Bartholomew lurched to a stop and became a perfectly humble gentleman.

"Why, you must be Crispin. I mean Lord Nottingham." Bartholomew fumbled with his coat and tried to straighten himself, obviously embarrassed. "I expected—" The words drifted away.

"Someone older, no doubt. Unfortunately, my father died and left the family's affairs in my young hands. Though I have full authority, some mistake my youth for irrelevance or ignorance." The young man strode across the room and bowed. Alexander had never seen such refined clothing before—the silken vestments, the tailored coat, and golden topped walking stick. "Crispin Nottingham, at your service. I trust you remembered our appointment?"

Bartholomew nodded vigorously, cowed like never before. Alexander remained on the floor, too mesmerized by this gentleman in his midst. He stood very tall, even taller than his burly uncle, but with a sharper musculature, steely blue eyes, and dark brown hair that curled around his face.

"Of course, I remembered." Bartholomew returned the bow. "You came about the investment."

Crispin frowned. "Indeed. Or should I say 'perhaps'? As you'll recall, I also came at the behest of the Royal Governor to look after your ward of the state."

"He's hardly just a ward. Why, he's my own blood."

Crispin arched a brow. "Despite what your report suggested when you refused legal custody? You were afraid of witchcraft. His Excellency takes such accusations quite seriously. Especially given the affairs here in Salem over the last few years. Thus, my requested involvement with the young man."

Crispin walked over to Alexander and reached down to help him to his feet. Alexander flushed at the touch of their hands.

"At any rate—" Crispin turned once again to Bartholomew. " — I've been advised to speak with him alone to assess the situation. If you don't mind, where could we speak privately?"

"The coop out back, I suppose. He's to clean out the eggs today, anyhow."

Without another word, Crispin, his posture erect, marched back to the door and spun around. He motioned for Alexander to follow him. Alexander glanced at his uncle for instruction, but he only glared at him and jerked his head for Alexander to go.

Alexander tugged at his jacket as they crossed the frozen yard. His uncle made it sound like a normal chicken coop, though he barely managed to keep two hens alive. Alexander lamented the animals that had been left behind on his father's farm, no doubt all dead by this point. Bartholomew refused to allow him to return for even a brief visit, though Bartholomew himself had pillaged whatever he wanted from the homestead, including the horses.

Crispin closed the door behind him, glanced around the horrendously kept coop, and coughed slightly. Alexander felt emotions he seldom grappled with in the presence of another person when he stood alone with Crispin, away from his uncle's prying eyes. As in his daydreams and night visions, his loins stirred, and he experienced an intense attraction like never before.

Crispin smiled confidently down at him. Then he frowned. "He beats you, yes?"

"A bit. As much as I allow."

This made Crispin chuckle. "Meaning?"

"Meaning if I stopped it altogether, he'd be worse. But I won't let him harm me too badly."

"You're a defiant one."

Alexander shrugged.

"Do you know why I'm here? Did he tell you before I arrived?"

"To invest in his mill. I wouldn't. He'll lose all your money."

Crispin laughed heartily this time. "I appreciate your candor." He grabbed Alexander's shoulders and squeezed them. Alexander felt dizzy at the touch. "That's only part of the story, I'm afraid. You see, as I mentioned to your uncle, the governor sent me to examine you. We must establish a relationship. Your mother died a witch. With all of the accusations and fears here, the governor decided to keep a close watch. There's fear your uncle isn't up to the task."

Alexander moved away. His face burned crimson again, but this time with anger. "Tis not true. She was no witch."

Crispin closed the distance again but cast his eyes to the ground. "According to your uncle, that is. Whether true or not, the rumors mark you as suspicious. I'm merely to ensure you're not a witch of your mother's doing. If she was no witch, you have nothing to worry about. I must connect with you so I can report back. Your uncle is convinced you'll cause the colony great trouble in time. The pastor thinks so as well and reprimanded your upbringing as churchless."

Alexander moved even closer to Crispin, intoxicated by this older boy's confidence and smell. "You're not a Puritan. I can tell from your clothes and the way you speak. You wouldn't attend church here, either, if you had to experience such a thing. All talk of the devil and depravity.

Enough to drive anyone to witchcraft."

Alexander expected a tongue-lashing but got the broadest smile yet. "So I've heard. And you're correct. I belong to the Church of England. We don't seem as alarmed about witches. They only appear to thrive up here."

"Only in the people's minds." Alexander suddenly worried his candor could put him at risk with this new person. He always spoke his mind, despite his father's constant warning about his words getting the better of him one day. Perhaps he needed to hold his tongue with Crispin, if for no reason but to protect himself. However, if they indeed had to form some relationship, better for Crispin to understand him from the beginning. Get on with the execution if need be.

Yet again, Crispin laughed. He once again took Alexander by both shoulders. "You're like the little brother I never had. I do believe we'll get along famously." Crispin took a lock of Alexander's long hair and tucked it behind his ear. "Your hair's a lighter brown than mine and your eyes green. Plus, you're a foot shorter, at least. Still, your attitude smacks of the brother I always wished for."

"You're not much older than me."

"Three years, if the records they sent are correct. Old enough to be your bigger brother."

Without thinking, Alexander stood on his tiptoes, leaned forward, and kissed Crispin right on the cheek. Instantly, the passion welled within him, but he forced himself back onto his feet and looked up into those glowing blue eyes.

Crispin froze for a moment before a smile spread across his face and he roared with laughter. "Well, young one, we'd better return you to your uncle. I'll talk to him about the beatings and threats. Our investment will come on the condition he treat you fairly and humanely. I'll come regularly to check on you myself. And to continue your lessons. I understand your father has you well educated, but there's much remaining you must learn. Now, if you're so inclined, may I return the favor before we go back?"

Alexander tilted his head, confused at the request.

Crispin winked, then leaned over and planted a lingering kiss on Alexander's cheek. He reached down then and tousled Alexander's hair before spinning around and striding back into the cold toward the mill. Alexander's senses tingled until he thought he would faint. He gathered his wits about him as quickly as possible and followed Crispin through the deep snow.

Chapter Three

Discovery

March 1693

Salem, Massachusetts

AT LEAST THE severe brutality subsided after Crispin came into Alexander's life. He had visited twice since his first visit a month ago, much less than Alexander hoped but enough to keep his uncle at bay. Crispin and his mother apparently made an initial investment, though small, and thus Uncle Bartholomew attempted more often than not to resist beating him, with the hope they would increase their funding.

Nothing stopped his uncle's ranting, however. Hints of spring's arrival surrounded them since the snow melted and the stream filled with water. They worked outside to repair the mill and fix the road so farmers could more easily bring their goods. They sweated despite the chill in the air as they moved dirt to try to fill the ruts.

Alexander tripped on a rock, sending his shovel of dirt flying through the air. Bartholomew made to come after him but stopped short. He slammed his own shovel into the ground and cursed. "The young uppity aristocrat is going to have to learn the value of a good beating to keep order in the young. What does he know of raising the son of a witch? Tells me not to use force with you. Besides, the pittance his mother and he laid at my feet hardly makes up for caring for you. It'll only last so long before I have to make my own way. Slave. You're a slave, and don't forget your place."

How could Alexander forget when his uncle reminded him every day? Yet he knew better than to believe idle threats from Bartholomew because he had no choice but to keep Crispin happy. Alexander learned as much, first from Crispin's explanation about why the governor sent him to monitor for witchcraft and, second, from Bartholomew's own lips when he ranted about his lack of funds.

They plodded along with their work in silence until Bartholomew had enough. Here came the tirade, as Alexander always anticipated. Since his uncle stopped the violence, he lashed out with his tongue.

"No good sister of mine. The whole family, rife with generations of witches. Don't think I don't suspect you too. Witchery doesn't die easily. And I don't have a lick of the devil in me. No, Satan doesn't have a place in my soul like he did with your mother's."

The air around Alexander became quiet and peaceful. He felt the cool breeze blow through his hair, noticed his arm strain at the heavy load of dirt in his shovel, and smelled the fragrance of budding trees and flowers in the air. His newest bit of magic drowned out his uncle's awful and hurtful words. He either complained about Alexander and warned he would cast him out, or worse — denigrated his mother and father as beasts of Satan.

The first time this new magic came to him, Alexander struggled for control. As the invectives flowed from Bartholomew, the room grew warm, his uncle's face disappeared, and Alexander only experienced loving thoughts and contentment. He stayed that way until his uncle dumped a bucket of cold water over his head.

Afterward, he learned to manage the power. He could lose himself in the magic and escape the hurt but maintain some sort of presence in reality so he instinctively knew when to listen again and engage in the true world.

Eventually, he came to command the ability altogether. He stopped relying on its spontaneous manifestation and called forth the tranquility. He did so in church simply to escape the boredom. He enacted it around his uncle to hide from the brutality of his wrath. At times, Alexander almost wished to return to the beatings because they hurt less than the condemnations of his parents.

And Bartholomew could go on for literally an hour once he started. "You know, your mother is responsible for the state of affairs right here at this mill. She is. My sister's witchcraft rubbed off on me. Her bad reputation caused the community to mistrust me too."

Alexander suspected it had more to do with his own vile

personality but never said as much. To avoid listening, Alexander dreamed of other places as he worked and lost himself in the alternate state.

He imagined an adventure with Crispin. Perhaps escaping with him to Boston or on a ship to some remote location. Or he merely envisioned another of their meetings, this time walking through the woods, and instead of Alexander reaching up and merely kissing Crispin on the cheek, he planted a kiss directly on his lips. How he longed to press their bodies together.

Alexander heard the approaching horse and thus brought himself out of the revelry and back to reality. Bartholomew stopped and leaned against his shovel.

A moment later, Crispin rode around the corner. He bowed solemnly to each of them, and they returned the greeting.

"I brought the next installment of our investment." Crispin tossed a small bag of specie to Bartholomew, who grinned. "I need to take Alexander on a short walk to gauge his current temperament."

They waited a moment until Bartholomew went inside, no doubt to count his money, and then walked down the road.

"You realize I only say such things for his benefit?" Crispin asked when they got far enough away. "I hardly worry about you whatsoever. You're my little brother, not my ward or job to monitor. At least, that's how I see us unofficially."

"I know." Alexander fell a bit toward Crispin to brush against him. "He stopped hitting me, for the most part."

They continued in comfortable silence. Unlike his previous visits,

Crispin asked few questions and seemed to trust that Alexander would relay anything important if needed.

"Ah, look there." Crispin pointed farther into the woods.

"At the bunny?" Alexander shrugged. "Good for stew."

Crispin laughed and walked toward the rabbit, which raced in the opposite direction. Alexander and he found themselves tucked away, a good distance from the road.

Disregarding caution, Alexander walked right up to Crispin, the same distance as the time he had kissed him on the cheek. Crispin stared down at him, smiling.

"You don't have questions of me, this time? Nothing you need for your report?"

"I'm satisfied you pose no danger to the colony."

"Then let me give you something to remember me by, so you may continue your monitoring of me." This time Alexander reached up on his tiptoes and planted his lips firmly on Crispin's.

Crispin jumped a bit at first and leaned backward, then pushed forward and smashed their lips back together. Too soon, the contact ended. The two boys stood looking at each other, Alexander with complete awe at the moment and Crispin with his sly grin.

"You shouldn't kiss me, you know. You very well could be doing the devil's work. Perhaps you're too brave for your own good."

Alexander smirked. "You kissed me back. And liked the taste of my lips."

"You've no way of knowing what I like or dislike." Crispin moved them back toward the road.

"It doesn't take a witch to know such things."

Heading back toward the mill, neither said another word about anything until they approached his uncle, standing in the road. Crispin again bowed and reported all seemed well. He asked if the funds proved sufficient, to which his uncle replied, "For now."

Too soon, Crispin headed away. Alexander watched him depart for as long as possible until he returned to his work and to his dream world. Except the kissing had become a memory, not a fantasy.

Alexander clung to the memory and often hid in the woods if he could escape his uncle's attention. The forest gave him precious moments to close his eyes and remember every detail of how Crispin's lips had felt and tasted.

He also hid out here to practice his magic.

One day, his tooth ached. Afraid Bartholomew would unceremoniously pull it, Alexander closed his eyes and called forth his magic to heal. He had no idea how he learned to control these powers because his mother had never taught him as promised. He suspected the final touch of their fingers somehow transmitted the knowledge to him, where it lay dormant until he grew old enough to manipulate the spells on his own.

He also got much better at the force of wind. He could aim air at a particular branch and send it crashing to the ground. He could cause gusts to irritate his uncle, though he seldom did so for fear he would figure out the witchcraft and come after Alexander.

Alexander almost felt guilty at his other power, to see the present, which he started using to monitor his uncle's whereabouts as a form of

protection, or to get a broader scene of the road and immediate surroundings to ensure no one crept up on him. The temptation became
too great, however, and so he also peered toward Boston.

Initially, such a long distance proved fuzzy, and he had no control
over where he looked. Over time, he taught himself to better command
the ability. He willed Crispin's essence into his mind and followed the
feeling to a grand brick house with servants and a woman with an imposing presence, and there sat Crispin at an enormous dining table, eating with this woman.

Alexander held the image for a moment before his guilt at such a
privacy invasion became too much.

"I need to collect firewood," Alexander informed his uncle one
day.

"Your ward comes to watch after you this morning. You'd best
stay here."

"Send him to me."

Bartholomew glared at Alexander, his face turning bright red at
the defiance. Yet Alexander knew today, of all days, his uncle could not
harm him because Crispin would see the evidence. Without another
word, Alexander headed for a quiet moment alone in the woods and
waited for Crispin.

He lost himself in the anticipation. He meandered about, watching the animals and breathing in the fresh smells of spring. Bored, he
raised his arms in the air and called forth the wind to whip through the
trees and descend upon him.

"Alexander?"

Alexander jumped and dropped his arms to the side. He forgot to monitor for anyone's presence and never heard Crispin's approach.

Crispin stood before him frowning. "What are you doing?"

"Nothing."

"Nothing?" Crispin marched across the distance and scowled down at Alexander. His authoritative walk, which so often caused Alexander to swoon, intimidated him this time. "Nothing? I repeat, what were you doing?"

Alexander stepped away. He went a few more feet into the woods and turned around. "I won't hide from you. Obviously, I can't. But I also won't apologize. At some point, they'll kill me for a witch, just as they did my mother. I can't do anything about their wrath. My magic is not evil, no matter what they say. I've no dealings with the devil, nor did my mother. If you want to be my guardian, you might as well know the entire story."

Alexander had no idea what took hold of him. He had always concealed his true nature so carefully. Secretively, he nurtured his gifts without his uncle or anyone suspecting. He learned about his magic and protected himself while also honoring his mother's dying wish. In one moment, he had thrown caution to the wind. What had gotten into him? He trusted Crispin more than anyone since his parents were murdered, but Crispin was here to watch him for witchcraft. Not only had he caught him manipulating the wind, now Alexander uttered the truth from his own lips.

Crispin pursed his lips together and continued to frown. But he moved forward and hovered above Alexander. This time, Alexander felt no sexual thrill as apprehension overtook him.

Crispin grasped him by the shoulders. "It isn't proper to do those things. You must promise not to do magic anymore."

"I never harm anyone."

"Listen to me. I can't protect you if anyone else finds out. I don't like your doing this, whatever the reason. I command you to stop."

Alexander started to protest, when Crispin pulled him close, took one hand and cupped it over his mouth, then kissed his forehead.

Crispin took his chin and held his face up. "For me?"

Alexander furrowed his brow, his emotions in turmoil. He had never done anything for anyone else since his parents died. Still, he wanted to please Crispin. "I'll take it under advisement." He spoke the only honest answer he could muster.

Crispin nodded. "Yes, please do so."

Crispin turned to leave, but Alexander grabbed his arm and spun him back around. If he had to consider this request and ponder allowing Crispin into his inner life in such a way, then he wanted to understand the stakes more completely. So he held tight, raised his head, and again forced a kiss. As before, Crispin flinched and then returned the kiss for a moment before breaking away.

"It's for your own good you think about stopping. We'll talk next time."

Chapter Four

Sexuality

April 1696

Salem, Massachusetts

ALEXANDER HARDLY BELIEVED three years had passed since his parents died; three years of sleeping in the dirty corner of a mill; three years at the beck and call of his violent uncle; three years of no hope for a future or means to escape the enslavement by his uncle.

Numerous times Alexander made to run away but one force kept him rooted in Salem. Crispin visited him and, by the power of his money and representation of the Royal Governor, held his uncle at bay from the worst sort of the violence. Without Crispin, Alexander would have used his magic and escaped long ago to any unknown fate, to take him away from this hell.

Crispin commanded the power to keep him in purgatory.

A year after Crispin had first started visiting, he sensed Alexander's escape plots. "I demand you stay here so I can see you. Otherwise, the governor may send a posse after you. I don't know if I could find you again."

Alexander knew in such a case he could use his magic to see the present almost anywhere and find Crispin, but then he would have to admit his continued use of sorcery and risk Crispin's dismissing him. Staying here was his best guarantee of their continued relationship.

One day, however, Crispin had annoyed Alexander with his refusal to discuss the subject. Alexander had lashed out when Crispin threatened him with the governor's wrath. "They stopped hunting for witches. I doubt the governor cares about me anymore. I could leave. We could figure something else out, perhaps. Do you need a personal butler?"

Crispin had shaken his head and laughed. "We can't. Perhaps someday. My mother watches too closely. Besides, did they really stop hunting for witches around here? Or did the governor's ending of the Court of Oyer and Terminer thrust their pursuits underground? You hear them. You listen. They fear witches, as they always have. And the governor could renew the court. It's too dangerous. In time, you'll leave. And perhaps I'll help. But for now, stay here for me. Your uncle would raise an alarm and accuse you of witchery. Whether true or not, they'd believe him and come after you. We both know they may have just cause."

Alexander had fumed but stopped bickering. But he pressed Crispin at every visit to do something, or at least give him a timetable. Nothing. For three years he waited, but nothing came of his patience.

Which brought Alexander to wonder what kept him so infatuated with Crispin? Why not flee him, too, if it got Alexander out of this misery?

He knew the answer. They continued to steal an occasional kiss. Those moments froze Alexander in place, waiting for the sound of Crispin's horse approaching, and the next time he could reach up and touch those beautiful full lips with his own.

Unfortunately, much as he longed for more, Alexander never pushed them further despite his strong desire. Increased intimacy scared even him, who usually let his emotions rule and who hardly feared a thing. He stared death in the face without a qualm, but Crispin paralyzed him.

And Crispin certainly never tried anything else. Alexander wondered if Crispin's mind could even take him to the places Alexander dreamed about going.

Yet fantasies about Crispin rooted Alexander in Salem. In the last three years, Crispin grew into a stunningly gorgeous man. His musculature filled out. His greater strength caused Alexander to swoon. His stronger jaw and stature allured Alexander.

To seduce Alexander further, on his last visit Crispin had commented how, though a head shorter, Alexander had developed a stronger body. "The physical labor your uncle has you do suits you well.

Perhaps there's a silver lining to the work." Yet he said nothing more or made no further moves.

If but a flight of fancy with the slimmest chance of transpiring, the mere possibility of Crispin holding him, of ever seeing Crispin lay naked in front of him, trapped Alexander in place.

To cope, Alexander found other distractions. Defying his pledge to consider Crispin's request for an end to his magic, Alexander pursued his witch's interests. He practiced and honed his abilities. He became more adept at seeing the present around him, increasing the distances he could view through the crystal. He could heal himself or even an animal more quickly. The wind obeyed him, not the other way around.

Alexander ventured deep into the woods, hunting for food for his uncle and him. He had learned to use the wind to fashion a weapon to catch almost any animal. Without explaining how, he demonstrated a keen hunting ability, and so Uncle Bartholomew allowed him on these day excursions because he liked the game for their table. He kept to himself how the actual hunt took mere minutes and used the rest of the time for exploration, from developing his magic to appreciating the manhood taking hold of his body.

By mere accident, he experienced his first orgasm as a dream in the middle of the night. He awoke to something streaming out of his penis and causing him to cry out in alarm. He stopped when his uncle threw a pot that hit him in the head.

Passion stirred in his loins on a constant basis thereafter, though he never experienced the same nocturnal emission. He sensed the feeling within himself, however, when he touched himself or his organ rubbed against his clothing. He learned to keep rubbing to induce a wonderful tingling sensation.

On his next hunt, Alexander practiced his vision magic to spy another teenage boy who sat alone in a latrine with his pants around his ankles. The boy was quite pretty, with long eye lashes, pouty large lips, and soft skin. Alexander had often enjoyed watching him during church. What he saw in the crystal mesmerized him. The boy grabbed himself and began yanking until huge globs of liquid erupted out of his penis. He moaned in pleasure.

Alexander reached down and felt his own hardness.

Alone except for a few creatures and the gentle breeze, Alexander concealed himself near a fallen tree and upon a bed of leaves. He set aside the musket he took to pretend he shot an animal, pulled down his pants, and began playing with himself as had the cute boy. Alexander shut his eyes tight and envisioned the boy with his nakedness and enchanting face. Alexander replaced the outhouse scene with the dream of Crispin's lips and his chest pressing against Alexander.

Before Alexander could imagine the sight of Crispin's nakedness, a passion roiled through his loins, commanding him to stroke faster and more urgently, until a stream of white liquid shot out of him and produced the most amazing feeling of pleasure Alexander had ever experienced, even better than the dream and original nocturnal emission.

Alexander breathed heavily, holding his manhood in one hand as he gently continued to stroke, while his other fingers played with the dense hair around his organ.

Alexander buttoned his trousers and stood. He saw the world through different eyes. Though his powers had strengthened over time, and he got better and better at commanding them, his sorcery had become more pronounced in one moment of self passion. He commanded his magic more so than ever before.

With a mere thought, he sent a small tornado through a rotten tree trunk and watched as the squirrel within scurried to safety. The wind tore at the log, so Alexander halted the wind, then reached over to heal the squirrel's broken leg with a touch.

He took out the small stone-size crystal his mother had used in the barn the night of her death. By glancing into the glass, he saw Crispin, laughing with a group of friends at some Boston pub. Alexander lingered over the image, longing to see Crispin in person.

Alexander had become the witch his mother promised dwelled within him. He was not an awkward apprentice learning his craft for survival; he had transformed into a full-fledged witch. He determined to change his life, once and for all.

Alexander raced to the mill, stole his uncle's horse, which was really his father's, and road far out of Salem. He ended up in Boston for the first time in his life. He gazed in awe at the buildings so close together and the tall ships in the harbor. People ran about everywhere. Even rats scampered through the streets, as if on a vital mission.

Alexander loved the city's energy.

But afraid of what to do with himself, he clung closely to the corners until he happened upon a pub and slunk inside. There he found a few soldiers, many sailors, and sundry other people enjoying a pint. He ordered himself one and paid with the money he had stolen from his uncle, bit by bit, in order to accumulate a war chest for his escape.

Alexander spent a couple hours drinking two pints and listening to the chatter of sailors and workers around him. He had no desire to speak with anyone; he enjoyed the liberation of doing something on his own without concern for his uncle, Salem authorities, or even Crispin.

His interest piqued especially at the stories he heard about pirates. Something about their concealed nature and disregard for authority mesmerized him. An officer nearby spoke of them with disdain, which only heightened Alexander's interest.

"I hear tell they control the Caribbean. Stealing from merchants. Not even afraid of His Majesty's Navy. Imagine? Oh, who cares if they take from the Spanish whores? Let them have at it. But at this rate, they'll win the seas entirely." The man pointed a finger across the table at his companion for emphasis.

The other man shook his head. "Always with the prophecies of doom with you, once you get into the ale. You forgot we have right on our side. Why, we haven't even gone after them yet. Those pirates will lose themselves in their wayward ways, and we'll strike. Wait until they get to port to fornicate and steal and spend their ill-gotten money. Then we'll round 'em up and own the seas for His Majesty."

The first man snorted. "They're not so careless."

A sailor at a neighboring table leaned over and joined the conversation. "But they are. I've seen them with me own eyes. Drunk and stumbling. Lost in their frightful world. Sucking at each other's knobs —"

"Enough!" another voice erupted. "Not in my pub! Don't be

encouraging pirate talk here. I'm warning you." The proprietor changed the subject and Alexander lost interest. He stumbled to the street, glanced at his crystal to see Crispin in a nearby home at a writing table, but resisted the urge to go to see him and rode his horse back toward Salem.

Chapter Five

Passion and Confrontation

August 1698

Salem, Massachusetts

NINETEEN AND MOVING toward his twentieth year, Alexander had enough of hiding in Salem and pretending to honor his enslavement to Bartholomew. He even grew weary of hoping something could develop further with Crispin. Other men younger than he possessed their own farms, started families, and came into their own. Why must he remain with his vile uncle? Why not strike out on his own?

To be sure, over the last two years, he had pushed Crispin to explore their pleasure and move beyond kissing to petting and further realms. That alone pacified him for some time. But Alexander needed more. With or without Crispin, life had to change. He was determined to use magic to better his life, even if Crispin disapproved.

Yet the physical connection with Crispin kept him rooted to this place. Alexander recalled the moment a little over a year ago when Crispin approached him in the forest during one of his hunts.

In the small crystal, Alexander spied him coming, knew when he approached, so sat down in the leaves and began rubbing himself to excitement. Crispin tied his horse near Alexander's and walked a few steps before he spied Alexander sitting there playing with himself.

Uncharacteristically, he said nothing but merely walked forward and sat next to the younger man. Alexander leaned into him and forced a kiss. To his delight, Crispin pressed back. Within moments, they both undid their trousers and fondled themselves, kissing passionately until both completed the act.

They said nothing afterward and redressed before conversing as usual.

"You know, the investment in your uncle's mill continues to lose money."

Alexander laughed. "I think I warned you from the beginning about my uncle's failed business. You could stop contributing."

"Then how would I see you? How could I make sure you're well?"

Alexander grinned. "Anything else you come for?"

"Shh." Crispin glanced around, as if ghosts spied upon them.

"Then help me run away so we don't have to worry anymore."

"We can't. Enough talk."

Alexander stormed back to his uncle's, not bothering to say goodbye, though his thoughts lingered over what he and Crispin did to each other in the woods.

They pleasured themselves together several more times before Alexander intensified the moment even more.

In an abandoned home, Alexander reached over and grabbed Crispin's curved penis in his own hand and manipulated him to climax. Then he did himself while kissing Crispin. After a couple more similar episodes, Crispin had the courage to return the favor.

They fondled each other, felt each other's bodies up and down, and added tongues to the kissing. If only Alexander could rid Crispin of the unease he felt afterward.

For a long time, they never even discussed the intimacy. But their bond felt so natural and easy to Alexander he finally brought up their sex life as casually as had the sailor in the bar who referenced pirates who had sex with one another.

"We could do it more than once, you know. Or next time get completely naked." Alexander had twirled a stick absently in his hand as he made the suggestion while sauntering around a lake.

"Shh." Crispin frowned at Alexander. "Someone may hear. One never knows. What we do isn't natural. Keep silent, or we'll have to stop."

Crispin made no sense to Alexander. "If our relationship is so unnatural, why are we attracted to each other? No one sees us."

"We need to be careful. We're best not to speak of these things."

Again Alexander disagreed but stopped pressing the matter.

Alexander came to love bringing up their intimacy, if nothing other than to tease Crispin. No matter what Crispin said, he too must have reveled in their intercourse because he visited more frequently, always led them off by themselves, and never resisted Alexander's advances.

Alexander determined to satisfy himself even more. And Crispin.

Bartholomew took to adding Crispin to his tirades, as he did today while they awaited his arrival. "Snobbery of the elite, doesn't mean he's smart. They barely give me a pittance and then suggest how I should handle you. I ought to throw his money back in his face."

Alexander drifted away to float on a quiet cloud, unaware of a thing his uncle said until he heard the horse hooves and opened his eyes to see Crispin riding up on a stunning young black stud his mother had purchased for his birthday.

"You're late." Bartholomew moved between Crispin and Alexander and snarled.

"Perhaps you don't want this, then?" Crispin got off his horse and held up the sack of specie. "I'd watch your tongue, sir, considering our investment has done nothing but lose money to this point."

Bartholomew grabbed the bag. "The biggest problem is I can't discipline this one, and you don't give me enough to make up for the problems he creates."

"You've done a fine job with him since I began monitoring."

Alexander winced at Crispin's words. He always apologized later, claiming he had to keep up appearances. Still, Alexander was infuriated.

"Now, I must meet with him in private. You can get back to your work." Crispin guided Alexander away from his uncle. Soon, they raced together on the horse, returning to the secluded and abandoned log home in the midst of the forest.

"Why doesn't anyone live here?" Crispin asked. It was the first time he'd ever spoken before their physical encounter. He usually got deathly quiet until they finished, even if Alexander chatted away.

"Indian raids. A lot of isolated farms and homes were abandoned because people couldn't protect themselves."

Alexander moved close to Crispin, reached his arms around his waist, and pulled them together. Crispin looked down into his eyes and smiled before they kissed.

They lowered themselves to the floor, never letting their lips part, and undid their pants.

At just the right moment, Alexander changed their typical behavior. Before Crispin could grasp his own penis, Alexander took hold of Crispin's but then scooted down their bodies and engulfed Crispin between his lips.

Nothing thrilled him more or tasted better than the moment Crispin released into his mouth and down his throat. Alexander never wanted to release the penis from his lips and masturbated himself to completion as Crispin's breathing steadied and his member grew limp.

Crispin dressed more hurriedly than usual and scurried outside before Alexander even pulled his trousers up. Alexander casually followed him and smiled when he looked into Crispin's astonished face.

"I know you liked it as much as I." Alexander walked to Crispin and stared into his eyes.

Crispin stepped away, then started down a path. When Alexander caught up, Crispin lurched to a halt, stepped a few feet away, and let out an exasperated breath. "You frighten me."

Alexander laughed. "Why? Because I'm a witch?"

"Don't say so out loud." Crispin grimaced. "And no, as long as you keep the magic under control, it's never bothered me. I keep coming back, don't I? It's what you do to me. How I feel about you. Those moments of passion. I don't know where you're leading us, but at some point we must stop this unnatural relationship."

Alexander again closed the distance between them and ran his hand down Crispin's chest. "There you go again with your nonsense about guessing what's natural or not. You sound no different from the Puritans who warn about magic being unnatural and witches threatening the community. You're speaking nonsense."

Alexander reached over and grabbed a plant from the ground. He enchanted the greenery and then rubbed it over a deep scratch on Crispin's hand, which healed at once. "See? There's nothing wrong with my power. Just as there's nothing wrong with our love."

Crispin jerked his head back toward Alexander and pulled his hand away. He clenched his jaw. He never could handle Alexander's references to their relationship or how he felt about Crispin. He certainly never reciprocated. "You use this magic, don't you? Despite my telling you to desist?"

"You're not my master any more than my uncle."

Some revelation appeared on Crispin's face. He started to say something, stopped himself, then motioned for Alexander to follow him back toward the horse. "It's you. All those repairs and problems with the mill. You're breaking the mill yourself."

Alexander grinned sheepishly. "No. The wind does damage."

Crispin slammed his fists against his sides. "Stop. Do you know how much money I've lost in the damn mill? It will ruin me! And every time you do harm I have to pay more. I should have known you would cause destruction." Crispin circled the horse, then came to a stop in front of Alexander.

"I don't like how hard he tries to make me work," Alexander rebutted. "I survive the best I know how. Besides, your mother pays for the mill. She has plenty."

Crispin ground his teeth together. "It's not my mother's. It's mine."

"I don't understand. I thought she contributed to the mill, and you came to check on her investment. Plus you visit at the governor's behest because of me. Even though I really am a witch." Alexander smiled.

His smile typically disarmed Crispin. This time, Crispin stepped back, the scowl firmly planted on his face. "I have to tell you something."

Alexander tilted his head, intrigued. He raised his eyebrows to prompt Crispin to continue.

"My coming has nothing to do with my mother. She refused to invest after my first visit because your uncle was too risky. I used my own money. It was my investment. And I never thought I would earn money. I knew the business was a pit from the beginning. I contributed to continue seeing you."

Though Crispin appeared agitated, Alexander's heart melted. He never before admitted such an intimate detail that came so close to expressing the emotion he felt toward Alexander.

"Why didn't you use the reason of coming for the governor? You didn't have to invest in my uncle's losing venture."

Crispin breathed deeply. "That's not true either."

"What's not?"

"After my first visit, I came of my own will every time." Crispin stepped closer to Alexander. "Don't you understand? The governor sent me one time amidst the witch hunts and because of your mother. I returned and exonerated you. Since your uncle watched over you, my report ended the matter. The governor never sent me back. I invented the excuse to force my mother to allow the continued visits. She couldn't defy the governor, though sometimes I suspect she knows about my ruse. And she despises my seeing you, for reasons I can't understand. The investment, the governor, I concocted those reasons."

The gravity of the revelation set in with Alexander. Not the loss of money or Crispin's subterfuge; the meaning behind the story became clear, which Crispin buried. "You invented reasons to see me."

Crispin stepped toward Alexander. "To protect you. Yes." Crispin nodded. "Because whether from your sorcery or some other force, you hold a spell over me."

Alexander leaned toward Crispin. "Me?"

Crispin stepped away. "Which is why I need you to stop using the magic. Stop causing damage. I can't protect you forever. We can't continue this way. This all—" Crispin waved his hand in the air as if to explain the ambiguity of his statement. "—must end. We have duties we can't ignore any longer."

Alexander wondered how to respond. He had always kept secrets from the world, even from Crispin, ever since his mother and father had died. Crispin often talked of duty and obligation, which Alexander understood on some intellectual level. He listened and sympathized with how the burdens affected Crispin. Yet no such compulsion governed Alexander. Such responsibilities for him had died with his parents. He survived the remainder of his youth and moved toward adulthood as a matter of course, always planning for the moment when he would strike out on his own. He wanted Crispin as a part of his future, but not to the imprisonment of himself in this puritanical society that held nothing but contempt for him. But how to communicate his sentiments to Crispin without driving him away? Or was their separation inevitable?

"We have different experiences playing into our future obligations." Alexander squinted at Crispin to see if he understood. "Either way, I think a vision can include a space for the two of us, together."

Crispin sighed. "Perhaps, though unlikely. Our best chance might be for you to embrace the gristmill with your uncle. Why aren't you learning the craft? The skill could serve you well." Crispin began one of his monologues. "You need to follow the rules. Society has expectations of you, whether you like them or not. And you have to conceal your magic. Being found out could get you killed. Do something useful, such as a trade. Why are you always so defiant?"

Alexander's mind drifted away, which he seldom did when with Crispin. But he hardly wanted an argument. The rage building within as he heard these words threatened to overcome him. To stem the tide, he closed his eyes and felt the force of wind blowing in the trees above him. He thrust a powerful gust up and away, to conceal the magic from Crispin but give himself a release from his growing ire.

"Alexander? Are you listening to me?"

Alexander turned his attention back to Crispin. He determined to say something despite his reluctance. "I'm alone, Crispin. I don't have the same obligations to people. There is no duty for me. You don't understand. I won't stay as a slave to my uncle. He would never apprentice me, even if I wanted such a fate. Your vantage point must make seeing my predicament impossible. I have nothing in this world."

Alexander felt the rising despair lurking around him. He shoved his fear deep inside, then turned and faced Crispin. "You're the only thing I have. I'm a little surprised you can't see this reality. I do love you, no matter how much you can't reciprocate or express the same. But I won't suppress my witchcraft or remain a slave on the off chance you'll visit from time to time, depending on where this obligation takes you in life."

Crispin stood quietly before he spoke. "Does what I say matter?"

"Your actions tell a tale."

"And unfortunately some of your actions endanger us."

Alexander glared at Crispin, wishing his power came with the ability to read a person's mind. "Do you think me evil? You say no. But you bring up my sorcery a lot. You're as afraid of my witchery as the Puritans."

Crispin stalked over and grabbed Alexander by the shoulders. He held him tightly. "You're not evil. I have no fantasy about you fraternizing with Satan. I'm trying to protect you."

Crispin let go and spun around. He stalked back to his horse and motioned for Alexander to follow. Having thus ended the conversation, Crispin returned Alexander to the mill, said a brief goodbye, and disappeared. Alexander's head spun, wondering what exactly they had achieved, if anything.

Chapter Six

Portia Nottingham

August 1698

Boston, MA

ALEXANDER HID UNDER floorboards of the old house, wishing he could more easily summon the magic to see the present. While he could use healing magic rather fast if given the right elements, and while he mastered the wind, for the most part, he struggled with the present and could do nothing to see the world without his mother's crystal.

The trouble being he had concealed himself quickly because he got so lost in commanding the wind he had heard the horse's hooves too late. He dove into the abandoned cottage and pulled up the boards, where the previous owner had built a hiding place before leaving this place altogether.

Crispin was not scheduled for a couple more days, and anyone else would either suspect something of him or have come to rob him.

Alexander heard the horse gallop toward him, and then someone jumped off. The person came directly toward the cabin and walked in. Alexander had never heard such a heavy footfall. Authoritative. In command. Confident. He even tried to hold his breath to hide himself. He thought such a powerful step might come right through the floorboards.

Only after he calmed did he wonder at who might so cavalierly come into this house. He noted the faint cologne that filled the air and listened to the breathing. Did such a manly footfall belonged to Crispin? He recalled hearing the forceful step when the two of them entered here together or when walking alongside him.

"Alexander, if you're here, we need to talk."

Alexander scurried from under the floorboards, peeking out at an astonished Crispin.

"What on earth are you doing?" Crispin asked.

"I thought you were someone else. I didn't expect you today." Alexander got up with a broad grin and went to Crispin, who allowed the soft kiss on his cheek. "Why are you here?"

Crispin walked away, but Alexander followed close behind. Crispin's solid calves made Alexander want to reach out and tackle him to the floor and ravage his body. Yet he held back because he sensed an unrest in Crispin. However, he did reach out and hold Crispin's hand.

Crispin stopped and looked down at Alexander. He squeezed the hand and let go. "I haven't much time. I shouldn't even be here. I've been called to meet with officials in Salem. I came to you first because I need for you to come to Boston and meet with me. I've changed our meeting to my house. I informed your uncle, so you'll have no problem borrowing the horse. Here are the directions." Crispin handed Alexander a sheet of paper.

Alexander almost said he had already been by Crispin's house a couple times but kept the secret to himself. "Is there trouble?"

"I have to go." Crispin turned around and walked toward the door.

Alexander reached out and grabbed Crispin's arm, spinning him around so they faced each other. He yanked them together and kissed Crispin's full lips, only feeling better when he returned the embrace and inserted his tongue into Alexander's mouth. Too soon, Crispin halted the intimacy. He pulled away but kept one hand cupped around Alexander's head, massaging his scalp ever so slightly.

"Return to the mill. Don't do anything else. Anything. For me. And you must come two days hence."

And so Alexander found himself riding into Boston on a fine summer day a few days later. He left early enough to take his time and enjoy the beauty as he rode along. The forest covered the road with a comforting shade, and the passersby seemed content and at peace.

Again, Alexander thrilled at the outskirts of Boston, which surpassed Salem in terms of its port and command of the colony. He loved the bustle of activity, all the fit young sailors running about, and the anonymity he so lacked in rural Salem.

He spent the last two days trying to ascertain what exactly prompted this summoning to Boston but had no idea despite using his ability to see the present to spy on Crispin a number of times. He only viewed him at some noble social gatherings or alone in his house, writing at a desk. He blushed at having spied on Crispin's naked body while bathing.

Despite a slight anticipation at seeing Crispin in his home for the first time, Alexander sensed something amiss.

Alexander grew a bit self-conscious as he rode down Crispin's street. Though he generally dismissed how others may view his working clothes and lower status, today he wondered more because he stopped to tie his horse outside one of these homes.

Crispin lived in a rather imposing brick house. The brass knocker alone probably cost more than all of Alexander's possessions put together. He owned hardly a thing, what with the government having confiscated most of his father and mother's belongings because of the charge of witchcraft and everything else going to his uncle.

Before he reached out to knock, he paused and closed his eyes. He sensed a force he had never experienced but that his mother's brief teachings warned him about. She said some used their magic for ill-gotten gains or to harm people. While she insisted over and over she and their ancestors were not witches and in no way in league with the devil, she also warned others took advantage of their power and perhaps did fraternize with him.

Alexander quizzed her about this possibility, but as with so many lessons, she left his questions unanswered. His learning about his magic and other revelations came with the hint of choices to make about when and how to use his abilities, and to what end. How many times had he envisioned the wind knocking over a branch or hurling a tool through the air, both of which landed on his uncle's head and killed him? An inner voice pushed Alexander in a different direction, one his mother would approve of and that made him feel less maniacal and more like a mere human with special powers.

Something in his midst today spoke of blackness and anger. Yet, what had such a thing to do with Crispin's home?

He shook the feeling and knocked at the door. A young man, no older than Alexander, answered and bowed. Alexander hardly knew what to do, so stood still for a moment before the other one spoke.

"Master Nottingham is expecting you." He ushered Alexander into a large foyer, with a rather imposing staircase. "This way."

Alexander followed him through a hallway lined with portraits and into an office. A large desk sat in the middle, the wall behind lined with shelves of books, and two chairs sat in front of the desk. The attendant disappeared so Alexander walked around the room, admiring the splendor and luxury.

After a few moments, he heard those footsteps again, pounding down the hardwood floor in the hall and coming closer and closer. Crispin turned the corner, and Alexander grinned.

Crispin stood rigid and merely nodded. "Please, sit." Crispin motioned toward one of the chairs and then walked around to the other side of the desk. He remained standing and leaned against the desk with two hands on top. He refused to so much as crack a smile.

Alexander frowned, growing nervous. A summons to Boston. The formal setting. And Crispin acting like the King of England, not the man who lay naked with Alexander only a couple of weeks before. He resisted the urge to drift away and ignore anything he heard. But he did marshal his magic to defend himself. Never before had he felt uneasy around Crispin. Again, that sense of a dark force nearby flooded Alexander's being.

"What is this about?" Alexander asked after the long silence unnerved him.

Crispin stood rigid, took a deep breath, then sighed. He tilted his head, and a hint of those caring eyes fought through the demeanor he had affected for the day. "I have three things to tell you. None of which you will want to hear. For your own good, you need to listen and accept all of them."

Now Alexander went stiff and sat straight in his chair. Much as he loved Crispin, he never followed random orders from anyone. He stared back hard.

Crispin had started to speak when the approaching sound of another person stopped him. He waited a moment until a regal woman walked into the room. She wore her jet-black hair up, a perfectly tailored dress, and her blazing, blue eyes seemed to stare through Alexander when she glanced at him.

Alexander ascertained two things in a split second. First, she was Crispin's mother. They had the same deportment, the same shape of their jaw, and the same erect posture. Second, the malevolent form of witchery he sensed upon coming to this house emanated from her. He gathered the wind above the house to prepare a defense if anything should happen.

She walked casually into the room and stood, waiting for Crispin.

"Alexander, my mother." Crispin motioned toward her. "Portia Nottingham. Mother, this is Alexander MacBeth, of whom you've heard me speak."

"Of course." She neither bowed nor smiled. She turned her head sharply toward Alexander and leered at him. "You may stop."

How did she know? She commanded him to stop the use of magic. Crispin looked puzzled but also seemed cowed in his mother's presence. "I came because I need to see your guest in my sitting room before he leaves. Alone." She lowered her voice at the last word, then turned and glided out of the room.

An awkward silence returned between the two young men.

Alexander had enough. "You were preparing to issue three edicts before your mother frightened you into silence."

"Don't start with the games today." Crispin folded his arms in front of him. He tried for rigid again, but the softness sneaked through his eyes as he peered at Alexander. "This is hard enough."

"Then just get on with your nonsense."

Crispin cleared his throat. "First, I received word from a minister in Salem he and several of the residents suspect you of witchcraft." Crispin held up his hand to stop Alexander's protest. "Nothing you say will do any good. They know I befriended you. I met with them and warned how the governor frowned upon such proceedings and would never stomach a trial. They understood but hinted that they had ways to protect themselves from a witch in their midst. You know how I feel. I'm merely trying to warn you. To protect you. It's becoming more serious."

The quiet returned as Crispin seemed to wait for Alexander to acknowledge the conversation. He refused to engage the topic, however. He knew for certain he must soon leave Salem, regardless.

"And the other two items?" Despite being near Crispin, Alexander wanted nothing more than to leave immediately.

"I've been commissioned in His Majesty's Navy. My duty in life has a firm direction. I won't be able to serve as your ward any longer."

Alexander rolled his eyes and stood, tired of the power game. "Did you forget you already admitted you never were such a thing? I have no need of a ward, nor would I accept one. I suppose you'll enjoy this royal obligation as it allows you to run away from your desire under the guise of duty."

Crispin's face turned beet red. "Hold your tongue."

Alexander smiled, unafraid, even as Crispin smashed his heart under his heavy foot. Alexander had suffered much worse in life. Indeed, escaping the clutches of Salem would be easier without the one force holding him there.

"Then continue. I'm growing tired of this."

Crispin came from around the desk. He started toward Alexander but stopped. His commanding presence appeared to wane, his shoulder slumping slightly. "I'm betrothed. My mother found and approved of the woman with whom I shall share my life. Do you understand?"

Alexander commanded the tear in his eye to retreat. He would never give Crispin the satisfaction. He snorted. "I should have known you could never stand up to the forces working against us. Duty. Obligation. They consume you. You hide behind those ideas. I wish you well."

Alexander turned to leave and walked toward the door but stopped when he heard the rigid tone in Crispin's voice.

"Stop."

Alexander turned around slowly. "Yes?"

Crispin straightened his posture and smoothed the front of his coat. "Perhaps we'll see each other from time to time. I'd like to. For friendship's sake."

Poor Crispin. Alexander understood him differently at this moment than ever before. He loved Crispin's masculine deportment, his commanding presence, and the way he took charge of a situation. His nobility made Alexander swoon. Yet Alexander was also drawn to the softer side of Crispin lurking underneath, which allowed a certain vulnerability, needed warmth, and a soft caress. The two personas strained against each other. Alexander saw the inner conflict in Crispin's face. These two traits warred against each other because society and those around Crispin only allowed the young man in charge to exist. They shunned the gentle side of him, which had brought him to Alexander.

Alexander determined not to burn the bridge. He walked closer to Crispin and whispered, lest a servant or someone else overhear. "I still love you, if that's what you're needing to hear. I'm sure I always will. Now, I'm to see your mother?"

Crispin walked Alexander in silence through the large house and knocked at her open door. She stood and then dismissed her son. Alexander felt the threat immediately.

"You're of poor stock." Portia eyed him up and down. "And your mother was a careless witch. All the talk of doing right. Look what that got her? Listen carefully." Portia closed the distance. She stood eye to eye with Alexander, who forced himself to stand his ground despite wanting to run from her. "Stay away from my son. You're not the only one who can peer a distance away. I will protect him with everything I can. You're vile with your seductive ways. I've set him on the right path. Caroline will be good for him. You, go. Never return here."

With her dismissal, Portia Nottingham turned her back on Alexander and walked away. He stared dumbly for a second before whipping around and hurrying through the house. He let himself out.

He soon found himself on the horse, riding not toward Salem but back toward the pub and the comfort of drunken sailors. He allowed himself to cry at the apparent loss of Crispin. He had combated the force of Crispin's duty battling against their love and lost. Alexander would mourn both the loss and the hole left forever in his heart.

Long ago, however, Alexander decided between total despair and life. At a tender age, he'd lost everything but chose the latter, at first for his mother, and over the years, for himself. He would allow a bit of sadness at the loss of Crispin, but never allow another person to dampen his potential. He would survive.

II: Dark Sorcery

Chapter Seven

Dark Sorcery

8 June 1700

Boston, MA

AS ALEXANDER RODE the short distance to Boston, he pondered the same question over and over, in an endless and depressing loop. Two years ago, Crispin had declared his love of duty outweighed his love for Alexander. Though Crispin denied putting the matter in those terms, Alexander felt differently. Alexander therefore determined to leave Salem, flee his uncle and the mill, and head out on his own.

So why had he stayed? Why did he pine for Crispin and await their fleeting moments together? He promised himself to run away and start anew somewhere, yet here he remained, in his early twenties, a slave and clandestine witch. Miserable. Alone.

Perhaps his two attempts to escape and their subsequent failure chained him to Salem.

The first, after a year of planning and preparing, saw Alexander flee westward until confronted by hostiles. He pleaded with them to accept him. "I'm an outlaw to the white people. I'm outcast, like you. They want me dead."

The Indian leader either spoke a different language or ignored Alexander because he said nothing. He turned and spoke to the others in a foreign tongue. Then he had pointed for Alexander to leave.

Alexander had stayed the night in a nearby woods, hoping to approach them in the morning with a better argument. His senses tingled an alarm so he got his mother's crystal out and saw several of them with painted faces, sneaking through a field toward him.

Alexander had scurried to his feet and run from them, using the wind to down trees in his wake until he got away from them. Then he hurried back to the mill.

"Where've you been?" Bartholomew had screamed.

"Hunting." Alexander resisted the urge to peer outside to see if they followed.

"Hunting, indeed. Where's your game? You were out at a Witch's Sabbath, weren't you? In the woods with Satan?"

Alexander ignored his uncle and slumped into his corner to sleep.

Alexander never told Crispin about the first failed attempt to run away.

But Crispin lay at the heart of his second failure. Six months after running toward the West, Alexander bolted toward Boston's harbor. Despite stories of merchant captains always on the lookout for sailors, two rejected him with a curt no.

Alexander next approached a Royal Navy officer. "Sir, may I join His Majesty's Navy?"

The officer looked him up and down, then laughed in his face. "Are you even twelve yet?" Alexander blushed. He started to explain his true age when the officer interrupted. "And what do you know of the sea? Can you tie a knot? Mend a sail? What could you offer my ship?"

Just then, Crispin rounded the corner. "Excuse me, sir. Is this man bothering you? I know him."

"Not at all. Fancies himself a sailor but looks more like a common dockworker to me."

"I'll take care of him." Crispin grabbed Alexander by the arm and pulled him off the street and into an alley.

"You're not meant for a seafaring life. It's too dangerous." Crispin lowered his voice to a whisper. "Besides, we might never see each other again if you travel off."

Alexander laughed but found himself in bed with Crispin in a rented room for the afternoon. Once satisfied, they argued about Alexander's behavior but came to no resolution and parted with their usual tension.

With Crispin monitoring his Boston escape route, Alexander had again returned to the mill with his tail tucked between his legs.

Suddenly two years had passed since Crispin announced his be-trothal and career in the navy. He remained engaged but unmarried, returning a few days ago from his first yearlong tour of duty.

So Alexander headed toward Boston after another summons from Crispin. He thrilled at seeing his lover at the same time he dreaded the meeting and wished for a clean break from their relationship.

More than anything, Alexander derided himself for staying in Salem. He had to come up with a better plan and, once and for all, sever ties with Salem, the Massachusetts Bay Colony, and his old life. What good was witchcraft if he could never use magic to his advantage? Not to mention the fact the Puritans continued to lurk, despite everyone thinking the witch persecutions had ended. They despised him and pre-sented a continued danger.

As Alexander tied his horse outside Crispin's house, he first felt the negative energy and then spied Portia Nottingham peering out the front window. According to Crispin, their tolerance for one another had grown more tense since the first meeting because Alexander continued to see Crispin against her wishes. The two witches could spark a fire from miles apart, but fear of exposure to Crispin and the outside world kept them at bay.

Before he could knock on the door, Portia flung it open and blocked his path.

"I thought we understood each other?" She folded her arms over her chest and glared. "Yet, you return."

"Your son called for me." Alexander concentrated on the wind around him, swirling the forces to his bidding. He feigned fear and then blew out a breath. "That's your hair? I thought a black cat had curled atop your head."

Portia waved her arm in the air, and the gusts at Alexander's disposal shot away into the clouds. "You're weak. Leave, before he sees you."

Alexander sighed. He feared her dark sorcery but felt some day he could learn to overpower her. "Why must we enact this charade? You won't do anything to me. Step aside, and go play in your dungeon."

Portia's face burned crimson and she started to speak when Alexander heard the forceful cadence pounding down the hallway toward him. He saw Crispin, sporting a wide grin, behind his mother. "Alexander!"

Portia stepped aside. "I was just coming to get you." She smiled at Crispin but turned around before leaving and stared daggers at Alexander from behind Crispin's back.

Alexander bowed low. "You summoned me, master?"

"Very amusing." Crispin grabbed a walking stick and led Alexander outside. "Come. I need a bit of fresh air."

"Fresh air? Or are you leading me toward a seduction? I suspect you seek something more carnal."

Crispin walked briskly ahead due to his longer legs, making Alexander practically jog to keep pace with him. As usual, he ignored Alexander's banter.

"Perhaps you're not interested anymore in what I have to offer, what with all the young, virile sailors at your command. You're an officer now, after all, and can demand their favors at your whim. Who needs a miller's slave?"

Crispin lurched to a stop and frowned at Alexander. "Will you stop? People may overhear. I've looked forward to seeing you again for months, yet you insist on tweaking me. Let me get this out of the way from the beginning. Your snide comments won't drive me off. You're completely wrong about what takes place aboard ship. I barely have a free moment to take care of such business from time to time on my own. And if you don't want to go with me, just leave. Why did you come if I so upset you?"

Alexander sauntered down the road, proud of himself for raising Crispin's ire. He turned down the street leading to their favorite inn and waited for Crispin to follow.

"I come because you seduce me. I know you claim you don't know any magic. But you do something to me. I love you, still, even though you cling to this false notion of duty and obligation. I only hope I never meet your fiancé. How long will you pretend you intend to marry her before she calls your bluff? You can't pretend it's because you don't have enough money to support her. So you use your naval service. Plenty of officers have a wife in port. She'll want the same."

Crispin continued to ignore him as he went inside the inn while Alexander waited outside. A few moments later, the back window to one of the rooms opened, signaling for Alexander to climb in.

Crispin pulled him into an embrace. "I don't know how long I'll be gone this time. We're leaving in a month because of the new law against piracy."

"I thought piracy was already illegal." Alexander snuggled into

Crispin's arms as they fell onto the bed.

"The monarchy wants to crack down even more severely. Thus the Act for More Effectual Suppression of Piracy. We no longer need to take pirates to London for trial and execution but can execute at sea. His Majesty wants the navy to become more vigilant in combating this seditious force. He will even pardon any pirates who surrender this year and return to royal service. My ship will sail to eliminate more piracy."

"Speaking of your ship." Alexander began unbuttoning Crispin's shirt. "When will you command your own?"

"I'm barely an officer and only have such status because of my rank in society. Anything else will take time."

"When you become a captain, will you take me aboard your ship?"

Crispin stopped playing with Alexander's hair. "Don't start this already. When I return, Caroline and I will be wed. I can't go gallivanting around with you. I've a duty to my family and new bride."

Alexander raged inside but determined to make his point in a different way. He ripped off what clothes remained on Crispin and then slowly removed his own. He ground atop Crispin, leaned down and kissed him, probing with his tongue and licking across Crispin's teeth. He bit at a nipple, licked down Crispin's hairy chest, and then took him in his mouth. Once saturated, he lurched up and impaled himself on Crispin.

Crispin's eyes went wide, and his hips thrust in and out. To the same rhythm, Alexander manipulated himself until he sprayed all over Crispin's chest. With a hard thrust and deep moan, Crispin tensed beneath him before Alexander slid him out.

They dressed in quiet before returning to the streets and heading back toward Crispin's house. Alexander often waited for such public places for his attacks because Crispin so feared a scene he rarely retaliated.

"She won't satisfy you in the same way. She won't know the pleasure of the mouth, won't be as tight as my anus."

Crispin leaned over. "Lower your voice."

"You can talk of duty and marriage all you want. But you really want me. I don't understand why you refuse to help me escape so we can figure something out together. I can think of a million options, but I need your help. I'm going to escape eventually, with or without you. Together, perhaps we could fulfill our dreams."

They turned the corner and Alexander saw his horse in the distance, waiting to take him back to purgatory.

"That's your confounded problem. You're always dreaming and avoiding reality."

"And that's your problem. You see one as reality and the other as a dream. Did you dream what happened in bed today?" Alexander waited for a couple of men to pass before continuing. "Why this sharp division between fiction and reality in your world? They aren't mutually exclusive unless you allow it."

"Enough. Stop." Crispin clenched his hand around the walking stick and balled his other hand into a tight fist. "I've barely returned. Of course I wanted to see you, but instantly you start up. We have a perfect situation." They stopped outside Crispin's home. Alexander's horse neighed at him. Crispin walked a few steps away from Alexander and then spun around. He marched toward him as he must to the lowly sailors aboard his ship. "We get to see each other. Perhaps we can continue. But not if you disappear."

"I won't stay there. I've already broken a promise to myself by remaining for this long. I'm going to force the issue. I won't play in your perfect little world forever. You're going to have to decide at some point. Mummy and Caroline, or me?"

Alexander lost himself in the moment. He twirled his finger in the air and a small tornado, no taller than the top of his ankle, swirled between them and toward the path to Crispin's door. Alexander flicked his fingers and a sharp wind blew Crispin's hat off his head.

Crispin's eyes grew wide with fright. He scampered after his hat, smashed it onto his head, and stalked back to Alexander. "We're in public," he hissed.

"Then you'd best run inside because if you stay this close to me I'm going to kiss you in front of everyone and force the issue."

Crispin spun around and walked briskly toward his front door. A torrent of emotion swept through Alexander. Why did he so antagonize the man he loved? On the other hand, why did he stick around in this futile situation?

Before Crispin got to the door, Portia stormed out. Loud enough so Alexander could hear her, she spoke to her son. "He's a witch. Did you see what he did, Crispin? He's in league with the devil. You have to believe now. Come inside, quickly, before he gets one of us. Hurry."

Portia pulled him along. With one hand behind her back, she

wiggled her fingers and what felt like a huge boulder smashed into Alexander's stomach. He fell to the ground with a grunt.

He took the opportunity to escape. He scurried to his feet and jumped atop his horse, spurring her out of town as quickly as possible.

Chapter Eight

Puritan Investigation

17 June 1700

Salem, Massachusetts

ALEXANDER FOLDED THE letter and placed it in his pocket. At this point, even if Bartholomew discovered the theft, stealing was the least of his worries.

Portia Nottingham had enlisted the assistance of his uncle to undermine Alexander and put him in danger. After their magical confrontation a week ago in front of Crispin's house, he had expected such a move. And, of course, Bartholomew had seized the opportunity. Alexander long suspected his use as a slave would wear thin on the bitter man.

Their collusion intensified Alexander's predicament and forced him into action. He figured, at most, he had a few weeks before they came after him, if not mere days.

Bartholomew had left a few minutes ago, which gave Alexander a safe distance from which to follow. He headed out the door and concealed himself in the woods as dusk settled over Salem. Despite the unsure footing, Alexander caught up quickly but stayed behind a safe distance and hid amidst the trees.

Bartholomew meandered down the road, whistling a soft hymn and swinging a stick in his hand. He appeared to have no suspicion Alexander followed, even after he got to the clearing and entered the village. Not once did he glance behind or even to the side.

Alexander thought Salem rather devoid of people but remembered the persistent fear of the night in this community, where they believed Satan lurked in the woods and knew the Indians could attack at any time. Most houses shuttered their windows, thus helping Alexander remain in the shadows until Bartholomew knocked on the judge's door. The pastor stuck his head out, allowed him entry, then scanned the night for signs of anyone else.

Alexander pulled out his mother's crystal but predicted the result. Nothing. Despite how adept he had become at using his magic, his attempt to peer into his uncle's business never worked when he went on these nocturnal visits to the village. Somehow they counteracted his power.

Alexander therefore crept alongside an old barn, sprinted across a yard, and barely missed the eye of the old dog tied up under the porch before concealing himself beneath a window of the judge's rather prestigious home. Thankful the black night camouflaged him, Alexander hunched over and peeked through a crack between the shutter and frame.

Bartholomew sat at the dining table, with the pastor, judge, and another hefty man unknown to Alexander. All of them wore the drab black suits the Puritans so loved. He could barely hear their discussion and read their lips.

"I'm grateful for the presence of another minister," Bartholomew said. "This business unnerves me. You're sure he can't use his power to watch us? He'll kill me in my sleep if he finds out."

The new minister patted a small wooden chest with its lid open, though Alexander could not see its contents. "The Church has powers of her own. We're upon God's business, and He has ways of concealing our activities from the Devil."

"I think we have enough evidence to go after him now." This time the Salem pastor spoke.

"Not so fast." The judge leaned back in his chair. He had his back to Alexander but sat closest to the window, so Alexander could hear him best. "Not even the sheriff will back us. The Royal Governor made his feelings abundantly clear seven years ago. No more witch trials. No more accusations. Even if Bartholomew has this documentation from a woman in Boston, it's not going to change the legal situation. I wish you had remembered the letter."

Bartholomew turned red with embarrassment and fumbled with

the hat in his hands. "It's securely hidden, I assure you. I'll have it when needed."

"Reverend Mather, you spoke against such proceedings yourself." This time the judge addressed the other minister.

"Publicly, of course, I had little choice, unless we wanted the governor to come after the Church. I had to protect Puritan autonomy, lest the Anglican Church become the official Church of the colony and once again chase us away from our home. Privately, however, we have duties to the people we serve. And God. Never forget, whether sanctioned or not, we must be about His business."

"Which brings us to the point of tonight's meeting." Salem's pastor seemed to smile, though the sound came out as more of a grimace. "Realizing the lateness of the hour, and the long and darkened journey ahead for our miller, let me explain. We've been investigating the young man for some time, since Bartholomew took him in after we proved his mother a witch. We've gathered various forms of documentation. We know he does damage to the mill, and therefore we know Satan resides in his soul. Or should I say he invited the Devil in? Bartholomew even spotted him leaving for days to attend a Witch's Sabbath in the woods. We need no further proof to justify whatever action we decide to take in the name of God."

"And the governor?" the judge asked.

"He provides a slight complication," Reverend Mather sighed. "Of course we can't compromise your position or risk this becoming another fiasco. The 1692 trials did more damage to the Church than any good accomplished, even with the purging of witches. But there are secret ceremonies and functions for our church to follow. With your blessing, naturally." He nodded to the judge. "We could hold the trial, convict the witch, and execute privately. The subterfuge would protect our community and be done in His service. But without the unwanted attention."

The judge got up and paced the room while the other three sat in silence. He added a log to the fire, straightened his jacket, and coughed. "Tell me again what this latest letter included to convince all of you to take action. Can we trust this woman? She's not a Puritan. What's her name?"

"Portia Nottingham." Bartholomew leaned forward. "I trust her. She believes Alexander has unnatural aims upon her son. He has sinful longings in addition to the witchcraft. She wants to protect her son and became alarmed when she learned, by chance, of Alexander's magic. He tried to use sorcery against her. Goody Nottingham warned me about his actions because she thought he endangered me most of all. About a week ago, Alexander went to visit this young man in Boston. That's when she saw him use his magic in public. He controls certain elements, such as the wind."

Salem's pastor gasped. "As did his mother the night we went to apprehend her."

Bartholomew nodded. "Portia said Alexander created a raging tornado right in the middle of the street. He almost attacked her son, had she not gone out to ward off the sorcery with a firm prayer to God. She explained the episode in the letter."

Again, the judge paced. He stopped and ran his fingers along the back of his chair. "He's taken to doing the witchcraft in public? Bold. Even in these times when so many disbelieve."

"Indeed." Mather nodded with vigor. "Combined with these lustful thoughts for men, he poses a risk to the community. Why, the sodomy may speak to punishment more than the witchery. We're begging for your cooperation. The sheriff already refused, as did your colleague. The four of us can do this together, however, and perhaps round up a few friends. But time is of the essence. Before Lucifer strikes an even more bitter blow."

The judge sat back down. "You're sure we can capture him, enact the ceremony, and hang him without anyone's knowledge?"

All three nodded.

"And the body?"

"Will be taken care of." The Salem pastor reached over and grabbed the judge's arm. "With no one the wiser."

The silence unnerved Alexander. He fought a rising panic and stayed glued to the crack in the window.

"Then begin the preparations." The judge folded his arms across his chest. "We'll have no record kept of this deed. But we will protect this community."

Alexander had heard enough. He turned and ran as fast as he could out of Salem Village, deep into the woods, and then slumped against a tree. His uncle had sold him out. Alexander struggled to understand why he was bothered when he knew all along of the possibility. His uncle seemed painfully predictable, as did the men's entire plot.

Of course, Portia Nottingham provided the last bit of evidence.

Alexander removed the letter from his pocket, then illuminated his crystal to reread the missive.

She reported to his uncle and his colleagues about the incident in the street the other day. True, her report contained accurate facts about Alexander's actions. However, she embellished the story. His tornado stood no more than a few inches off the ground and never endangered anyone, let alone the man he loved. She perhaps prayed to some unseen force for help, but all Alexander remembered was her return use of magic against him.

The light went out and Alexander sat alone in the dark, contemplating his quandary, worse than any he had confronted before. He could combat his uncle's hatred. And as long as Crispin's care for him persisted, Portia had limited powers against him.

But the judge and those ministers told a different story. They had authority, the means to come after Alexander, and now the will to apprehend him. They had discussed execution, in secrecy, and with no attempt at a fair trial.

Alexander had always contemplated fleeing for his own happiness to a situation where he could more readily use his magic, away from the mill and his vile uncle, and, if lucky, closer to Crispin. Now he ruminated not whether he should run away or even how to create the best circumstances. No, he had to decide how to escape from Salem, with little delay, to save his life. He wondered if he would ever see Crispin again.

Certain problems presented themselves. Alexander had no future. He cursed himself for not taking these things more seriously in the past.

He had no money or valuables whatsoever. He had limited skills at any craft, to the point no one even wanted him aboard ship as a grunt. He could never settle anywhere else because, at best, he knew rudimentary farming he'd learned from his father.

Alexander closed his eyes and concentrated on the wind above the trees, softly blowing through the leaves. He rubbed the crystal between his fingers and felt the powerful presence of his mother, begging him to survive.

When he got up to return to the mill, he had restored his confidence. He could outmaneuver the bunch of stale old men. He would need to stop tuning out his uncle and pay more attention, but Alexander had no doubt over the next few days he would escape.

His life depended on it.

Alexander spied regularly on Bartholomew, the judge, and ministers. However, Alexander had now learned Mather carried a box used to enact magic, often to block Alexander's view of their meetings. Alexander had witnessed a myriad of hypocrisies in his life, but perhaps none as bold as the pious minister employing the same magic for which he accused others. This time, before Mather hid the proceedings, Alexander had ascertained they planned nothing specific against him as of yet. Otherwise, Alexander ignored Bartholomew, refused most tasks when ordered, and spent most of his time away from the mill in the woods, figuring out what to do and where to go.

He could no longer worry about his failed attempt to flee west and the fact no one wanted him aboard a ship. No matter, because the sea continued to call to him. Something deep within prodded him to move toward the water and a ship, to sail far away, never to return to this oppressive place. With nothing more than a hunch, he decided to become a sailor, regardless of what others thought about him. He fancied the sea. Such determination had suited him well in the past when he learned magic, fended for himself at the mill, and grew into a man on his own. It would surely work again.

Besides, in the back of his mind he kept hearing those conversations in the Boston bars about pirates. They seemed the type to accept anyone if Alexander could only find them.

He gathered his most treasured belongings in a small satchel. He possessed a few papers from his father and mother, wanting to keep a couple of personal effects, stole a knife and other supplies from his uncle, and even dared to pinch a few coins from Bartholomew's obvious hiding place under a rock. Though Bartholomew hardly knew how to run an efficient mill, he kept track of his wealth meticulously. Alexander had learned this fact the hard way when he'd previously took money as a treasure chest for his eventual escape. His uncle almost beat him to death until he'd forced the wind to push the man away. His uncle stopped attacking once Alexander returned the coins. Alexander never stole from him again, so he would need to flee before his uncle discovered the latest missing specie.

Alexander woke the next morning, grabbed his pack, and slipped outside as his uncle slept off another night of heavy drinking and cursing about Alexander's parents and Crispin. Last night, unlike other times, Alexander had stayed in the moment and listened, in case Bartholomew let something slip in his drunken stupor. Alexander learned nothing but remained vigilant lest the others come for him without his uncle's knowledge. No doubt they tolerated Bartholomew more than they respected him or needed him in this endeavor. If Alexander used his magic to escape into his more peaceful spiritual realm, he might give them a perfect opportunity. They could strike without warning, as they had against his mother, regardless of how much he watched them through the day. He often wondered how she failed to see them coming, if she indeed had the same power as Alexander. Without an answer, he wanted to be vigilant to protect himself.

Fearing people may know about his hiding place in the old abandoned house in the forest, even under those floorboards, Alexander took to concealing himself in more random places, including his parents' old barn. Their homestead lay in ruins. No one wanted to purchase land owned by a witch, and his father had an increasingly difficult time yielding enough from the land, anyway. Even he had contemplated moving before his death.

Alexander climbed up the ladder to the loft and nestled himself into the now moldy hay near the same spot where his mother held him in her arms before she died.

He had retreated to his childhood spot in hopes of clearing his mind. Within the week, he intended to run away for good. Yet he had to formulate a clearer plan. So far, he decided to head for the ocean. But where exactly? And how? Not Boston because Crispin might block him again. Alexander did not want to risk convincing Crispin to help him against his holy call to duty. With all due respect to their love, Alexander would not gamble his life on Crispin doing right by him.

Alexander wondered if he could get to a place such as New York City or another colony. And where could one hook up with a band of pirates?

As he started to despair at what to do, he heard an approaching horse.

Alexander reached for his mother's crystal but barely calmed himself enough to use its magic before the door creaked open below and someone strode into the barn. The boots seemed to pound upon the dirt floor and rocks. Alexander breathed a sigh of relief when he recognized the footfall.

"If you came to sentence me to death, you're too late. Others already condemned me to die," Alexander called down. He had not seen nor heard from Crispin since the incident with the tornado.

"Where are you?"

"Up here. My old haunting grounds. I've used this as a hiding spot my entire life. Only my mother knew about it."

Alexander heard Crispin walk to the ladder and begin to climb. When his head peaked above the floor, Crispin wrinkled his nose. "It smells of rot up here."

"All the better to ward off unwanted attention."

Crispin crawled over and soon sat, almost snuggling next to Alexander. Alexander leaned his head into Crispin's chest.

"I have something to tell you." Alexander fought the emotion welling within him, fighting the tears that threatened to burst forth as he spoke. Why did this man hold such sway over him?

"I came for the same reason." Crispin rested his chin on

Alexander's head. "Shall I go first?"

Alexander assented to give himself time before he announced he had to escape.

"I learned something inadvertently from my mother. She explained afterward you two have some feud. I don't know any more about your issues with her, and I don't want to get in the middle. But she's afraid of your magic and what you intend to do to her. Whatever you think of her, promise not to use any witchcraft against her. She can't harm you."

Alexander bit his tongue. Crispin had no idea about his mother's secret power, and getting into an argument with him would only make the inevitable parting worse. Although, he hardly wanted to acquiesce to the nonsense. "Did you come to tell me I don't like your mother? I already knew."

Crispin actually laughed. "No." Then he seemed to choke on a sob, so Alexander looked into his eyes, which started to tear.

"What?"

Crispin breathed deeply. "She admitted she dislikes you. I overheard her talking to your uncle and demanded the truth. Imagine my surprise to find him sitting in the parlor with her. I had gone for the day to organize provisions for the ship but returned unexpectedly because the captain had already completed much of the work himself. Bartholomew left rather abruptly after I came home, so I asked my mother what they were meeting about. Oh, Alexander."

Crispin wrapped both arms around Alexander and pulled him close. He leaned his head down and planted an impassioned kiss upon his lips. Tears streamed down both their faces.

"You don't have to tell me." Alexander ran his hand down Crispin's chest. "I know. I learned for myself."

"You know they intend to try you for witchcraft and secretly execute you?"

Alexander nodded.

"Then why are you still here?"

"I don't know where to go. I've been stealing supplies and wealth from my uncle for the journey. I figured I needed a better plan before I fled into the wilderness."

Crispin scrunched his brow. "I don't think you know everything."

Alexander tilted his head. "What?" His stomach turned in a knot of panic.

"The trial takes place two days hence. They intend to apprehend you, *after* the trial, and put you to death. You don't have time to plan. I came to warn you."

Crispin's news shocked Alexander. "I need to leave immediately. Can I have your horse? I can go to New York."

Crispin shook his head and stood. "No. I can't be implicated."

Alexander raged. "Of course, we wouldn't want you messed up with helping me. Or saving me. Why don't you execute me? Right here." Alexander jumped to his feet and jabbed a finger toward the floorboards. "Immediately. I think I'd rather die at the hands of my lover than the Puritan demigods."

Crispin got up, walked over, and clutched Alexander in both his hands. "Listen to me. If I gave you my horse, my mother would surely know I helped you. They could then interrogate me. What I'm trying to say is we have to get you away more cleanly. For your safety, as well as mine. We don't want them to know anything is amiss until after their trial when they can't find you."

Alexander relaxed in Crispin's grip. "Can't you use your connections? They don't have the right to execute me. This isn't a legal trial. Go to the governor."

"I can't." Crispin continued to hold Alexander. "They're doing this with or without royal sanction. I don't have time to use official channels."

"But I'm not an evil witch. You have to believe me."

"I do. I do." Crispin kissed Alexander again.

Despite the urgency, Alexander went limp in Crispin's arms. He wrapped his hands around Crispin's neck and pulled him into a deeper kiss. Soon they lay naked in the hay, and Alexander gave his body once more to the man he loved.

His mind drifted with every sense of pleasure to the thought he may never again experience this utter bliss and passion. One last time he felt Crispin deep inside him and climaxed to the rhythm of his lover's motion. They lay together for several minutes afterward.

Neither spoke as they dressed. Neither wanted to verbalize what they so feared.

Down in the barn again, Alexander peered into Crispin's eyes, desperate for some sign he would at least help him get away. "I don't have anyone but you. I realize I sound rather dramatic and sorrowful. I'm simply explaining they've trumped up extra legal charges against me: sorcery and cavorting with the devil. They intend to hang me like one of the witches from the past, to come after me as they did my mother. I can get out of this on my own, I think. But I might fare better with your assistance."

Alexander took several steps away, trying to break the emotional connection with physical distance in a futile attempt to protect his heart. He hated any feeling of dependence upon another person. Never in his life had he allowed such a thing, and he really didn't need emotional comfort. Unfortunately, he felt a longing toward Crispin.

Crispin stood rigid, the sailor returned, the duty set in his countenance. Yet a flicker of emotion lit his eyes. "I won't sit idly by and watch you die. I'll return tomorrow. Meet me here, in the morning. If you intend to go to New York, then I'll help you get there."

Alexander nodded.

"I must go." Crispin started toward the door.

"Crispin! Wait!"

Crispin turned around.

Alexander ran a speech through his mind, a pleading for Crispin to abandon his obligation and fiancé, his mother, and the Royal Navy, and flee with Alexander. But it would fall on deaf ears. Alexander choked back more tears, determined to meet Crispin's stoicism with his own.

"Whatever happens, thank you." Alexander took a deep breath. "I'll always remember our love."

Crispin pressed his lips tightly together. He stood even straighter, nodded, and turned to leave.

Alexander watched him walk out of the barn and, in a matter of seconds, heard the horse race away. He remained in the barn for several minutes, thinking of his father, then his mother, and finally Crispin. But he shed no more tears.

He thought to himself of all that he had survived. Losing Crispin would hurt, but Alexander had overcome much worse. If anything, their love gave him hope for a better future that somewhere, something out there would provide an improved life for him. He would survive.

Chapter Nine

Trial

19 June 1700

Salem, Massachusetts

ALEXANDER REFLECTED ON what he mistakenly learned moments ago. His enemies were gathering.

After Crispin rode away that morning, Alexander left his family's barn and spent the day in the woods, refining and preparing his magic for his escape the next day. He checked the supplies in his pack and decided he had no reason to return to the mill. He wandered around because he had nothing else to occupy his time.

As night fell, he found himself on the outskirts of Salem and saw

Bartholomew walking briskly down the road. Alexander followed Bartholomew until he entered an old meeting house, followed by the judge.

Alexander became alarmed. Something was amiss.

Next, Alexander spotted Reverend Mather walking down the road with his little chest. Before he could enact the spell, Alexander grabbed his crystal and spied into the meeting house. Portia Nottingham and the pastor already waited inside.

Alexander scrambled toward the back of the building, slowly opened the back door, and slipped into the shadows, away from their prying eyes but where he could hear them.

Soon enough, Reverend Mather entered, greeted everyone, and opened his mysterious box. After several minutes, he announced they were protected from Alexander's magic and could proceed. Alexander felt the crystal in his pocket shudder, as if the magic to see the present drained out of it.

The judge coughed. When he spoke, Alexander heard the edge in his voice. "We had the arrangements made for a trial in two days. We secured the location, including the execution spot. We can't be ready tonight. I realize we plan to thwart the governor's wishes, but we must follow some modicum of the law. I won't tolerate vigilantism."

"Goody Nottingham, tell him!" Alexander heard a chair creak and then someone rubbing their hands together.

"I trust you won't judge my son harshly for this. He means well. He has an unfortunate malady which leads him to try to save every rotten soul he passes. He's taken to trying to save Alexander, for God, of course, no matter how useless the endeavor. I've told him a number of times we lost the boy to Satan a long time ago."

"Get to the matter at hand," the judge instructed.

"I learned from my son about Alexander's plans to escape. He has some elaborate ruse he wouldn't even explain to Crispin. He leaves tomorrow."

"Which means the trial must take place immediately." Alexander heard Reverend Mather speak. Alexander peeked around the corner to watch. Mather sat beside the judge and placed a hand on his forearm. "Surely you see the urgency?"

A silence fell over the room as the judge sat in contemplation. Alexander feared they might hear his own breathing in the complete quiet. The judge glanced at each of them, then tapped his fingers on the arm of the chair. Finally, he got up and rearranged the furniture, then repositioned the various people around the room.

Alexander wondered why no one questioned this behavior until he recognized the basic arrangements of a courtroom.

The judge even pulled a gavel out of his robe. "This court is now in session." *Whack.* "Marshall?"

Salem's pastor stepped forward, apparently playing the role of either sheriff or prosecuting attorney or both. "Your Honor, before the court we have the case of Alexander MacBeth, charged with the high crime against humanity of witchcraft. And, if we fail to act upon this knowledge, it threatens God's wrath upon us all. God will not tolerate sin in our midst."

Alexander hardly believed his eyes as the farce of a trial continued. They read a whole list of alleged crimes, all concocted. He never saw a witch's familiar in his life, let alone a little yellow bird flying around the mill and pecking at his uncle upon his command. He never denounced God publicly, nor did he call forth demons to torment Crispin or his mother.

The judge and Reverend Mather sat stoically through the proceedings. Uncle Bartholomew and Portia Nottingham served as the witnesses, while the good pastor played all other parts in this drama except judge.

With little fanfare, the trial wound down after the prosecution rested its case. No one asked for the defense to step forward. The judge glanced through a variety of documents and then turned his attention to Reverend Mather.

"Reverend Mather, can you verify for the court the religious danger of these accusations and sanctify the validity of the evidence from your clerical point of view?"

Mather cleared his throat. "The evidence weighs heavily against the accused. He practiced witchcraft in the open. He torments his relatives. According to all available sources, he displays several signs of cavorting with the devil. The Church recognizes the facts presented at this trial as valid religious proof of his witchery, and therefore his danger to the community. If I might add, the Royal Governor may have put an end to the witchcraft trials as a legal means of defending ourselves in 1693. He hardly expelled Satan from our midst."

Again, the judge pondered in complete silence. With another hard *whack*, he smashed his gavel upon the desk. "For the high crime of witchcraft, I therefore sentence Alexander MacBeth to death, to be administered at once."

Alexander fought back a whimper of dread. Could this really happen? Could they do this to him? Even if they determined to defy Colonial law and the edicts of the Royal Governor, what of their ethical beings? Alexander suspected his uncle and Portia had no such morality within even an ounce of their soul. But these other men paraded about as righteous figures in the community and God's representatives on earth.

Alexander pressed back against the wall and deep into the shadow, afraid someone may decide to exit through the back door and see him. He held his breath for fear of making the least sound.

After hearing them shuffle about and formally bid adieu to Portia, Alexander grew worried at the stillness in the room. He peeked around again and saw the men staring down at Reverend Mather's open chest.

With wild eyes, Mather shot his head up and stared at Alexander. "There!"

The four men launched across the room toward Alexander, running into each other and toppling over chairs along the way.

Alexander, younger and sprier than the portly gentlemen in his pursuit, got to the door before they reached him. He burst outside and hit the ground running. He sped into the woods, but too quickly, for he missed seeing the branch sticking out of the ground and fell flat on his face.

Alexander glanced back and saw his uncle and the judge bearing down on him, with the pastors struggling to catch up from behind.

Without having to think, Alexander commanded the wind as he scrambled back to his feet. Before they got to him, a large branch came crashing down, barely missing their heads.

Alexander again ran through the forest but heard their continued chase behind him by the cracking of sticks and crunching of leaves. He lurched to a stop, spun around, and called forth his power, remembering the times he practiced in these very woods. The wind whirled around him and the trees swayed back and forth as if a mighty hurricane invaded the area.

Alexander gazed straight ahead, and the four men caught up to him but stopped, Bartholomew and the Salem pastor with eyes wide with fear. Even Reverend Mather stepped back with his arms up in surrender.

Wanting to frighten them away, Alexander glared in their direction and affected how he thought a demon might appear before killing them. He raised his arms high in the air, then twisted them around in front of himself.

No small tornado appeared this time. A blackened swirl of cloud, wind, and debris spun in front of him and moved toward the self-righteous fools. They ducked and ran the other way as the tornado pursued them.

Alexander had no idea if the tornado injured or killed any of them because he took off deeper into the forest. He ran as fast as possible but more under control so as not to fall.

The environment around him calmed the farther away from Salem he got. The night sky reappeared above him, with the stars twinkling down. The wind abated into a tranquil night in Massachusetts.

When he could run no more, Alexander stopped and leaned

against a tree, waiting for his heavy breathing to subside. After several minutes he regained the energy to slump down along the tree and land on his butt.

He had almost fallen asleep from exhaustion, when his head fell forward too quickly, and he woke with a start. He sat right in the open, vulnerable to anyone who searched for him. No doubt those fools would come after him again, and next time with Reverend Mather's magic at their disposal. Alexander willed himself to continue moving.

He struck into the wilderness, paying no attention to his direction.

The night grew even darker, and Alexander became disoriented. When at last he had to rest or fall over where he walked, Alexander spied a hollowed out tree trunk laying on the ground, big enough to house even a man. He forced himself to ignore the stench of other animals that had used this log as their shelter and latrine, and refused to acknowledge, in his own mind, the bugs and vermin that would soon crawl over his body.

He shut his eyes tightly and drifted away to sleep and to his imaginary place where he could command the situation. Instead of a log in the middle of the forest, and running from the authorities who wished him dead, Alexander found himself in a warm bed snuggled next to Crispin. He could feel Crispin's hard stomach pressed against his back, his muscular arms wrapped around his chest.

He could worry about going into hiding and escape in the morning. For now, he must replenish his energy. No better way existed than in this fantasy realm where he lay as Crispin's lover, Crispin's one and only duty in life to protect and love Alexander in return.

Chapter Ten

Confrontation

28 June 1700

Massachusetts Wilderness

ALEXANDER'S EVERY MUSCLE ached when he woke from beneath the pile of leaves and rocks he used to hide himself through the night. For ten days he had run around the Massachusetts wilderness between Salem and Boston, concealing himself from others and pillaging to survive.

He never saw any of the men he assumed searched for him but remained vigilant. His glances into the present to find them yielded little results or showed them simply milling about Salem.

At least his sore muscles diverted his attention from the extreme hunger that weakened him further every day. He stayed alive on the few nuts and berries he scavenged and by drinking from any source of running water he passed. He contemplated hunting but worried a cooking fire might expose him.

Twice, he nearly came into contact with other humans, but he fled the other way and averted them. His power to see the present kept him safest, for he could spy upon anyone approaching and find abandoned areas in which to hide. He worried about the nights when he went to sleep, however.

He knew he remained too close to those who had sentenced him to death. He could never reach New York on foot or anywhere else safe without better transportation. He almost stole a horse, figuring saving his life outweighed the economic loss for the farmer, until the man appeared. Alexander lost his nerve and left.

For the last ten days, mere survival took up his every waking moment. He spent too much time climbing into trees and disappearing mentally into his magical realms. He lost track of reality so he could mentally and physically recover from his shock.

He checked a variety of times to see if Crispin would come for him but saw an argument between Crispin and his mother the day after the trial and thwarted execution. He assumed she told him what happened, or at least her version, so Crispin gave up on coming for him.

However, his situation had become clearer over the last couple of days. Alexander figured out his first and second course of action. No more drifting away into invented worlds within his mind. He hatched an official escape plan.

He would first try to sneak into Boston and meet Crispin away from his home and mother. Perhaps he could steal a horse and head to New York. Failing that, whether because he could never find Crispin alone or because Crispin refused, Alexander would push his way onto a ship, either as a known sailor or a stowaway. The sea beaconed once more.

Alexander meandered through the forest toward Boston, sure of his direction, both literally and figuratively. He kept to the shadows and away from the roads, going so far as to climb a tree once when he heard voices nearby. The two men laughed and bumped into each other as they traveled farther into the woods. Alexander wondered why they came into the woods alone. Did they have a relationship like his with Crispin and want to get away from prying eyes? When they disappeared, Alexander climbed back down and continued on his way.

Alexander could almost hear the bustling activity of Boston when he stopped to pull out his mother's crystal. He peered into the glass, watching as the stone disappeared and the tiny city of Boston materialized before him as if he glanced down from the heavens. He willed the scene to descend toward the residential area of Boston where the upper sorts resided, then move over to the street and above Crispin's house. Crispin sat alone in his office, reading some book but tapping his foot against the floor.

"You can put that down."

Alexander jerked up, scared to death. He dropped the crystal and stepped back when he saw Portia glaring at him from five feet away.

How had she arrived without him knowing?

"You're not the only one watching the present. I've known every move you made since you escaped your sentence. Clever of you to hide in the meeting house to spy on us. And you generated an impressive storm. I noticed you saved the theatrics for after I left."

Alexander kept his eyes on her but leaned down and picked up the crystal, before placing it carefully back in his pocket. "You've been spying on me?"

"Of course." Portia rolled her eyes. "Do you think me a fool?"

"On many counts, yes. But not in regard to using your magic for ill means."

Portia's smile vanished. "It's hardly ill means to monitor the doings of a convicted witch who means to imperil my son in his vile ways."

"I don't know what you mean." Alexander stood straighter, preparing to use his magic to defend himself if necessary. True, Portia controlled her own witchcraft, but Alexander had confidence in his ability to protect himself. Her inner rage made her dangerous, but also careless.

Portia stepped closer until she stood eye to eye with Alexander. Her loathing oozed off her skin. "Like you, I can see what happens in this world around us. You think you possess a unique gift. And you make me sick." She poked Alexander in the stomach. "The way you manipulated Crispin into kissing you, another man. Risking my family fortune if someone ever caught you in the seduction. I've seen where you place your lips. I've experienced how much you enjoy when Crispin treats you as a woman. I'll do anything to defend him from your sorcery."

Alexander stepped away. "You twist reality to match a story of your own making. You failed to add how much he enjoys me and instigates our sex. I have no power to make him want me. The longing is his."

"Hold your tongue. You should flee while you still can. Alone."

"Because you can't stand the thought he cares for me more than you? Or because he so defies you with the way he worships my bum?"

Portia slapped Alexander across the face, but he smiled in return.

"You're smug. You may want to reconsider your attitude." Portia walked a short distance away, leaning over to pick a flower. She twirled the blossom in her fingers for a moment before taking the petals and smashing them between her thumb and index finger. "I'm willing to let you escape, in exchange for a promise to never again contact or see my son."

Alexander scrunched his brow. He contemplated accepting the offer since he doubted he could get Crispin to go with him anyway. However, if but a remote chance, could he give up so easily on him? And how could he trust a thing Portia said? That settled the matter.

"You won't be able to control him forever. If not me, he'll find someone else. You found Caroline, but she'll never satisfy him."

"Haven't you learned yet he never goes against my will? He does my bidding. Think how easily I thwarted you. After I spied upon your little plan for him to assist your escape, all I had to do was explain to him they spotted you fleeing. He thinks you left without waiting for him to help."

"But you told the judges he informed you of my plans."

Portia arched an eyebrow. "My lying to those fools surprises you?"

Alexander's heart dropped. She did have the upper hand with Crispin because of her lie. Crispin thought he escaped alone? Maybe this made their parting easier. Except, Alexander would never yield so easily to this woman.

"Whether I go or not, you can't win," he repeated his assertion. "For how long and in how many ways can you protect him? You're trying to make him into something of your own creation, not the man he would become. You've imprisoned him. But I see more in him than a puppet to your machinations. I see a man waiting to assert himself. You'll eventually lose."

The corner of Portia's mouth lifted slightly. "I always win. Besides, I have the law on my side, now more than ever. No more silly underground trials and convictions. No more trifling Puritans with their religious ways and fears of witches."

Alexander hesitated.

"Shall I explain?" She arched a brow.

He nodded.

"Careless of you, like your mother, unable to conceal your magic from the world. Unable to understand how to survive and at the same time use your power to your advantage. Your last tornado killed the judge. Your uncle lies an invalid in his bed. And the Salem pastor lost his ability to speak, when a branch smashed into half of his face. Unfortunately for you, Reverend Mather survived intact. He witnessed the whole affair. To be sure, and again unlike you, he kept the witchcraft and sorcery to himself. But it took little imagination to come up with the story of your beating your uncle senseless, followed by the minister, and to concoct a story you murdered the judge when he came to apprehend you for the crimes. Even Crispin will see and believe the warrant for your arrest on the charge of murder."

Portia walked toward him with her arms outstretched. A crackle of lightning flickered between her fingers. She raised her arms in the air. A bolt struck Alexander, who fell to the ground with a hard thump.

The vines in the dirt came to life and spun around Alexander's legs and arms, tying him to the ground. Alexander sat passively, stunned but unafraid. His mother and experience had taught him that calm and careful thought prevailed, not panic.

Portia leered from above. "Let me explain something to you." She knelt in front of Alexander. "Crispin turned eleven when his father caught him and another boy in the attic, doing something unseemly with each other. He beat the other boy senseless while shoving Crispin off and punching him in the face. By the time I got to the attic, the young man had died. And Crispin's father had turned to do the same to him. I flung myself between them, using my magic to incapacitate my husband while telling Crispin to run. Once Crispin fled down the stairs, I unleashed my full fury and killed my spouse."

Portia stood up. "Do you understand? By the end of the day, Crispin's father died of a tragic accident when a beam broke loose in the attic and crashed down upon him. Authorities found the other boy in a back alley of Boston, the apparent victim of a fight or robbery gone bad. And Crispin was safe."

She walked behind Alexander and again knelt, whispering so close her lips brushed against his ear. "Crispin's one vice I can't get out of him, despite his obedience and love for me because I'm his mother and saved his life, is assertive young men who seduce him. If I killed his father and allowed the death of a ten-year-old boy to protect him, what do you think I'd do to you?"

Alexander sat stoically through this tale. As predicted, and as his mother promised, the answer came to him as he relaxed and let his mind contemplate. These roots had healing elements. The mere thought of those properties turned them into a salve, and his chains disappeared.

Alexander jumped away from Portia, who stood back up. She tilted her head and clapped. "Wonderful! Finally, a worthy adversary."

When her hands went back in the air, Alexander fled. Not on foot, but with the wind. A gust came swooping down through the trees and lifted him several feet off the ground. As if flying with the birds, Alexander moved through the air and landed several hundred yards away.

He took out his crystal to spy upon her, but she had vanished. He gazed back to Boston and saw Crispin wandering through his home, calling for his mother.

Portia Nottingham materialized in her bedroom, opening the door and calling back to her son. Before she went into the hallway, she looked straight into the air as if she could see Alexander and winked at him.

Chapter Eleven

Suicide

28 June 1700

Boston, Massachusetts

ALEXANDER SEETHED AT Portia after she winked at him from the confines of her bedroom. She claimed to love her son and to protect him and his legacy. Except, she had jailed him in a life of propriety and doing her bidding. Crispin stood no chance against her.

Yet Alexander could spend little time reflecting upon Crispin's fate if his love could never challenge her or his sense of obligation. Alexander even dismissed his combat against Portia Nottingham. In all her stories, the most important detail for Alexander came in the news he had murdered a judge. Regardless of his real intent, Reverend Mather held the power there. Alexander no longer fled from hysterical Puritans but from the King's Office.

None of this news altered his original plan. Portia or not, he wanted to give Crispin one last chance before he headed out to sea. He bided his time until evening, when Crispin and his mother left in a carriage. He watched them travel toward Caroline's house for a tranquil dinner with the fiancé and her parents.

Taking his opportunity, and assuming Portia focused her attention on those assembled around her, Alexander concealed himself in Crispin's bedroom. He had never been inside there before, except by spying through the crystal from afar. Portia had clearly decorated the room as another one in the house, nothing personal to Crispin, or to give away the sense of the man who resided there.

Alexander opened a drawer and pulled out one of Crispin's shirts. He held the cloth to his face, smelling the man's essence even on this clean garment. He decided to place the item in his pack as a memento. He paused when he saw on a dresser the little figure of a bunny he had carved as a gift for Crispin not long after they first met.

Alexander occupied himself for a while with such things until he sat in the darkened corner to wait. The crystal indicated a slow dinner, and so Alexander had time before Crispin's return. He tried to fight off the fatigue but fell asleep.

Alexander jumped to his feet when a lantern illuminated the room. His heart sank when he spotted Portia standing in the doorway, not Crispin. She walked into the room and set the glass lantern on a dresser. Backlit, she appeared more a demon than ever before.

"Crispin had to check on his ship. Or at least he uses the excuse to get away from time to time. I allow the subterfuge. If I controlled him too much, he might rebel, which is why I allowed him his dalliances with you for so long. You see, I do understand him. But I never guessed your power. I figured you out too late."

"Because you're too confident. You make mistakes, like you did earlier today when I got away."

Portia nodded. "Clever of you. I admit."

"So what's your plan? To kill me in his bedroom and leave the body as a token?"

Portia walked to the window and peered down at the yard below. When she turned around, her countenance had darkened completely. "Because we fight for my son's soul, I understand why you despise me. I appreciate your power and strong will, despite how much I hate you. I did indeed underestimate you. See, I thought perhaps a fling with a nobody from Salem might sate his appetite but otherwise keep him under control. And he would have continued that way of life if not for you. You had to push for more. You had to seek what you desired." She shook her head. "You act aloof and disengaged. In truth, you're calculated and devious. However, your weakness will always be the moral compass that guides too many of your decisions."

"Toward goodness?" Alexander laughed.

"Call your aims what you will. But a real witch would have killed his uncle and taken over the mill, or sold it and fled."

"You know I've killed. I have no qualms there."

Portia held up her finger to stop him. "No. You killed to save your own life. The murder came as incidental, not intentional. The same hesitation led you to foolishly resist our fight to the death, which will inevitably come."

"You think murdering is a virtue?"

Portia shook her head. "I consider such outcomes a reality of life. I'd do anything to protect Crispin."

Alexander shook his head in return. "That's not what you're doing or what you want. You have some other motive. You mask your desires, perhaps even from yourself. Forgive my bluntness to a lady, but your soul is rotten."

Portia nodded. "And so I've made a decision. Only a worthy opponent could bring me to this. It's a sign of respect to you, see?"

"What are you talking about?"

Alexander heard a horse gallop to the house and suspected Crispin had returned.

"This." Portia swept her arms out in front of her. "Our final battle. There's one way to ensure my victory."

The front door creaked open from far away.

Alexander stared at Portia Nottingham, confused but ready to spring into action to protect himself or Crispin.

Yet the force of the wind surprised him. Someone else controlled the elements, not Alexander.

Too late, Alexander understood her move. A gale force crashed through the doorway and shoved furniture in her direction. Objects blew through the air and pummeled her. As Alexander enchanted a counterwind, a vase knocked her in the head. She closed her eyes and appeared more tranquil than ever before as the blast of air sent her body crashing through the window.

Alexander raced over and peered below to see Portia Nottingham's dead body lying in the dirt next to a bed of roses beneath her son's window. At the same moment, he heard those footsteps pounding up the stairs and marching down the hall.

Alexander spun around to see Crispin enter the doorway, an expression of complete surprise and then anger on his face.

"Let me explain." Alexander held up his hands and moved to stand between Crispin and the broken glass.

"Explain what?" Crispin said curtly. He brushed by Alexander and headed for the window. His eyes went wide when he looked down and saw his mother. Crispin whipped his head toward Alexander and stared daggers through him. "What have you done?" he spat before pressing his lips together.

"I didn't do anything." Alexander barely whispered as he pointed toward Portia.

"You and your uncontrolled magic." Crispin spun away and hurried out of the room.

Alexander followed, struggling to keep up with Crispin's longer stride. They ran through the hallway and down the stairs, Crispin taking them two at a time. He stormed through the first floor, out a back door, and Alexander spotted him stoop over and pull his mother into his arms.

Tears streamed down Crispin's face when Alexander reached

him, Crispin sitting on the grass with the limp body in his arms. "You're a wretched beast. How many times did I plead with you to stop the witchcraft? I thought your magic endangered you too much. Clearly, I should have worried about other people more. Why? Why did you do this to her?"

Alexander stood several feet away. "I didn't," he whispered.

"What?"

"I didn't." Alexander spoke louder. "She killed herself. Crispin, listen to me. Not everything is as it seems. There are things about your mother you never knew. Please, believe me. I'd never do anything to hurt you. She hated me because I loved you. And she did this to herself to get back at me."

Crispin hesitated. He brushed hair out of his mother's face. For the first time, Alexander noticed the trickle of blood coming out of her mouth, and the other wounds leaking a crimson stain over Crispin's white shirt.

Crispin shook his head. "She would never commit suicide. She wouldn't just leave me."

"She was a witch." Alexander's words came out more coldly than he intended.

Crispin scowled at Alexander. Then he gently laid his mother's body on the ground and stood. He stalked over to Alexander and glared as he jabbed a finger toward his window.

"I know you command the wind. I've seen you practice. You created a small tornado right in the middle of the street. I recognize the signs. I know who could manifest the tornado to whip through my bedroom, destroying the place. I can see the same wind pushed my mother to her death."

Alexander stepped back a few feet. "Someday, maybe you'll learn the truth."

Crispin began to speak when the sounds of a carriage halting in front of the house diverted his attention. Seconds later, a beautiful woman came around the corner. She wore a stunning dress, carried herself with exquisite posture, and a servant followed her. Her blue eyes glistened as she smiled when she spotted Crispin. Her curly blonde hair fell gently upon her shoulder.

"Crispin," the woman said. "You forgot your walking stick. I brought it as a chance for a moment alone—"

Caroline choked on her words when she noticed Alexander standing nearby. Thus Alexander came face-to-face with his nemesis for Crispin's heart. Could the night grow any worse? Caroline took a step forward, but Crispin lurched ahead and turned her away. Too late, however. She gasped when she saw Portia Nottingham's body lying on the ground.

"There's been a terrible accident, my dear." Crispin moved her away, but Alexander stayed rooted to his spot. "Don't move," Crispin spat at Alexander and pointed to him as he continued to guide Caroline toward the front yard.

Alexander wondered why he obeyed. Perhaps he should take his chance and run. Portia had won, after all. Yet Crispin told Caroline an accident took place, not a murder. Should Alexander have hope?

A few minutes later, Alexander heard the cadence that at one time had made him swoon. Crispin marched around the corner and back to Alexander. Despite Alexander's slight hope, Crispin remained as angry as before.

"I should have you arrested. I heard today you also murdered a judge?"

Alexander slumped over and cast his head to the ground. "They were coming to execute me."

"So you admit you murdered them?"

"I inadvertently killed the judge, trying to protect myself since no one else would. I had nothing to do with her." Alexander pointed toward Crispin's mother.

"Her? Did you say *her*? She happens to be my mother." Crispin was shouting when he finished speaking, then started crying. "Get away. Just get way." He pointed toward the street.

Alexander stepped forward and pulled Crispin into his arms. Despite his words, Crispin went limp. Alexander held him for a long moment before Crispin pulled away.

"Someone may see. And I have more obligations now than ever before to this family's legacy and to Caroline. To my mother's memory. I can't continue to see the man who killed her." Crispin folded his arms in front of his chest. "You should go."

"You'll allow me to leave?"

Crispin nodded.

"I don't understand."

"Neither do I." Crispin continued to stare at Alexander, though not with the same hostility.

Alexander turned to leave. He thought of asking for a horse or assistance but had already pushed things too far. Still, he paused. Impulsively, he turned around and hurried back to Crispin, who remained planted in place.

"I love you. If you ever discover the truth or find me again, remember how much I love you." Alexander stood on his tiptoes and planted a kiss on Crispin's lips.

Did Crispin almost return the kiss?

A moment later Alexander ran down the back alley and away from Boston to return to hiding.

III: A Witch's Flight

Chapter Twelve

A Ship Arrives

1 July 1700

Massachusetts Coast and Woods

THUNDER CRACKLED. NATURE conspired with Alexander over the last three days to conceal him from the many authorities now in pursuit. Since accidentally killing the judge and maiming a minister and his uncle, the forces against him had moved from an underground and extra-legal band of Puritans to the full backing of the Royal Governor for the crime of murder.

He kept a close eye on his own surroundings and monitored what he could through his crystal. However, Reverend Mather worked to block his attempts to see the present and concealed what else he and the authorities were attempting. Fortunately, they appeared to possess no way to find Alexander.

Alexander welcomed the three days of rain and storms because most people remained hidden indoors, out of the elements. The saturation never bothered him, because he could hide here and there, finding a dry place to sleep through the night, but otherwise had at his disposal a more powerful wind than normal. The rain also helped to cool him amidst the steamy July temperatures.

Alexander ventured around both the urban setting of Boston and the more desolate countryside.

The one time a soldier spotted him in Boston and raised the alarm, Alexander sprinted away. Once around a corner and a safe distance from them, he generated a storm. The torrent of rain concealed him from the pursuers, who eventually gave up and sought shelter from the large hail crashing down upon them.

For his part, Alexander remained on the other side of the storm, a thin line separating him from his creation and those who wished him harm.

Another time he blew over the cart of a farmer who spied him in a tree and aimed a musket in his direction. The man ordered Alexander to come down because he trespassed upon his property. Alexander could not even see the man's face, with his hat pulled down low, dripping with rain. He could not tell if the guy wanted him off the property, recognized him as a fugitive, or meant to hurt him.

With one spell, Alexander called forth a gust of wind to carry him out of the tree to another one close by while also toppling the cart and the farmer with it.

As the man cursed, searched the sky for Alexander, and then took to repairing the mess in front of him, Alexander made his escape.

What intrigued Alexander during the storm came from the crystal's vision of the nearby coast. A sloop had arrived, brazenly heading toward Massachusetts despite the elements. When most ships stayed out to sea and away from the possibility of a shipwreck upon the rocks, this one came closer. More puzzling, it stopped short of any port and anchored.

Alexander barely saw the various figures board the row boats and head toward the shore. Strange how they sought to alight upon this desolate and rocky shoreline, so far from either the Salem or Boston port.

Even more interesting, the crystal insisted upon showing Alexander one particular figure. Though too far away to see his features, he seemed to command this bunch. Alexander typically told the magic what he wanted to see. Why did his sorcery change course and present this man to Alexander? Why had the witchcraft taken control? Whatever the reason, Alexander trusted the message. He paid close attention and wondered if this man and his ship offered his rescue.

Alexander returned to his wooded shelter and set up a small camp for the night. He secured his pack under an evergreen, out of the rain, and even built a tiny fire for the rabbit he caught earlier. He doubted anyone would venture out as the storm intensified and lightning flashed.

The meat, nuts, and berries filled him more than he had felt in weeks. He rested against a tree, a sense of confidence sweeping over him. His crystal glowed by his side. He picked it up to see the same vague scenes as before. The ship, too close to the shore during this tempest, the row boats secured on land, and the people moving about in the shadows, like himself.

Again without his bidding, the crystal zoomed in on the taller of the figures, who now sat with them under the trees, laughing and passing around a jug. A band of men who would frighten anyone else in the Massachusetts Bay Colony called to Alexander. The one, in particular, seemed to stare at Alexander through the crystal with amazing blue eyes and a handsome face. He fell asleep, excited to learn more about these men in the morning.

Alexander spent the next day watching the boat and shadowy figures disembark in an unorthodox manner upon the shore. The storms abated, bringing the hot July sun beating down and drying up the landscape. In monitoring them, Alexander assumed a few of the mysterious band snuck to Boston, others toward Salem, and most scattered about the woods to scavenge and steal supplies. The whole thing intrigued Alexander.

As he moved toward these sailors this morning, a Colonial search party took up camp between him and the shoreline. Alexander knew these men hunted for him, so he moved away lest they find their prey. He noticed they also came close to seeing these other men who hid as swiftly from them as did Alexander.

Reverend Mather rode into the midst of the official searchers as Alexander spied upon them through his crystal. The pastor tipped his hat and conversed a short time before moving on. Alexander thought he spied Crispin among them but remained true to his promise not to search for his former lover.

He worried the sailors might depart before he could meet them but watched closely and knew several milled about, two of them way over in Boston. He doubted they would leave anyone behind, so he would monitor and not panic about getting to them unless they headed toward the boats.

Between watching the pirates and scrutinizing the men hunting for him, Alexander never allowed himself to drift away or contemplate life. The moment had come for him to end in either liberation or death.

His surveillance and need to hide brought him to shelter in an old barn left to rot. Alexander remembered its story well, once told by his father as they traveled through the countryside. Even before his father's time, one of the first Indian attacks came at this very location. They stormed a farm, killed a man and his three sons, then captured two daughters and the wife.

The early settlers thereafter formed tighter communities and left this place to decay. Strange, the close proximity of the old farm to Salem and Boston, yet the utter and complete isolation in the event of an attack.

The Royal Governor's men had combed this area already. They'd searched every inch of this barn but found nothing, not surprising, given how Alexander had never been here since the day with his father. Once they departed, he felt safe to climb into its rafters and watch the events from here.

Alexander's crystal glowed if something required his attention, while at other times he watched various people or events for lack of anything better to do. Keeping close to the crystal gave him plenty of time to decide his response when one member of the governor's search party broke from the rest and headed toward the barn.

Alexander allowed his heart a weakened moment. He stayed put.

Soon footsteps approached the barn, pushing through the brush and hitting the ground so loudly Alexander could hear the boots hit the hardened soil.

Alexander looked down upon the erect figure below as he scanned the barn. "I assume you were watching us. I know you well enough, and your power, to double back to find you. What I'm saying is if I intended to capture or harm you, I would not have come alone. Alexander? Come out."

Alexander made a commotion to signal his presence and climbed down the ladder. His emotions swayed back and forth, from realizing the very bad idea to see Crispin to wanting to fall into his arms.

They stood several feet apart, staring awkwardly at each other.

Crispin cleared his throat. "Because I know you best, they put me in command of the search for you. I have a number of soldiers at my behest. To make appearances, I'll have them scour this region for you for two more days. Two days hence, I'll declare we didn't find you and move us to a new area. Once we go, you must flee. Get away from Salem and Boston. Remove yourself from this colony. Do you understand?"

Alexander nodded. "I intended to do as much."

"Yet you remain here." Crispin stepped forward again but stopped himself. "Do you have a better plan? Where will you go?"

Alexander paused before answering. He thought of telling Crispin about the men he would approach about joining their expedition. But Alexander remembered their conversation about Crispin's next call of duty. A new act, to hunt more decidedly for pirates and execute them on the spot at sea. Alexander had no idea how his presence on such a ship would play out in Crispin's eternal battle between what he wanted and the duty that bound him. Better to keep his intended plans from Crispin.

"I know my destination and means of escape. I don't want to place you in the awkward position of knowing, should they suspect anything of you. I'll be gone. I can watch and get away as soon as you clear your minions out."

Crispin smiled. "Minions. You have no respect for anything."

"That's not true." Alexander stepped closer but, like Crispin, kept a safe distance. "I don't respect arbitrary authority, or most people, for that matter."

Crispin laughed aloud and nodded.

"I'm surprised you came to me." Alexander shifted back. "Or, I'm surprised you didn't want to apprehend me." He almost added "because you think I murdered your mother" but even he avoided going too far.

"And so I would have at one point."

Alexander tilted his head and scrunched his brow. "But not now?"

"Now? I'm torn." Crispin rubbed his hands across his face and looked up to the hole filled barn roof for guidance. "I went through my mother's possessions. Papers, family heirlooms, everything. I found certain items very confusing."

Alexander smiled, despite the situation. "I should imagine a women's undergarments would confound most men. Most especially us."

"Indeed." Crispin smiled for but a second before his thoughts troubled him again. "Listen, this is very awkward. I want to tell you the truth. And the truth is I don't know what to believe or think anymore."

"What did you find?"

"Evidence to put my mother's story in doubt and give credence to what you said. I can't make it all out, and she only left bits and pieces. I destroyed every one of them. She at least dabbled in witchcraft."

Alexander allowed himself a smile. Portia, careless? After her admonishing of him?

Crispin shook his head, wiping away Alexander's smile. "I didn't necessarily figure everything out. I have no doubt this witchcraft had something to do with your feud with her. But why would she kill herself? And the wind. Only you could command the wind. Then again, maybe you defended yourself? Maybe you told me the truth about her committing suicide? I don't know."

Alexander turned away and walked to an old plow. He ran his finger over the metal, unsure what to say or where else to go with the conversation. He decided to proceed with caution and move them toward their parting.

"Thank you, then, for coming to warn me and for giving me a chance to escape, even though you think I might have killed your mother. I didn't. I realize my words won't settle the matter for you. I feel the need to defend myself. I would never have done that to you, much as I wanted to get her out of the way."

"I was afraid you'd yell at me again." Crispin's eyes welled with tears, bringing the same to Alexander's.

Alexander shook his head and moved closer again.

"Anyway," Crispin straightened himself and wiped at a tear. "I came for two reasons. To make sure you fled for good this time. For your own protection, you understand?"

"And so I shall." Alexander nodded. "And the second reason?"

Crispin sighed. "A rather more delicate matter."

"We've dealt with as much before."

"True. I want to emphasize henceforth we must stop all activities together."

"Activities?" Alexander laughed. "I never thought of our affair in such a manner. I suspect my flight from here alone will accomplish your request without the need for discussion. Why torture ourselves over the matter?"

"I don't want to think you're watching me, hoping for something. Or you may suddenly appear somewhere and decide to start up again. Whether I ever figure out what really happened in my bedroom, you and I must go separate ways. I will be wed to Caroline and must devote myself to her. My obligation will also fall upon His Majesty's Navy. Our interaction imperils everything."

Alexander stepped back and mimicked the proper posture standing before him. He nodded sharply and even saluted. "I will obey."

"So flippant."

"I'm not the one permanently terminating us."

"Meaning?"

Alexander moved forward, close enough to reach up to Crispin and kiss him. "Meaning this. I always wanted you to fight for us. I dreamed at some point you could become the man I know lives inside of you, the one aching to lash out against the duty, obligations, and expectations. The one I fell in love with the first day in the chicken coop, who gave himself over to a kiss despite the danger. The one who created ruses to return time and again to me, and eventually to my bed."

As Alexander gazed into Crispin's eyes, he again saw the emotional fight raging within. Crispin nodded. He turned to leave, stopped, walked forward again, and then returned to the same spot right in front of Alexander. He started to reach out, then flopped both arms to his sides.

"I can't," Crispin whispered.

Alexander, too, lost all words. He began to lean forward, then caught himself. He determined to have the last word. Crispin usually did, simply by calling an end to their interaction and running away or ordering Alexander's silence. If they would never meet again, Alexander refused to depart with a whimper.

"Hear me out." Alexander watched until Crispin tilted his head. "Crispin, fight. Whether or not we ever see each other again, fight. Fight for yourself. Fight against all that would enslave you against your will. If you can't combat those forces for us, now, then at some point battle for yourself."

They stood in close proximity for what felt like hours before Crispin nodded, turned, and walked out the door. He stopped outside the barn but did not turn back.

Alexander admitted Crispin tore his heart out. All the bluster and promises to himself, all the denial halted in an instance. Alexander never doubted he would recover quickly, as always, but for this last second, he gave in to his desire and longing.

"Crispin! Wait! I'll always love you. No matter what. Even if I never see you again. Part of me will always hope you'll decide to fight for us."

Alexander's heart sank as Crispin walked away. He watched him go, hoping he might turn around or signal something in return to Alexander. Crispin did glance back once, his firm countenance written on his face, his lips pressed together.

Alexander stood rigidly until Crispin disappeared. Then he fell to the barn floor and wept like he had never cried before. For his mother and father. For his lost life. For the loss of Crispin.

When he got up, he glanced into his crystal to further monitor the situation and move forward. He was done mourning. He was moving toward survival.

Chapter Thirteen

A Pirate Captain

4 July 1700

Coastal Massachusetts

ALEXANDER SURPRISED EVEN himself with how rapidly his emotions evolved after the angst-ridden parting with Crispin. He expected more heartache and longing but found peace of mind.

Truth be told, he had said goodbye to Crispin long before, despite any lingering hopes to the contrary. He'd demonstrated such resilience his entire life. By the time he woke the next morning, he directed his attention to the future and grew excited at the prospect of leaving Massachusetts forever.

While Alexander monitored the comings and goings of the soldiers patrolling for him, Crispin stayed true to his word and kept them away from the barn and areas already investigated, allowing Alexander to keep most of his attention on the other men lurking in the same region.

He weighed his options and the danger involved in approaching them, realizing he might as well commit suicide as to just saunter into their midst and expect a warm welcome. He decided a one-on-one meeting suited him better, if he could isolate one of these gents and convince him to take Alexander to meet the rest of the crew. He recognized he was about to deal with pirates, an often vicious and deadly lot. Who else sneaked ashore, went different directions, and then pilfered for supplies? While he suspected as much, from the first time he spied their ship lurking along the coast, Alexander had no doubt whatsoever about their calling in life at this point.

And the more he watched them, the more he thought the captain gave him his best chance. The tall blond figure must lead them, as he appeared to command them about, and individuals often solicited him for directions. Alexander took to watching him the most: with his tall frame, his tanned muscles, obvious when he reached out his arm to point, the piercing blue eyes, and the long, wavy, blond hair sticking out from behind his hat. The captain ran his fingers through his hair when he removed his hat to wipe at sweat or glance around the landscape.

Perhaps Alexander could seduce him? He watched the captain and how his gaze trailed across the other men's bodies. He glanced at people as Alexander did, not out of curiosity but with an apparent lust.

But if not seduction, then Alexander would plead his case and hope a captain's authority would get him onto the boat as a new sailor.

Of course, any approach risked death. Pirates had gained a ruthless reputation for a reason. When they would take cover, Alexander would spot them readying to fight if caught. True, they hid in the shadows and avoided contact, but they also clutched knives and drew swords. Alexander would need to imperil his life in order to make first contact, which meant he must ready his witchcraft.

Thus arrived that fateful morning for Alexander's best chance at escape, the day Crispin had promised to remove his forces.

Right on schedule, Alexander pulled out his crystal and noticed the soldiers already scurried about their camps, doused breakfast fires, and packed up tents and supplies. A few times Crispin came into Alexander's view, ordering men around and monitoring their progress. Alexander never dwelled on him and instead moved his view to others, making sure no one remained behind. Before noon, they had gone. Alexander observed the entire company until the last person marched down the road toward Boston.

Alexander turned his attention back to the pirates, many of whom returned from parts unknown and their various missions, carrying goods and greeting each other. Each reconnaissance party first reported to the captain and then joined their fellow mates.

Alexander particularly scrutinized the comings and goings of the captain. He stayed near his men most of the time, especially the few who concealed and guarded the supplies before they put them on the long canoe and moved them to the main ship.

Though the captain did surveillance at regular intervals throughout the day, at least a couple of times he meandered off farther than usual, always by himself. He appeared to be daydreaming or enjoying peaceful moments taking time to sit upon a log or rock. When the captain moved off alone, Alexander studied this man even more.

He had an enticing presence that commanded a space, even with no other people around. He sat erect and walked with a swagger. Despite his torn and tattered clothing, especially the ripped up trousers, he held the air of an assertive leader and someone accustomed to success and getting what he wanted.

In preparation for his escape, Alexander positioned himself close enough to the pirates for contact with the captain when he next went on one of his lone walks. He set his pack down and took out his crystal. He had honed his skill to the point where, within seconds, the magic directed its attention to the pirate captain. He walked among the sailors and cavorted with them before pointing to something and heading off alone.

Alexander scrambled to his feet, grabbed his belongings, and hurried through the forest to get in line with the captain's path. He wanted to get there first, without making a sound to alert him to his presence. Alexander called forth a breeze and directed the wind toward the captain. It blew briskly enough to rustle the trees and create noise to cover Alexander.

Alexander reached a small clearing and threw his bag against a tree. He half lay on the ground, with the pack and tree supporting his back and head, where he untied his trousers and pulled them lower on his hips. He peered into the crystal and saw the captain approaching, turning his head side to side and listening but content he was alone in the woods.

Just before the captain got to him, Alexander whistled a hymn to signal his presence. He placed his crystal in hiding, so he could only guess at the captain's reaction. Unfortunately, he only knew Christian hymns and hoped such pious music would not scare his prey away.

When a twig cracked and the leaves moved nearby, Alexander pretended the sound startled him. He stopped whistling, jerked his head about, and feigned grabbing for his pants. "Who's there? Show yourself!"

Silence answered him.

Alexander looked at the source of sound and stared into those steely blue eyes.

Thus exposed, the captain strode into the clearing with his sword drawn. Alexander lay motionless, except to tilt his head, look the captain up and down, and smile.

The man squinted his eyes and sneered as he continued to move closer. Then he lunged forward and placed the sword at Alexander's neck as he hovered above.

Alexander flinched but remained calm. "You don't look like a Puritan." Alexander held the captain's gaze, the cold steel pressing against his neck. "Most of them don't carry swords or lurk about in the forest. Or hold a weapon to my throat."

The captain smiled, staring right at Alexander, but pressed his sword ever so slightly into Alexander's skin. Despite his predicament,

136 -   Damian Serbu

Alexander swooned. The man tilted his hat back with one hand but kept the sword in its position. His eyes glowed even more beautifully in person. His commanding presence might even outdo Crispin. His biceps bulged because of the tense pose, his strong legs flexed at the ready in front of Alexander's face. Then, he smirked.

"Truth be told," the captain said, "you don't strike me as much of a Puritan either. Not with those clothes. Not hiding here alone in the woods. Not with your drawers undone."

Alexander grinned despite the sword at his throat. "You caught me. An exile, hunted and wanted by those very Puritans."

"Wanted? For what?"

Alexander threw caution to the wind. This was his only chance to convince the captain.

"Murder. And sodomy."

Alexander smiled again when the captain raised his eyebrows in disbelief.

"I'm telling the truth. They tried to execute me for sodomy, and then I accidentally killed one of them to get away."

This time, the captain roared with laughter. He released the sword from Alexander's neck and stood tall, clutching the weapon as he stepped back but continued to chuckle.

"Aren't you worried about my being a killer?" Alexander stayed motionless. The captain may have stepped away but his body language remained tense.

"I have quite a few acquaintances who've had to murder here and there. Why, I myself have done so. Out of necessity, mind you, much like yourself." He pointed with his free hand at Alexander. The captain had lost a bit of his initial edge as he stood staring down at him. "You don't strike me, on first glance, as someone who belongs to those ranks."

"You don't believe me?" Alexander asked.

"How'd you do it?"

Alexander paused. How much should he reveal, and how fast? "My murdering is a long story, which happened while I ran away from the authorities."

The captain walked over and knelt in front of Alexander, the sword held tight in his hand, but at his side. "I've experienced stranger things in my life than a young beauty sitting in the woods by himself, on the run from religious folk. But this is certainly unique."

"I've had an odd life. I'm searching for a new direction. Maybe take to the sea."

The captain scratched his head. He sat down. "Explain yourself."

"Well, I can't stay around here, waiting for them to hang me. I've always fancied the sea. I figure maybe I could find a ship and make a new life. I've thought about becoming a pirate."

Alexander studied the captain's face during the long moment of silence. He knitted his brow but again his posture relaxed. He placed his sword on the ground, but his hand moved to the handle of a knife in his waistband.

"What might draw you to something as nasty as pirates?"

Alexander had gotten excited at their proximity, so he moved a bit to show himself. "For one thing, I hear pirates have different rules. A lot more freedom to act as they may."

"You talking about sodomy again?"

"Maybe. What do you know of such things?"

"Sodomy or pirates?" The captain laughed heartily, reached out, and placed a hand on Alexander's calf.

Excitement welled through Alexander. He closed his eyes to enjoy the moment, opening them to see the captain adjust himself below.

"I'm Alexander." Alexander moved a foot toward the captain and touched his leg. He stopped when he gripped the knife more tightly.

"Henri," he barely whispered and squinted at Alexander. "What's your game?"

Alexander blushed. "I don't know what you mean. Are you speaking pirate talk?"

"Why would you think I'm a pirate?"

This time Alexander laughed. He sat up, his face a few feet from Henri's. "I've been watching you. I know."

Henri clutched tighter at the knife and started to pull it out. Alexander reached over and touched his hand to stop him. He shook his head and smiled, then leaned forward and planted a kiss directly on the captain's lips.

When he pulled back, his face inches from the captain's, he lost himself in those magnificent blue eyes until Henri spoke.

"I'd like a moment with you. But any funny business, and I'll be the murderer today. Understood?"

As an answer, Alexander kissed him again.

The seduction worked as well, if not better, than all those years ago with Crispin in the chicken coop. Henri pushed harder into

Alexander and his tongue darted out. He let go of the knife. Alexander lay atop him. Alexander fumbled with Henri's clothes and released his manhood, wrapping his lips around a penis much smaller than Crispin's but tangy and sweet. He sucked until Henri tensed and released himself into Alexander's mouth.

Alexander fumbled at the same time to push his pants down the rest of the way. He held Henri's softening dick in his mouth as he pumped at himself until he sprayed all over the ground between them.

The instant they finished, Henri jumped back, did up his pants, grabbed his knife and sword, and turned to leave. Alexander almost panicked. Had he served as nothing more than a temporary whore and lost his advantage? Fortunately, during their encounter, he noticed an infected gash upon the captain's right leg.

"Wait!" Alexander implored.

Henri stopped and turned around.

"I can heal your wound." Alexander pointed to the man's leg.

"You're a doctor too? A murderer, sodomite, and a healer?"

Alexander shook his head. "A witch."

Henri stepped back toward Alexander.

"Please, sit next to me."

To his surprise, Henri sat on the ground and stretched out his leg near Alexander, though he once again held his weapons at the ready. Alexander smiled. He had to get this right and prolong the interaction.

"I've heard this place housed witches. But you won't harm me, will you?" Henri said it more as a statement than a question.

Alexander shook his head, reached for a nearby flower, and

winked at the captain. He closed his eyes and mumbled an enchantment as he rubbed the flower between his fingers. First, the blossom disintegrated, and then the magical properties took hold, transforming before his eyes into a white ointment. The substance tingled on his skin.

Alexander caressed Henri's leg with his other hand and then slowly rubbed the ointment into the wound. Henri flinched at the first touch to his puss-filled gash. For Alexander's part, he struggled to focus on the healing because he grew aroused again at feeling this man's calf, covered in light-blond hair and with a tight muscle, not large like his upper body, but well defined and beautiful.

Lost in the moment, Alexander almost missed the second the leg had healed. Not only did the puss evaporate, but the laceration grew together, any scar disappeared, and the fine hair again covered that area of his leg. Alexander let go and looked up at the captain.

Henri studied him. His brow again scrunched together, he flexed his calf back and forth, then sat quietly on the ground, his previous tension released. His weapons remained nearby but not in his hands. He reached down and pulled up his shirt, revealing a slight belly but otherwise muscular stomach, again with the light-blond hair. Below his pectoral, Alexander spotted another scar.

"This one healed but hurts sometimes." Henri pointed to the raised and whitened area of tissue.

Alexander went back to work with the ointment remaining on his fingers. After massaging the scar, Alexander bent over and licked along the area while he mumbled the enchantment. He also grasped Henri's penis through his pants. The chest scar, too, disappeared as Alexander peered into Henri's ice-blue eyes.

"Much obliged." Henri tilted his tricornered hat as a sort of thank-you. He made a move to stand, but Alexander grabbed him by the arm to stop him.

"Wait. Please."

Henri sat back down.

"Take me with you."

"You're pretty." Henri ran a finger along Alexander's cheek. "But I don't have room for decorations on my boat. I need sailors. Despite what you said, you're hardly a murderer. Wet behind the ears. Find your way to a city or something. You don't want to take up with the likes of me and my crew."

Alexander gripped Henri's arm tight. "You're my only chance for survival. I'm not as weak and sheltered as I look. I can do this. I can contribute. Can anyone else heal wounds?" Alexander pointed to Henri's leg.

Henri betrayed a conflict of emotions as his eyes danced over Alexander's body, his brow knitted, and then he wiped at his forehead with his hand. "What else can you do?"

Alexander seized the moment. Unlike the rest of his life and the constant concealment, he had no intention of hiding anything from the pirate captain.

When Alexander jumped to his feet, Henri lurched back and took his sword in hand. Alexander held up his hands in surrender. "I only wanted to show you this." He stepped several feet away from Henri.

A slight breeze blew above them on this hot summer day but

nothing most people would even recognize amidst the stifling heat. Alexander closed his eyes and held up his hands for effect. He could control the wind without the theatrics but needed to convince Henri, so he sought to manufacture visual proof of his ability. When the breeze gathered and rushed into Alexander's arms, he swooshed them to the side. The wind caught a nearby tree and battered it about before disappearing into the atmosphere. Next Alexander called forth a violent blast of air, forcing the large boulder beside them to roll several feet before he stopped and allowed the atmosphere to return to normal.

"You did that?" Henri pointed to the large stone.

"And the burst of wind before." Alexander nodded. "I can rule the wind. I want you to know, though, in terms of the ship and sails, the power comes and goes. I can't always sustain the wind for long periods of time. But I think in crucial situations I could be of service."

"What else?"

"I can see the present. From miles away."

"What the hell do you mean, see the present? So can I. Presently, you're standing right in front of me."

Alexander laughed despite the tension. "No." He shook his head. "Like this." He pulled out his crystal and gazed at the other pirates. "Your comrades are taking stock of what they have on land and placing the goods into one of the canoes to go to the main ship. The skinny one looks in charge. The one with the parrot on his shoulder."

Henri's eyes lit with recognition and then turned stoic again. "Let me see."

Alexander held the crystal out to Henri but he frowned. "Looks like a fancy stone to me."

Alexander glanced down and saw the pirates working away at storing their wares. Only he could see the magic. "Let me prove myself another way. Go into the forest where I can't see you and do something. I'll tell you about your actions afterward."

Henri spun around and walked back into the trees. After a couple minutes, when he had disappeared from view, Alexander pulled out his crystal. He spun around. Henri had circled him and now stood several paces off, behind a tree with his sword raised. Neither could see the other from their current position.

"Please, put your sword down. I want to join your side, not get attacked."

Henri plowed through the brush and stood in front of Alexander.

"So you can mess with the wind and see what's going on around you."

"And heal." Alexander held his breath, waiting.

Henri took off his hat and scratched the top of his head. He glanced to the trees, then stared again at Alexander with those beautiful blue eyes. "Here's the thing. I want to take you with me."

Alexander jumped up and clapped his hands together two times, but Henri held up a hand to stop him.

"But some won't like your presence. They're a superstitious lot. As captain, though, I have to recognize what might help my crew. So here's the deal. I can't commission you onto the boat. We vote. I'll back you and convince them of your worth. But you keep quiet about this witch stuff, hear me? I'll decide what to tell them and when, and I'll decide what we'd best keep secret. In fact, bring some plants and stuff so we can pretend you heal them with Indian remedies and such. Understood?"

"Yes!" Alexander nodded.

"Especially keep that shit about seeing the present to yourself. You would scare the piss out of them. Many are a might bit afraid of spirits and ghosts and bewitching."

"So you'll take me on your ship?"

"I said I'd take you to the crew for a vote. Best I can do."

Alexander squinted at Henri. "I thought you were the captain?"

"So I am. By election. And that's how we operate. I can plead your case, help them understand what you'll offer. Then it's up to them. And you." Henri pointed at Alexander.

He turned and started walking back toward the pirate camp when he halted. Alexander caught up to him and stood at his side. Henri reached over with one arm, pulled Alexander against him, and brushed his lips against Alexander's ear as he spoke. "Unlike them here Puritans, nothing wrong with a bit of sodomy between the willing on my boat. You'll be mine."

Alexander blushed and leaned into the pirate. "I'd like nothing more."

Henri tilted his head back and roared with laughter.

As they walked along an old trail, almost hidden under dense growth, Henri continued to talk. "Lost a good bit of my crew recently. Scurvy got some of us before we could resupply. We found a couple men in Boston, another in Salem. We're still down about fifty."

"So how many of you are there?"

"About a hundred, give or take."

The large number surprised Alexander. He had spied around twenty or so milling about on land. Crispin never indicated so many men lived aboard his ship. This large number came after Henri told him that they lost fifty men.

Already, Alexander grew more and more comfortable in Henri's presence, despite his masculine appearance, quick use of weapons, and seeming continued watchfulness around Alexander.

"You were very cautious when you first found me in the woods. What changed your mind?"

Henri stopped and turned to Alexander. "You ask a lot of questions."

Alexander grinned.

Henri barked another laugh. "At first, I was making sure you weren't out to get me, either as some damn lost Puritan or hidden soldier. Then I had to make sure you weren't a robber wandering around. All sorts of people can lurk in the woods, but seldom do you find one alone up to any good. One momentary lapse, and you could've slit my throat."

"And I could have, while we —"

Henri chuckled and started them moving. "No words for it, huh? A taste of my manhood is what you're getting at. Don't be too confident. One wrong move and I would've been carrying your head in my hand, with your nice little body behind us, rotting in the woods. After I used the bum right properly."

Alexander contemplated the meaning of Henri's comment but decided not to clarify. He turned them in a new direction. "But you came to trust me?"

"Not yet." Henri shook his head. "Enough to bring you this way and vouch for you. Not enough to let you out of my sight."

"You seem to like me." Alexander looked over and smiled.

"Yeah. You're my kind of man."

They walked in silence until they crossed a worn road and headed into even denser foliage. Alexander recalled, from monitoring the crystal, they approached the pirate camp when he saw the row of rotted tree stumps nearby.

"You came ashore to find more men?" he asked Henri.

"No. We came ashore for supplies. Food, mainly. Of course we take anything else we can pillage. But we had to replenish our ranks, so we watched around for some men too."

When Alexander could hear the whisper of voices and spotted one person ahead keeping watch, the captain held out his arm and stopped Alexander from proceeding.

"So I admit I kind of like you. We could use your power, whether they like your power or not. We need more sailors, to be sure. But let me handle this? If you get cocky and too sure of yourself, that's all well and good until you open your mouth and convince some of them you're more trouble than your worth. At this point, if we don't vote to bring you aboard, we'll have to vote to execute you. I'd hate to kill you."

Henri pressed his hand against Alexander's back, and he moved forward with a lump in his throat.

Chapter Fourteen

Pirate Rendezvous

5 July 1700

Coastal Massachusetts

AS ALEXANDER AND Henri made their way to the pirates, Alexander was lost in infatuation. He became almost comfortable with courting a pirate until he remembered that the gang of men would either vote to accept him or execute him on the spot. Yet he felt safer than with any of his past dealings with the Puritans. At least pirates spoke upfront about the situation.

Alexander expected the vote and debate immediately upon their arrival. Instead, Henri grunted a greeting to his men and demanded a jug of rum. As they fetched the alcohol, he pointed to Alexander. "He's with me for the night. We'll talk about him in the morning."

Thus ended the introduction. The men steered clear of him for the rest of the night as they drank, ate, and guarded the provisions. Henri stayed close to Alexander, even sleeping mere inches from him. While Henri talked to the other pirates, no one spoke to Alexander, not even Henri, and he remained quiet.

Not until the next morning did attention turn toward Alexander as a newcomer.

He stayed next to Henri even after he woke, afraid to get up for fear of interacting with one of the pirates and defying Henri's orders. A nice breeze blew over him that cooled the heat from the rising sun. He lifted his head when Henri stirred next to him.

Henri reached over and placed a hand on Alexander's shoulder. He sat up and surveyed his surroundings. "Stay here."

A moment later, Alexander heard Henri give an order to assemble the men on shore leaving a skeleton crew to watch the ship. "Do so with haste. We have votes to take, and we leave tonight. I don't want so many of us off the ship more than necessary. We've stayed here long enough."

Alexander was laying on the ground, staring into the trees, when Henri came into his view. He had taken off his hat, so his long, blond hair fell into his face, but Alexander could see him smiling.

"Come." Henri held out his hands and helped Alexander to his feet.

Alexander noticed a few pirates organizing provisions and could hear others pushing a canoe into the water. But before he could see anything else, Henri pulled him along, back to the clearing where they initially met.

"I didn't want you around them until right before the vote." Henri stood a few feet from Alexander, peering down. Alexander felt short next to him, in part because he stood a few inches taller but more so because his presence gave an illusion of height. "Some of them will know about you. God only knows how. So you remember not to say anything? Let me lead."

"Yes." After remaining quiet for so long, since the night before, his own voice sounded strange to Alexander. Even alone he usually talked to himself, to the animals, or to the elements around him. Henri had ordered him to blend into the background, and so he obeyed.

"Good." Henri nodded.

"What are we doing here?"

"Waiting."

"Waiting for what?"

"The assembly." Henri walked over to Alexander after pacing in a circle. "You always ask so many questions?"

"I don't like being in the dark. And even when people try to keep secrets, I can usually figure out by watching them in the crystal to see what they're up to. Your warning me they may decide to kill me made me nervous yesterday."

Henri leaned over and kissed Alexander on the cheek. "Well, you should be. I told you, you should run away from this band of Satan's hellions." Henri pointed toward the encampment.

"I explained I have little choice. I will die if I stay here too. Besides,

I don't want to leave you." Alexander knew nothing about pirate mating rituals but neither had he ever held back regarding such feelings. Only Crispin ever before inspired such passion.

Henri's response gave him little to go on. "Good."

They said nothing else but stood in the woods for a long time before Henri headed back toward the coast. He waved for Alexander to follow, which he did, walking behind the captain in their renewed and uncomfortable silence.

Alexander almost said something to break the monotony, before he looked up to discover their arrival with the other pirates. He had expected a handful of men milling about, but Alexander walked toward an assembly of close to the hundred pirates who sailed on Henri's ship.

Alexander had never seen such a conglomeration of humanity in his life. Pirates came in all shapes, sizes, and colors. Some with long hair, some short, and others were bald. Their eyes matched the colors of the rainbow, their skin different hues. Alexander had seen few Africans in his life, all of them enslaved. Here they stood among the others as peers. The majority of them appeared fit, most likely from the labor aboard ship and perhaps the lack of food.

Alexander spotted a handful of attractive men, while others repulsed him.

A glance at their teeth displayed the same variety, with some mouths full and some seemingly without even one tooth. Most of the teeth looked yellow. Various pirates missed sundry limbs or had scars on their bodies and faces. A few with hardly any teeth also had blackened legs or fingers, a sign Crispin once told him meant scurvy, which

Henri had mentioned.

In all, Alexander's heart sank at the unfavorable opinion he formed of this motley crew. They held none of the allure he daydreamed about upon first deciding to become a pirate.

Yet he forced the fear from his mind and concentrated on the more fascinating aspects of the people in front of him. He loved how so many had rings in their ears. While some wore nothing on their head, others donned tricornered hats like the one Henri wore, and even more had various scarves tied on their heads. They displayed a wide variety of pants and clothes, some that looked like old uniforms, some common clothes, and some in such tatters Alexander could hardly recognize their origin. A lot of them wore short, blue jackets and checkered shirts, with baggy canvas pants or red waistcoats. Some had smeared black tar across their clothes.

More exotic than anything, Alexander peered upon the tattoos. A few sailors in Boston exposed such body art, but never so many and in such colors. Amidst the dirt and grime, dragons, birds, and other symbols of the sea showed through.

The squawk of a parrot brought Alexander out of his appraisal.

"Well, so King James has brought this assembly to order." Everyone laughed at Henri.

"King James has brought this assembly to order," the parrot chirped back.

Henri laughed too. "Spittle, shut him up now."

Alexander recognized the man to whom Henri spoke. Not only from the parrot sitting atop his shoulder, but because he seemed to command the crew in Henri's absence. He wore an orange checkered shirt and long pants. His slight, but muscular, build contrasted with many of the other, more stocky men. He also had less facial hair than the others, causing Alexander to wonder at how a man seemed to shave while others failed to do so for a long time.

Then Alexander paused at the name. Spittle? And someone had named the parrot King James? He had never wondered about pirate names, but then recalled the various nicknames he heard the night before and decided pirates must choose their own name or got one from each other. At any rate, no one had said a common Christian name since Alexander came into their midst.

Spittle whispered something and reached up to pet King James, who stopped mimicking those around him.

Henri nodded. "Good. First item of business. We got some new blood to join our ranks. Vote 'em up or down." Henri spoke with more of an accent and lost his proper English when in front of the men, apparently an affect used for his leadership.

One by one, four different men came forward. They gave their names, and then one or more of the pirates vouched for them. In every case, a chorus of "Ayes" filled the air without any dissent when Henri called for the vote.

"We need the men, for sure. Good thing we found them. Last one here. I'm vouching for him. Come forward."

Alexander moved in front of the captain and held his head high. He stared into the eyes of each man as he glanced through their ranks. "Alexander MacBeth. I'm running from the Puritans."

"Shall we vote? All in favor?"

As the usual chant in favor began, one voice rose above and screamed. "Halt!"

Out of the masses stepped forward a towering figure of a man. His bald head brandished tribal tattoos right down to his cheek, where the markings eventually wrapped around his neck. Alexander peered upon the largest biceps he had ever seen and bulging thighs the size of a tree trunk. His white skin glowed a deep brown from the sun. A scar above his left eye took away half his eyebrow, and he wore no shirt, exposing a hairy chest. He scowled at the men.

"What, Beast?" Henri spoke with a warning and a hint of loathing.

"I vote to keep this one here to die."

Henri stepped between this god of a man and Alexander. "On what grounds? I already vouched for him."

Beast squinted at Alexander. "He's a demon."

"I sensed the curse too!" another pirate chimed in, one whom Alexander did not see.

Thus erupted a chaotic debate about Alexander's status. He readied the wind above him for assistance, lest this get out of hand and force yet another escape for his life. Some pirates defended him as innocent looking or proclaimed their trust in Henri's counsel. A handful joined Beast, saying they sensed Alexander's otherworldly powers.

Henri allowed the deliberation for some time before he held up his hands and shouted for quiet.

"Enough. This one's no danger. I think you feel his ability to heal, which is why we need him aboard. Here, look at this." Henri moved his pants aside and showed them his healed leg. "Most of you know the gash I had. He healed me because he's learned how to use plants for their healing properties."

"He's lying," Beast growled.

Henri stepped forward and stood mere inches from Beast and his five-inch height advantage. "You want to do this here, finally?"

Alexander braced for a fight, but Beast fell back into the ranks.

"The vote. All in favor?"

Almost all the men affirmed the decision, though with less volume than before. But when Henri asked for those opposed, Beast screamed out with a few compatriots.

"It's done. Welcome aboard," Henri said to each of the new men.

When the throng began to quiet again, apparently to take up more business, Beast shouted. "Hey, charlatan!" He looked right at Alexander. "Do you know why we call him Henri the Twisted? Or do you think him just a gentile guy who goes by Henri?"

"Shut it, Beast." Spittle glared at the man and spit at his feet.

Beast again blended back into the crowd.

"Shut it, Beast!" King James parroted, much to the delight of the pirate assembly.

Alexander began to understand something of pirate hierarchy, without a formal lesson. Beast physically could snap Spittle in half but respected his authority. The same for the fact he had backed down when Henri challenged him, though Alexander suspected Henri could and would have fought him well despite the size difference.

"Next. We're renaming the ship." As Henri spoke, Alexander and the other new pirates slipped in with everyone else. Alexander stood as close to Spittle as possible, already trusting he and the captain shared a similar outlook.

"Why?" someone asked.

"Cursed. The old name is cursed. We lost too many before we got the right provisions. May lose more before we're done. We got to change our fortune. And I have the name to put us on the right path and provoke fear in those who would challenge us. Are you ready?"

The men rang out with a chant of yes.

"Are ye sure? For this name comes from Satan himself to protect us. We mustn't cower in the face of our reality as others will."

Again they repeated their enthusiastic assent.

"One last chance to turn back. Are you sure you can handle the moment?"

"Yes!" the men bellowed.

Henri stretched out his arms and motioned to the ship, bobbing in the ocean not far from shore. "Behold! You are about to set sail on the vilest ship to ever float upon the waters. Grown men will weep at the sight of her and tremble in fear. His Majesty's Navy can never defeat Her. I give you the strongest ship on the seas, protected from all who would harm her by the worst elements you could imagine. Only the mighty will dare board her now. Gentleman, you set sail tomorrow aboard — *All Hallows Eve!*"

The pirates roared their approval.

"I'll take that as your vote of approval, then." Henri smiled when the gathering shouted in agreement.

After a minute of revelry, Henri held up his hands to silence the men. "Since we woke the dead, we'd best get on our way. These here Puritans might not appreciate a pirate throng taking up their holy ground."

As the men dispersed, Alexander stayed put, wondering what to do. Most of them returned quickly to the boats and headed back to the ship. Others went about the land, gathering various things and packing the last bit of supplies.

As Beast stepped into a boat, he turned around and glared at Alexander, staring into his eyes. For the first time since taking up with the pirates, Alexander remembered the man's sorcery when his senses tingled and the crystal in his pocket vibrated.

Beast had no soul. Whether or not the true man lived somewhere inside, something foul lingered about him. Possession. Alexander realized a demon or the dead controlled him. A smile spread across Beast's face as these revelations came to Alexander. He held up an arm and pointed directly at Alexander as his eyes danced with delight.

Alexander jumped when Spittle came up to him and spoke. "Don't worry about him," he said. "He won't defy Henri. Come, I have much to teach you."

Chapter Fifteen

Pirate Codes

5 July 1700

Coastal Massachusetts

ALEXANDER NEEDED SEVERAL minutes to calm his nerves after Beast pointed at him from the canoe. A demon aboard ship hardly offered Alexander the escape from Massachusetts he desired. He concentrated on Henri and his own ability to protect himself, but something about Beast alarmed him more than an angry spirit possession.

Spittle tried to engage him a couple times but finally patted his shoulder. "Gather yourself. I'll be right back."

Alexander closed his eyes and meditated. He saw his mother,

imploring him to survive. He thought of everything he had already experienced in life, and the fact he came out of each dilemma stronger, smarter, and more prepared than ever for the next adventure. When Crispin appeared in his vision, Alexander dismissed him, and up popped Henri, with his piercing blue eyes, muscular demeanor, and authority with the pirates. Soon Alexander regained his confidence and found the willpower to combat whatever Beast may throw at him.

He opened his eyes to see Spittle walking briskly toward him.

"We don't have much time before sailing, so I can only give you the basics."

"Give you the basics!" King James tilted his head as if inspecting Alexander.

"Meet King James." Spittle pointed to the bird on their shoulder. "He's a pain in my ass." Despite his words, Spittle reached up and petted the bird on the head. "Quiet," he said in a commanding voice.

Alexander smiled. "I like your bird."

"Thanks. Like I said, he's a pain in the ass but keeps me company. And the other men too. Somehow, he became a smart ass." Spittle sat next to Alexander on the log. "Anyway, captain ordered me to give you some basics about the pirate codes we have to follow. Says you've never been on the seas, but to keep the information between us."

Alexander nodded. "I'll do whatever's necessary."

"We leave soon. I'll teach you more, maybe tomorrow when we're floating around. For now, these are the basics. First off, don't go by Alexander. No one on Henri the Twisted's ship goes by their actual name, except Henri because he doesn't like constant reminders about the twisted part of his nickname. Anyway, we'll come up with something for you soon enough."

Alexander wanted to ask how Henri got his name, how he would obtain his own nickname, and even why they called him Spittle, but Spittle launched ahead with the lesson.

"We should go over chain of command. Captain's obviously first. Then me, his first mate. You'll meet the second mate, warrant officer, gunner, and others soon enough. You'll be low in the ranks, and men will test you. Best for you to follow orders from anyone until you get the lay of the land, so to speak." Alexander's head began to spin with confusion at the information Spittle threw at him. "On our ship, there's no gambling. Captain enforces this rule rigidly because gambling leads to fights. If we go to port, you can do what you want. Get your gambling fix then. You don't want to know what happens if someone violates the laws of the ship. You'll learn soon enough because we have several who can't help themselves. Everyone votes on decisions, including you now. The crew will decide our destination once we get aboard, though Henri often has suggestions. All these and more rules are written out, if you need to review them. Captain will have each new person sign them when you get on the ship. What else?" Spittle thought for a second. "Everyone gets the same rations, including liquor, and booty gets split evenly among the crew. Even Henri, despite being entitled to more as captain. This lot of men has more superstition and fear than any I've sailed with, which is saying a lot because all sailors are superstitious. I guess you experienced their beliefs when we voted on you. Watch your-self. I heard some wonder if you're bewitched."

"I'm not—"

Spittle held up his hand. "Captain explained you have power but aren't an evil witch. Your secret's safe with me. One last thing, speaking of people not liking you. If you get in to too serious a snit with someone, be prepared for a duel."

Spittle stared at Alexander for a moment, then looked him all over, as if checking him out. "You don't have any weapons."

Alexander shook his head.

"Good for you the captain has taken a shine to you. He'll help you out. He likes you."

Alexander smiled but had no idea how to respond. He never discussed his sexual appetites with anyone, not even Crispin because they danced around the matter, regardless of the fact they lay naked in bed together.

Spittle roared with laughter. "Listen, mate, there aren't many secrets aboard a pirate ship. Everyone already knows about Henri's leanings. Some will be mighty jealous you got to him. He's resisted many seductions, despite an occasional dalliance."

"Fair enough. Do you—you know, um."

"You've got to learn to speak in plain language. But no, I don't bugger. Anyone. Any time. Not interested. With either sex."

"I've only been with one person before. He joined the navy and left me." Alexander already felt comfortable with Spittle and confessed his past with Crispin. "Anyway, you're right. I like the captain."

"He seems to like you too. We don't need to tell the others right away. It's good to have some secrets from the men. Everyone has a secret or two."

"You have a secret?"

Spittle laughed again. "You've no idea. Now come, time to get aboard *All Hallows Eve*."

Too quickly for Alexander to process or entirely gain his bearings, Spittle led him to one of the fishing canoes they used to get to land from the sloop. "Last ones, right?" Spittle looked at the men getting aboard. "We didn't leave anyone behind?"

An older pirate with no teeth and several missing fingers smirked. "Only ones who almost got left were you two, chatting like gossipy women on the log."

Alexander clutched his bag as he climbed the rope ladder up and onto the ship. A couple of pirates helped him over the top. He scanned the crew and saw most men scrambling around. Henri stood high above them on the top deck next to the wheel, shouting commands.

"Sit over here and stay out of the way." Spittle moved him to a crate and pushed him onto it. "If Henri or I tell you to do something, obey. Otherwise don't move. You'll be in the way."

"I thought you said I should obey *anyone*?"

"Unless the first mate or captain tell you otherwise, which I just did." Spittle hurried off.

Alexander scanned the ship. At first he felt disheartened. It was dirty and smelled. Various animals scampered about, including a three-legged dog. He had learned enough about boats to recognize this one as a single mast sloop. Crispin once explained various ships to him, particularly scolding Alexander for calling anything with less than three masts a ship and not a sloop. Before Crispin prepared to leave to hunt pirates, he talked extensively about pirate life and ships. Pirates preferred the single or dual mast sloops to larger ships because they moved faster through the water. Speed mattered.

Alexander found himself drifting away mentally, something he had not done much since escaping from life with his uncle. But the talk of knots, riggings, sails, and pirate language for preparing to set sail confused and unsettled him. His body stayed put and ready to move if ordered, but his mind hovered above.

He stayed in his dream state as the Massachusetts coast disappeared behind him. Finally, he had set sail and escaped. Why then, did he feel a pang of regret? Not for a home that so mistreated him; not for the people, who so despised him. No, he was experiencing a final tug at his heart for Crispin, whom he would never see again.

"You sick?" Spittle drew him out of his other realm with this question.

Alexander smiled. Unlike his instant disdain for Beast, he trusted Spittle. Both his natural instincts and supernatural senses gave him a positive impression, like he already had a friend aboard. Alexander, who went through most of his life as a loner, could not remember anyone other than Crispin who fit such a category.

Alexander shrugged. "I'm well."

Spittle rustled his hair. "The captain needs to see you in his quarters to sign the code."

Alexander followed Spittle across the ship. Without knocking, he pushed the door open and Alexander followed. Spittle nodded to the captain, then took his leave.

Alexander stood frozen near the closed door.

Henri grinned. "You're bashful all of a sudden? What happened to the lad laying on the ground and losing his pants in the forest?"

Alexander smiled. "I suppose the presence of the captain of a ship in his quarters at sea has a certain aura."

Henri laughed. "Remember, this is a pirate ship. I sleep here. These are my quarters, but men can come and go in here. Pay no attention to my pirate rank. With but a vote or bit of turmoil, they could cast me out of office."

Alexander thought Henri modest, given the obvious command he demonstrated over his crew.

"Come here. Sit."

Alexander joined Henri on a bench at a small table. He leaned into Henri to feel his strong physical presence. A bunch of papers were spread out before them.

"These are the codes the men established aboard *All Hallows Eve*. Spittle told me he went over them with you."

"For the most part. I don't know if I remember everything."

Henri waved his hand in the air. "You will in time. Besides, I have other plans for you. A special assignment."

"Plans?"

"Your powers can help us. They'll eventually give you a special place aboard ship, once the men learn what you can do and see you don't imperil them. I'll have to manage news about you carefully. With your help, of course. But I talked to Spittle about making you a special assistant to me. Not first mate. Spittle performs the best I've ever seen as first mate, better than anyone else sailing the ocean, pirate or not. But you can become someone who works with me. Mind you, we have to get you involved in the other ship activities, too, so people won't get suspicious or jealous. I'm sorry, but despite what you say, you don't strike me as a hardened sailor."

Alexander winced. How many times did people have to tell him? Here, he at long last came aboard a ship, but he continued to have to fight against some softened image. Yet as he watched the sailors scurry about as they set sail, part of him hoped to avoid some types of work. He decided to embrace the persona Henri described.

"I'll do whatever you think best." Alexander lay his head on Henri's shoulder.

"Then sign this so we can get on with the day."

Henri dipped a quill in ink and handed it to Alexander. Alexander signed his name underneath the other pirate signatures. "Hardly any Xs. I'm surprised."

"Don't be. Almost all those men are literate. The damn snobs and authorities try to paint a picture of us to make us look bad."

Alexander replaced the pen in its stand when Henri's strong arms wrapped around him. He took off his shirt, and the warm skin pressed against Alexander's back felt wonderful.

Alexander closed his eyes and enjoyed the embrace. He grew excited when he felt Henri's lips brush across his ear.

"Get over here."

Alexander started to stand and was dragged over to a bed in the corner. He turned to face Henri and yanked him closer. Henri used his weight to push Alexander onto the bed. Their lips locked together and Henri sucked at Alexander's tongue. He grabbed at Alexander's clothes and started to remove them, then the rest of his own.

When he licked his finger and moved his hand downward, Alexander spread his legs and guided Henri's arm the rest of the way. At the same time, Alexander reached down and grabbed Henri's penis in his hand, sliding his finger over the precome and watching Henri squirm above him with excitement. They played around for a long time until Henri snatched both of Alexander's legs and held them in the air. Henri took charge and sent Alexander into a couple of hours of absolute passion before they fell asleep in each other's arms.

IV: Life Among Pirates

Chapter Sixteen

Cooking and Salt

6 July 1700

Atlantic Ocean

ALEXANDER WOKE THE next morning to the sway of the boat sailing across the sea. He felt exhilarated at the motion, and at being finally aboard a ship and moving toward his new destiny. He lay in silence for a long time, happy to have escaped Salem and enjoying the sounds of sailors on the other side of the door as they went about their work. He also pressed against Henri to feel his hard presence. Never before had Alexander spent the night with anyone in the same bed.

When Henri stirred, Alexander slid down his naked body and

took his limp penis in his mouth. He swirled his tongue around the tip and grew excited himself as Henri's cock came to life. He sucked in, then slowly moved out until the head hit his lips, then he thrust down again. After a minute of this movement, he felt Henri gently grasp both sides of his head and encourage him. When those thick thighs went firm and Henri clutched his hands against Alexander's ears, Alexander tasted the semen spurting over his tongue and down his throat.

Still learning the nature of their relationship, Henri surprised Alexander when he got up and pushed him back on the bed. Henri grasped Alexander's penis and put it in his mouth, returning the favor. Alexander grew so excited, in mere seconds, he shot his own seed.

Henri stood and started getting dressed. "You best get ready too."

Once clothed, Henri paused at the door and yanked Alexander into his arms. "I like you. Don't go forgetting me today." They kissed and then Henri opened the door.

The immediate view gave Alexander a good sense for the upper deck of the ship. He saw several barrels and again noticed the large number of animals milling about — some pets, some kept for slaughter. He had no idea how to tell the difference.

Alexander smiled when he heard Spittle shout a couple of commands repeated shortly after by King James.

Henri strode by the wheel and down the steps, then stood underneath, looking up at the pirates in the crow's nest. He shouted something at them Alexander could not hear. In his awed state the night before, Alexander failed to notice the twenty cannons lined on either side of the deck.

Alexander wondered for the first time how Henri and this lot of pirates had commandeered this sloop. Again he relied on what he had seen on his trips to Boston and the lessons from Crispin to understand he stood on a ship originally designed for war, though he could not tell its nation of origin.

Questions like this, along with how people acquired their nicknames, kept swimming through Alexander's head. Perhaps he could ask Henri or Spittle.

"Where's the other new one? The one captain favors?" Alexander wondered who was shouting, when he heard the same thing again.

"Where's the other new one? *Squawk.*"

"Captain's quarters, I suspect. Where else?" One of the sailors standing in front of Spittle smiled when he spoke.

"Watch yourself." Spittle spit at the guy's feet. Alexander started to figure out how he may have come by his nickname. That was at least the third time in less than a day Alexander had seen him expectorate a warning volley at someone's feet.

"Watch yourself!"

"King James, time for a little quiet." Spittle looked up and spotted Alexander. "There you are."

Spittle charged through a group of men struggling with a barrel and came up the stairs. "I promised you more lessons later. But first you'd best eat something and then captain assigned you to Tacky today."

Spittle pulled him along, toward a small room near the captain's quarters.

They passed a rather handsome pirate, with long straight black hair, an earring, and a shapely body apparent beneath his clothes. As Alexander moved past him, he reached over and pinched Alexander's ass. "If you get tired of the captain, I can give you something you've never experienced before."

Spittle halted and spun around. "Right. It's called disease, and he doesn't want any."

The men around them fell into peals of laughter as Spittle grabbed Alexander's hands and yanked him along.

"This here's Tacky." Spittle pointed to a short Black man, a shaved head, and deep brown eyes that danced when he winked at Alexander. "Tacky's the cook. And this is Monkey, the cooper." Monkey stood about Alexander's height, with long red hair and lots of freckles. "Tacky because he's the cook and serves way too much fucking hardtack. Monkey because he had a monkey when he came aboard, but we ate him. Anyway, Tacky will feed you. And captain said for you to help out here for the day as best as possible."

Spittle turned to leave and then stepped back into the small room. "You remember the chain of command, right? Captain, me, second mate. Ah, fuck it. These two here will kind of be your bosses when the captain assigns you to them and you're not helping him or me."

"So they rank after you?"

Tacky and Monkey laughed.

"No." Spittle shook his head. "They aren't on the list."

"What?"

Spittle waved his hand behind his back as he walked away, too busy to answer.

Tacky walked toward Alexander, limping badly, and put his arm around Alexander's shoulder. He moved him behind a couple of barrels. "Cooks have special status. I don't have rank, but I'm not any other sailor either. They have to respect me, or they'd starve to death. Got this here limp in battle, which is how I became the cook. Don't have any toes left. And Monkey," Tacky pointed at the other man, "is a master cooper. Without him, our barrels would rot away and fall apart, and we'd have nothing to keep our stores in. You can't imagine how lucky we are to have a cooper. First ship I ever sailed aboard, outside of the merchant vessel I escaped from, with a cooper. Pirate ships usually can't afford such a one because they're hard to come by."

"Yeah, lucky you." Monkey rolled his eyes. "Henri used his charms on me. I make a lot more here than on those damned navy vessels. Pirate life suits me better. A pirate code I can handle. Some fool ordering me about who doesn't know shit about making a barrel was for the birds."

"So a cooper is in charge of the barrels?" Alexander asked.

Tacky shook his head. "More. He makes them. Repairs them. It's an art, not something you slap together. Because they can't leak. And then they warp and change and need to be fixed."

Monkey rolled his eyes. "He makes my job description more glamorous than the actual work."

Tacky laughed and motioned for Alexander to follow him. "Let me show you around." Tacky first pointed to a row of barrels along the wall. "We keep the food up here, where it's dry. If you're lucky, you won't have to go below deck very often. We keep some animals down there but can usually send someone to get them, even have them slaughtered for us. Up here, got to watch for the worms, spiders, and rats because they'll spoil our food. We got plenty to eat right now but it runs out faster than you'd think if we're not careful."

Tacky limped over to three fireplaces. "We put the kettles over here. But we can't use them if it's too windy. This here's one of the most dangerous parts of the ship, when we're not attacking another boat." He chuckled. "One spark goes the wrong way, and this boat goes up in flames and we die. We've got some salted veggies and salted meat. Quite the luxury we commandeered while ashore. I started salting as quick as possible to keep the food from rotting. One of the last times we were out, we came upon a ship hauling salt to port. A lucky find. Better than all the treasure in the world. I need your help with the salt for a while."

"Over here." Tacky moved Alexander to another part of the kitchen. "Spices." He smiled and wiggled his eyebrows. "Use them once the food starts to go bad, so it's tasty. Plus, of course, we get some fish. Anyway, here—" Tacky handed some hard tack to Alexander. Alexander had heard of this flour- and water-based bread but never tasted it before. Not bad, though a little bland. "—breakfast. Ready to salt away?"

Alexander spent a quiet morning in the kitchen helping Tacky put inordinate amounts of salt on the rest of the vegetables and meat the pirates confiscated in Massachusetts. Monkey left them after fiddling with a couple of the barrels. Tacky worked in silence for the most part, though plenty of noises filled the air from outside the confines of the kitchen.

Men shouted at each other, laughed, and a few argued. One disagreement got quite intense before Alexander heard Henri roar with anger. Tacky giggled.

As he grabbed the last basket of meat, King James drifted into the kitchen.

"You here to steal some provisions?" Tacky asked the bird.

"Steal some provisions." King James laughed, if a bird knew how to laugh. "Message to deliver. Message to deliver."

Alexander looked to Tacky for explanation.

"If Spittle's busy, he sends the bird."

"Sends the bird! Message to deliver. Message to deliver."

"Yeah, yeah. What's your message?"

"Alexander to follow. Alexander to follow."

King James turned and started to fly away, landing on a barrel near the door and looking back at the two men.

"You're supposed to follow him. First mate's calling for you."

Alexander trailed the bird toward a stairwell, descending below deck. He understood why Tacky warned against wanting to come down here. If an assortment of unpleasant smells filled the air on the top deck, they wreaked of a latrine below. First, a musty dampness filled his nostrils. Alexander spotted water dripping from above and could hear waves sloshing against the sides of the boat. Hardly any light filtered down, despite the bright sun above. This made temperatures hotter below deck than if he stood directly in the sun.

Glancing to his side, he saw a number of hammocks hanging from the rafters.

"Over here," Spittle called, just as he'd started to lose his nerve.

Alexander found Spittle standing near a pen of a few animals, including a huge pig. The location stunk worse than all the other putrid smells filling the air since Alexander came aboard.

"This here's part of the kitchen, so to speak. Come here if you ever get sent for an animal. Be careful to get the one you want and not let the lot of them run free. The men who have to sleep down here will cry heaven and damnation at the chaos and shit and piss they'll leave everywhere."

Spittle picked up a jug and took a swig, then handed it to Alexander.

Alexander almost coughed the liquid back up. After anticipating water, he was surprised to take a huge gulp of some alcohol he had never tasted.

"Some of the best rum we've had in a long time." Spittle grinned.

"I noticed men drinking a lot."

"Yeah. Regular drunkfest aboard a pirate ship, so long as the liquor holds out. Makes us hum a happy tune. Unless we've got to attack, which calls for sobriety, at least from most men. Whiskey Breath's a different story, but you probably could gather his truth from his name." Spittle leaned against the wall, taking another drink. "How was the kitchen today?"

"Fine. Good."

"You adjusting to life on the high seas?"

Alexander grabbed the jug and took another drink, though smaller. "Yeah. I like being here."

"Any questions? Let me know whenever I need to teach you. Captain assigned me special to you. Usually a new pirate has to learn for himself. But he wants me keeping particular watch out for you."

Alexander again fell quiet but smiled. "I hope to make him happy for a long while so he'll keep the privileges coming."

Spittle laughed. "It's good you recognize them as privileges. Henri the Twisted doesn't take to too many men. Especially for longer than five or six minutes. I doubt he'll dump you all of a sudden."

"He's quite fine." Alexander's tongue loosened as more alcohol seeped into his system.

"Right." Spittle giggled. "I don't really need to learn anything else about you two. So, anything else I need to teach you?"

"I have a question. Am I safe? I didn't like the way my vote went." Alexander had kept the fear to himself but felt protected with Spittle.

"I get your worry. Once you're voted on, you're voted on. The vote's final. You'd have to kill one of our own or steal from someone, something drastic to kick you off. Besides, Henri's protecting you."

"Do I need protecting?"

Spittle grew silent for a moment. He chugged the rum and handed the jug back to Alexander. "Beast took a disliking to you. But Beast dislikes most of us. I think he even hates the captain but has to respect how the other men chose him. Don't worry too much about Beast. He has his little group who listen because they're afraid of witches and ghosts. Most of the men ignore him. Beast doesn't really have much power.

Well, he has power in his little corner of the ship, but overall we control him."

"Why does he stay around? And why keep him on the crew?"

"I don't know why he floats with us. Most likely because he's a complete ass and has a hard time getting aboard a ship. So once he gets one, he stays. As for why we keep him, I can give you an easy answer. You'll see his value in battle."

Alexander shook his head when Spittle offered another drink. His head already spun too much.

"Anything else? You're kind of my special keep. Like my brother."

Alexander smiled. "One more thing. What about my name?"

"What about it?"

"You said not to go by Alexander. But I don't have any other name. How will I get one?"

Spittle scratched his head. "Depends. Some men arrive with their nicknames. Others choose their own. Most get one from the other men, if they don't already have one. The name can be good natured or cruel, hard to say. Plus they change. Tacky had a different name before he lost his toes, acquired the limp, and had to become the cook."

"How soon will I have one?"

Spittle shrugged. "Depends too."

"On what?"

"Well, anything. On something happening. On someone starting to call you something. Any number of things might get you labeled. Don't try to force the issue. Let one come naturally."

To hell with a spinning head. Alexander drank more and nodded.

"We could call you Henri's Whore."

Alexander started to protest the offense when he saw Spittle smiling widely. He burst into laughter.

"Kidding, mate. Kidding. If someone tries to call you a whore, King James and I will take care of them. Not to mention what Henri might think."

"Where is King James?"

"He hates coming down here, so usually stays above deck. Besides, he's on assignment."

"Assignment?"

"Yeah." Spittle nodded, as if there was nothing out of the ordinary about giving a bird duties like one of the pirates. "He's going to tell me if Beast is up to no good."

Chapter Seventeen

Storm Clouds

21 July 1700

Florida Coast

FOR THE FIRST time, Henri summoned Alexander not for pleasure but as the captain of the vessel. The morning ring around the sun signaled bad weather, and later they saw the storm clouds brewing.

"Stay right here." Henri pointed to an exact spot near the wheel. "I'll always know where you are, and you can hang onto these ropes. We may be fine and steer clear. Or the storm may slam into us." Henri frowned at the horizon and black sky bearing down on them. "I know you mentioned you can't always control the wind to your exact command, but if I ask for your assistance, do what you can."

Alexander nodded as Henri trudged across the deck and down the ladder, ordering the sails taken down and commanding other men to various tasks.

The sea already heaved the sloop about with the force of waves. Alexander spotted some of the men crossing themselves, others scurrying around doing some task, but every man serious and concerned. Not since they left Massachusetts had they walked about so sober.

Remembering the colony, Alexander hardly believed he lived aboard the ship for but two weeks.

Alexander had spent the first week settling into his new role, especially learning to assist Tacky with the cooking and sometimes Monkey with barrel repairs or other carpentry. He learned Henri protected him from the life of a common sailor among the pirates.

Most of the pirates accepted him, though Alexander detected some resented his special status — given so easily by Henri.

"Sometimes, this gets old." Tacky slammed down a spoon, the gruel flying across the kitchen.

Alexander paused before responding. "What does?"

"Cooking."

"Oh. I thought you liked to cook."

Tacky shook his head, then smiled, and contradicted the first reaction by nodding his head. "I do, I do. But slaving over the fires gets old. I used to be one of them." Tacky pointed toward the pirates on deck. "Fighting. Helping sail the ship. I became the cook because I lost my toes. That's how most pirate cooks get their jobs. Not because they want to, but because the only option left is to cook. I limp around too much. I'm a liability everywhere but here."

"So I'm the exception? I cook despite being perfectly fine?" Alexander reddened a bit when he understood this fact.

Tacky grinned. "I suppose. Better remember you got the job from Captain."

"Can I ask you something else?"

Tacky had cleaned up his spoon and gone back to whistling while he prepared a meal. "Sure."

"Beast approached me again today."

"Best to stay away from him."

"I do. Trust me. But sometimes he seeks me out. Seems like he, or one of his followers, come to me at least once a day. Do you think I should do anything?"

Tacky stopped stirring and looked at Alexander. "You listen to Spittle and Captain. I know what they told you. They're watching, so stay away from them. King James keeps an eye out."

"I wonder if my avoiding him made the other pirates question me."

"Don't worry. Captain and Spittle ordered you to keep away from him. No one here, or at least very few, question obeying the captain."

Tacky reached over and took a sip of his rum. Of all pirate life realities, Alexander struggled most with the drinking. He had too many bad memories of his drunken uncle. Alexander shook his head when Tacky offered him the bottle.

"You don't like the stuff?" Tacky asked.

"I do. My uncle drank a lot and then beat me into oblivion. Alcohol pretty much destroyed him. Plus, Henri got pretty pissed the other day when I got so drunk one night I refused to get out of bed the next morning. I mean, I *like the way rum lightens my head and tingles. However, I want to stay out of trouble."*

Tacky laughed. "You wouldn't get out of bed?"

"I couldn't. Not without barfing."

Tacky doubled over, which got Alexander to laugh too.

"You have no tolerance."

"I know. Some of these men drink constantly, yet never seem drunk. Or they exist in a state of intoxication and do all their duties fine nonetheless."

Tacky smiled. "Welcome to the life of pirates."

By his second week aboard, Alexander drifted into a comfortable routine. He spent most of his day cooking or gathering supplies for meals, between various lessons from Spittle and making sure he knew enough aboard the pirate ship to survive. "There will be more to learn," Spittle said one afternoon, "but we're done for now. Until we need to ready you for battle or to visit some port, there's nothing else you need to know."

"What about the ropes and sails?"

Spittle laughed. "Not your worry. Captain says stick to cooking. A few men questioned your assignment, but he told the guys you'd prove your worth at sea soon enough."

The first spray of rain hit Alexander in the face and brought him back to the moment. He remained rooted to his spot. A second later, Henri came over and lashed himself to the wheel. "Ready?" He smiled at Alexander, every bit the part of an adventurous pirate.

Here came another moment in which Alexander learned why these men so revered their captain. They faced the most danger since Alexander came aboard, and instead of worrying or becoming more rigid, Henri relished the challenge.

The storm arrived soon enough. The ship listed hard to starboard, so Henri spun the wheel and barked orders, some of which men relayed from the captain, near the back of the ship, to men in the front.

For the first time as a pirate, Alexander feared for his life. The waves tossed the ship around like a small toy, despite everything the captain and men did to maintain control. A few animals fell overboard, and the sea nearly claimed one sailor until two others caught him by the legs and yanked him back.

Alexander's mind wanted him to drift away to his peaceful and secluded location whenever faced with serious stress. The powerful storm was leading him away. He stayed there for but a second, however, before forcing his mind back to reality, lest Henri call for his assistance. A pirate could ill afford to allow his brain to float away in the middle of a tempest.

"Alexander!" Alexander could barely hear Henri, though he stood a couple feet away. "Do you got anything for me?"

"Like what?" Alexander almost choked as a cascade of water hit him in the face.

"Fucking magic! Be a witch, Goddamn it!"

Alexander let his mind study the wind. She blew in every direction and had no regard for the vessel. Then a possibility hit him. He grabbed his crystal, called to see the ship from the sky, and studied the clouds until he spotted the most direct path out of the storm.

"Captain! Turn us around!"

"Into the heart of the storm? Are you mad? I thought you could control the wind!" Henri almost slipped and fell but stayed upright because of the rope strapped around him and the wheel.

Alexander pointed to his crystal. "The fastest way out is behind us. I think I can give us a push when needed if we go the other way."

Henri frowned but screamed orders and started to yank on the wheel. As the ship turned to port, Alexander caught a draft of wind in the storm and pushed the front of the ship to tilt more sharply.

Alexander questioned his decision when an enormous wave rose high above their sloop and crashed down on the deck, sending men and supplies everywhere. But seconds later, Alexander smiled at what he realized. He commanded his power to grab a violent gust of wind that lifted the boat up over another gigantic wave and then shoved them toward the back of the storm. Several minutes and more machinations by Henri and his pirates later, they steadied the ship and put the storm well behind them.

After the men secured the provisions and got things back under control, the alcohol flowed even more freely than usual. The men shouted and cheered their survival. Only Henri's appearance on the deck overlooking the men got their collective attention.

"Listen here, mates. A damn fine job managing the storm. Damn good. Impressive."

The crew cheered as the captain called out a few sailors in particular, including the two who had saved one of their own. Alexander realized Tacky had been one of them, despite his difficulty in walking.

"And one more deserves credit. Some of you didn't want him aboard. Some have questioned his role since he joined our ranks.

Resented him, even. Well, if you look hard at the situation, I think you'll recognize we performed a dangerous maneuver, turning this boat around and heading directly at the center. I think most of you felt the change happening, but this one here turned us around with his power to control the wind. Call him what you will. But he brings needed power to our side. *All Hallows Eve* thanks you for your service on this fine day. And a special thank-you to our very own pirate witch."

Alexander noted, once again, Henri kept from them his ability to see the present and concentrated on his control of the wind.

Henri winked down at Alexander as a roar of approval filled the air. Soon enough, the pirates returned to their individual celebrating and drinking.

Yet Alexander winced when he heard a few men whisper his magic might bring unnatural forces to bear against them. They stared in anger at him, but Spittle stepped between.

"Pay them no mind. They're jealous because Captain never applauds them. They're generally worthless, except adding another body on ship."

King James landed on Spittle's shoulder and ruffled his feathers. "*Squawk!* Beast approaching! Beast approaching!"

"Shit." Spittle rolled his eyes.

"Shit! Shit!" King James repeated.

"Go get Henri," Spittle told the bird.

King James flew away as Beast stumbled into their midst, drunk. Alexander grew nauseous, peering into Beast's eyes. The demon inside could hardly control them with the alcohol coursing through his veins.

One eye glanced left, the other toward the crow's nest.

Beast pointed at Alexander. "We should throw him overboard before he causes trouble."

A couple of his friends stood behind him, glancing over his shoulder and nodding approval.

Spittle stepped forward, unafraid despite Beast towering over him. "Move along, Beast."

"I mean what I say. He's a witch." Beast reached around Spittle and poked Alexander in the chest.

Spittle glared at Beast. "He knows some magic he used to save us, including your sorry ass. *Move along.* I called for the captain, and he'd best not discover you harassing him."

"His lover? They're unnatural together too. Bestiality."

Before Spittle could offer a rebuttal, the men parted as Henri stalked toward them.

"Come on." Spittle grabbed Alexander's hand and pulled him along. "Let's get you out of here while this blows over." They walked through the men, and Spittle grabbed a jar of rum, and led them to the captain's quarters, shutting the door behind him.

Alexander spotted a deep cut on Spittle's lower shoulder, the blood seeping through his orange checkered shirt. "When did you get the laceration?"

Spittle frowned and covered the wound with his hand. "I've had worse. I'll attend to myself in good time."

"Let me heal you." Alexander reached for some of his herbs and prepared his mind for the magic, but Spittle jerked away when

Alexander approached him.

"We usually don't have a doctor aboard. I handle myself."

"I'm not a doctor. But I can help. Please?"

Alexander sat beside Spittle, who turned away. Alexander wanted to heal his friend who had done so much for him, so he determined to force the issue. After chatting for a moment about the lack of doctors on most pirate ships, Spittle began to relax. Alexander leaned over, pushed the torn shirt aside, and smeared the ointment on the wound.

Spittle lurched away but not soon enough to avoid the magic healing. And not soon enough to prevent Alexander from having spied down the torn shirt and learning Spittle's secret.

Spittle's lips pressed tight together, his face turning bright red.

Alexander jumped to his feet and went to the captain's chest. He knew he had precious seconds to right the wrong he had committed. Spittle was already clutching a saber.

He reached in and grabbed one of the shirts Henri had showed him, won at a card game but too small for him. He meant for Alexander to wear them.

"Here, put this on." Alexander handed the blue-and-red-striped shirt to Spittle. "You'll need better cover for your chest with your shirt torn. Or from me tearing it."

Spittle sat motionless, covering the wound but also grasping the weapon.

"Please. I didn't mean anything." Alexander sat down and laid the shirt on Spittle's lap. "I meant to help you, to heal your wound. I've never had a friend before. Crispin was my lover. And I'm not sure what to call Henri. But you're the first friend I've ever had in my entire life. You've helped me more than you could imagine. I'd never betray you or your secret."

Spittle put her sword down and unbuttoned her shirt, and for the first time in his life, Alexander laid eyes on a set of breasts. They were small compared to what Alexander had envisioned on most women, and Spittle had them strapped down with a couple layers of bandages, though the strap had also been ripped open. With the new shirt on, she sat down next to Alexander and placed her hand on his knee.

"Is your wound healed?" he asked.

Spittle nodded. "Thank you. Not even a scar. A broken crate slammed into me during the storm. You really are an amazing witch. I know you controlled the wind for us. And you healed me."

"I did my duty aboard this ship."

Spittle sat quietly for several minutes. "No one knows. Not even Captain."

Alexander wondered how she concealed her secret for so long from these pirates.

"Like you, I had to flee. I refused to marry or act like a proper woman. My father beat me, and my mother would have nothing to do with me. I got scolded most severely when I ventured out with a musket one day to hunt. To save myself, I gathered up a disguise as a sailor and went on a couple of journeys on a merchant ship. I got bored, so I escaped my contract and became a pirate. I've lived as a man ever since the day I walked out of my home for good. I never told anyone before.

No one ever knew, until you."

Alexander understood what had happened between them a couple days ago. He had shared his entire history with Spittle during a drunken revelry, from his mother and father dying, to the years with his uncle, his love affair with Crispin, and why he sought out the pirates. He had waited for Spittle to reciprocate, but she never did. Now he knew why. The threat of exposure risked everything for her.

Alexander smiled at Spittle and held her hand. "More than anything, friendship is based on trust. Or at least I imagine so. You know lots about me. Everything, really. And you still like me. Same here."

"You won't tell Henri? He thinks women aboard ship would make us weak."

"Nonsense. You make us stronger. And the men respect you."

Spittle nodded. "Thanks. But he won't agree."

"Well, he won't find out from me. Are you a him or a her? What do you prefer?"

Spittle tilted her head in contemplation. "I never had to consider before. I was a woman until I chose to be a man. I guess I feel like a her, but with an inclination to dress and act the part of a man. Do I make any sense?"

Alexander nodded. "Yes. I appreciate your choices and will honor them too."

A loud rap at the door startled them, and in walked Henri.

"There you are! I put Beast back in his place. He's scrubbing the toilet."

Spittle and Alexander laughed. Alexander perhaps liked going to the bathroom least of anything else aboard the ship. In a secluded spot on the leeward channel where the sloop had no rigging, you could pee over the side or sit on a scratchy wooden box to poop. Too many of the men had poor aim, and Henri used such cleanup as a punishment.

"Ah, scrubbing the seats of easement. A good task for a villain." Spittle laughed and moved toward the door. She stopped before exiting. "Captain?"

"Yes, first mate?" Henri chugged a large amount of some whiskey he kept stashed below his bed.

"Your mate there —" Spittle pointed toward Alexander. "— one of the finest sailors I've ever had the privilege of sailing the sea with, saved our asses today."

Henri nodded. "That he did. And I'll reward him kindly right now."

Chapter Eighteen

Medusa

23 July 1700

Atlantic Ocean

ALEXANDER MARVELED AT how many forms the ocean could take in a matter of days. Two days ago they almost lost the sloop at sea, and tonight they drifted on the most tranquil water imaginable. The ocean looked no different from the clear glass ponds of Massachusetts. Stunningly beautiful. Alexander appreciated this band of men, enjoyed the serenity, too, and thus voted to relax for a few days before heading on a mission.

In fact, the pirates had yet to determine their exact course of action or destination. Henri had them vote a number of times, but other than heading in the general direction of the Caribbean, they elected to enjoy the abundance of supplies they currently possessed and float along peacefully, or as peacefully as one could expect among the drunken revelries.

Alexander moved toward the leeward deck. Some pirates seemed to hold their pee for days on end, no matter how much they drank. Not Alexander. The minute he gained a buzz and felt the subtle tingling pass over his body, nature called. Around the corner from the seats of easement, which the pirates concealed somewhat with a batch of barrels and other chests, Alexander spotted King James, one of the only sober beings on the ship.

"Greetings, Kind Sir. Greetings." King James squawked this louder than his usual tone.

Alexander laughed and returned the sentiment. Odd. King James seldom engaged anyone except Spittle in conversation. Usually someone had to speak to him first, and even then he repeated whatever was said.

Not a second later, Spittle rounded the corner, tucking in her shirt. King James flew to her shoulder and pecked at her ear.

Alexander looked around to see they were alone and smiled. "He stands guard, doesn't he?"

"During the most dangerous time for me."

The alcohol made her comment funny, for some reason, and Alexander and Spittle broke into laughter at the parrot having to guard whenever she went to the bathroom.

"Coming here must be difficult. Going to the bathroom adds a layer to everything you do."

Spittle contemplated and then shrugged. "I got so used to dealing with the reality. It hardly phases me anymore. When you're done, come find me. I got us a special stash of wine we took off a ship once. I reserve vino for special occasions."

"What's the occasion?"

"Friendship."

Alexander sat down to pee, afraid he'd topple overboard if he tried to stand up. The gentle sway of the boat almost put him to sleep right there, but he wanted to get back to Spittle as soon as possible.

He headed toward the main deck where most of the pirates gathered for a party in honor of the calm sea. This crew liked to declare a reason for every celebration, though Alexander figured regardless of the circumstances, they would always come up with an excuse to drink themselves into oblivion.

Before he came around a pile of foodstuffs, a hand yanked him between a section of barrels, then slammed him hard into them. His head hit solid wood, and Alexander saw stars. He called forth some magic to protect him, but either the rum, the injury, or a combination of both incapacitated his sorcery.

Alexander looked up and stared into the angry black pits serving as eyes for the demon inside of Beast. Drool slid down his chin as he smiled down. "Not so powerful out here, are you?"

"Here? What do you mean?"

"On the ocean. Sailing around, trapped on a boat and drunk."

Beast held Alexander by the shoulders and squeezed until it hurt so badly Alexander thought his head might pop off.

Still no magic came to him.

Beast laughed. Not the laugh of a pirate or drunken sailor, not even the laugh one might expect to hail from Beast's mouth. He let out a sound from another realm that terrified Alexander even more. Then the noise turned softer, almost feminine, an incongruous sound coming from this hulk of a man, and in a tone Alexander recognized but could not place.

"You don't recognize me, do you?" Beast grinned as saliva dripped onto Alexander's cheek.

Alexander struggled in absolute panic against Beast's hold on him. Without his magic he would never survive the encounter. He saw in those eyes and heard in the voice for the first time what demon had taken over Beast.

Beast slammed him against the barrels again and smiled. "Hello, Alexander." The feminine voice, falsely soft, concealed a powerful witch and was especially frightening coming from this beast of a body. "Did you think I'd given up when you last saw me laying in the bed of roses?"

"I left Crispin. He's with her. Why did you come for me?"

Beast tilted his head. Or should Alexander now call the man Portia? "Perhaps revenge? Simply to torment you? I had to make sure you'd really left. And I have some vague notion not all is safe with my son so long as you walk this earth."

"Beast? Let go." Alexander peered to his right and saw Monkey.

Monkey walked up to them and grabbed Beast by the wrist. Then he held up a knife of some sort, which he used as a cooper, and threatened Beast. Alexander thanked his luck Monkey hated drinking because his sobriety likely assisted him in confronting a drunk demon.

Beast released his grip and silently walked away.

"You all right?" Monkey asked.

Alexander wiped at the sweat on his forehead. "Well enough. Thank you."

"Of course."

Alexander walked away, not wanting to discuss the matter or risk breaking down in front of Monkey.

But he decided to tell Henri Beast had threatened him. Alexander searched the deck and went to the captain's quarters but found no trace of Henri. He headed below deck, despite the fact his drinking made the smells even more difficult for him.

His heart sank when he rounded a corner of crates and found Henri leaning against the ship wall with another sailor on his knees in front of him. Henri winked and blew a kiss to Alexander. Alexander turned to leave, but Henri called him back. Alexander hesitated, his instinct wanted him to flee, but his pirate self needed to obey the captain and, truth be told, explore what Henri desired.

Henri pushed Alexander down and commanded the two men to work on him together. Alexander grew excited when he understood a rather slight but incredibly handsome sailor knelt next to him. He tasted of rum and rubbed their tongues together. He had luscious green eyes and full lips. Unlike most of his compatriots, he hardly smelled and tasted of sweetness.

"I'm Rummy." Alexander stifled a laugh, finding formal introductions odd while they lapped at Henri's dick.

The combination of Rummy with the tang of Henri's manhood compelled Alexander to suck more vigorously at everything his lips brushed across. Henri tensed and released himself on their faces. Then he watched as they licked and cleaned each other up, giving them instructions and pointing if they missed a spot. Alexander and this lovely young man also grabbed at each other so they, too, came on the wooden floor.

When they finished, and the little one disappeared, Alexander's head spun in a thousand directions. He stood and a tear trickled down his cheek.

Henri pulled him into a hug. "There's enough of me to go around. We never want things to get stale, do we? Know this. You're my boy. Only you, no matter what." Henri kissed him on the forehead and walked away.

Alexander took a moment to gather himself. They'd never promised exclusivity, and Alexander had no idea why he ever anticipated such a thing. Henri, as the captain and not his lover, explained the situation to him quite clearly. He should revel in his special status and enjoy the pleasures of life the openness might bring. And he had. The sexual excitement matched almost nothing he had ever experienced.

Yet the moment gave him pause. He also disliked how they never discussed the matter, but rather Henri issued an order, after having sex without Alexander's knowledge. His hurt feelings kept him from telling

Henri about Beast.

The emotional turmoil with Henri also prompted him to clamp down on the wild fear Beast had sprung within him. It was one thing to deal with a mad pirate who despised him, but quite another to confront Portia Nottingham again. Alexander had no idea how to combat her so ignored her presence altogether.

Alexander pulled the crystal out of his pocket, hoping a vision might transport him to another realm or at least divert his attention. There, somewhere on the ocean, he saw a large British warship patrolling the waters of North America. Crispin stood on deck, monitoring the men, his firm countenance set on his face, wind almost blowing off his hat.

Survive, Alexander. He heard his mother's plea yet again. And he had survived, countless situations, new circumstances, and the ups and downs of his existence. Most of the time he embraced life despite some of the horrendous events he confronted. The latest episode with Henri paled in comparison to other losses and offered the potential for excitement. He had fought Portia before and won too.

Alexander shook his head and shoved the crystal back in his pocket. He was Henri's now, with a special status aboard a pirate ship. He took the episode with Rummy as another pirate lesson, steeling himself by shoving the emotion deep down inside, then went to find Spittle and her special bottle of wine.

Spittle smiled when she saw Alexander after he came above deck and searched for her. "Get over here and help me drink this wine, or I'll drink the whole bottle myself and regret it later."

Alexander grabbed the bottle and took a drink. He and Spittle liked to laugh and joke during these times together. "Can we play with King James again? He plays my favorite game."

Spittle giggled. "Yes. I'll start. King James, please inform Stub over there he smells like warm piss in a bucket of slop."

"*Squawk,* Stub smells like warm piss in a bucket of slop!" King James flew off. Spittle and Alexander watched as he perched next to Stub and repeated the message. Stub cackled, then looked over and flipped Spittle off.

When King James returned, Alexander went next. "Go tell Monkey he's an uptight prude."

"*Squawk,* Monkey's an uptight prude!" King James ventured over to Monkey. But he stayed a moment longer before flying back.

"Message from Monkey! Message from Monkey! Alexander's an opportunistic slut! *Squawk!*"

Alexander glanced at Monkey, who looked back with an enormous grin, then both fell into peals of laughter. As he and Spittle regained control of themselves, Alexander sat up to see who else needed a visit from King James. But he flinched when Beast stood up unsteadily, clearly drunker than before, and called for everyone's attention. "Listen up! Listen up!" His group of minions also shushed the crowd until Beast had everyone's full attention.

"Time for a new pirate nickname!" Beast called out. Then he turned and pointed at Alexander.

Spittle scrambled to her feet and started toward Beast. She spit at his feet.

Beast reached over with his leg and smeared the spit with his boot. "I mean no harm. I want to name one who has no name, as far as I can tell. I'd like the honor of bestowing one."

The pirates cheered, too drunk or cavalier to care about the tension.

"What with the witchery and other-worldly power, if we must cope with its presence on our boat, then I propose we label him as accurately as possible. The one who lies with the captain is henceforth known as Medusa for the magic he brought aboard."

The men cried in agreement, some excitement welling within the ranks at coming up with a new nickname.

Alexander winced for a number of reasons. He thought of voicing his first objection when Spittle stepped in.

She screamed at Beast but had lost the attention of most men, who went back to their jugs and personal conversations. "You're such a fucking idiot! You make no sense! Medusa was a cursed monster, not a witch. You've got your mythology scrambled like that head of yours without a brain."

Alexander appreciated Spittle's effort but could tell they'd lost the battle as several pirates, including those he liked very much, congratulated him on having a name.

Besides, Alexander wanted to put as much distance as possible between Beast and himself. He had no stomach for fighting Portia tonight, nor any theory on how.

Alexander reminded himself to survive the latest irritation with his name and threat from a demon. Never mind that Beast intentionally chose a feminine name to emasculate him, or intended to remind the other pirates Alexander was a dangerous witch.

Then Alexander searched for Henri to see his reaction. Henri stood on a platform above, watching over his kingdom. Henri smiled and winked at Alexander. He too determined to go with the nickname and choose his battles.

When the hot guy from below deck, Rummy, tripped because of his drinking and landed in Alexander's lap, Alexander held him. They kissed and Alexander hardly flinched when Rummy whispered Medusa in his ear and then laughed before crawling off for more alcohol.

As a sign to himself that he embraced this new life, Alexander drank the last of their wine and then pulled Spittle close to him. He pointed across the way to one of the pirates who manned the crow's nest.

"How did he get that?" Alexander asked her.

"His scar? In a nasty battle last fall with a Spanish frigate."

"No." Alexander shook his head. "In his ear."

"The earring? Why, you need the hardware and we jam whatever you choose through your lobe. Easy enough."

"I want one. I must start looking more like a pirate."

Spittle laughed. "We can arrange to pierce you. Maybe we better wait until you're sober, and see what Henri thinks."

Chapter Nineteen

A New Kind of Love

28 July 1700

New Providence, Bahamas

FOR FIVE DAYS Alexander went about his business aboard ship without any contact with Beast. He told no one about their encounter or Beast's true nature, though Spittle suspected something as she kept asking him about Beast. Alexander planned on avoidance until something clearer came to him. Nor did Alexander spend much time thinking about the nature of his relationship with Henri, until Henri informed him to come along when he went ashore in New Providence.

Thus Henri pulled Alexander through the crowded and dirty

streets, the first pirate port Alexander had experienced. He'd grown accustomed to life aboard ship as they sailed along but now encountered his next lesson in pirate life. Sometimes they ventured ashore for supplies, other times because they needed another diversion.

This stop combined the two. They needed fresh water and possessed enough in trade to resupply their foodstuffs. Spittle had gone off with another contingent and a chest of various treasures, including an anchor, some cotton, and ivory, in order to barter for more pistols, swords, and gunpowder barrels. Monkey went to ensure any new barrels would survive transport to the ship.

The last few days at sea arguments arose and became intense a couple times. Some complained about the restriction on gambling, and of course, the alcohol flowed freely. Henri confided to Spittle and Alexander they needed to come to port to release the tension.

New Providence offered the perfect respite, with crowded bars, gambling in the streets, whores, and anything else a pirate might want to spend his plunder on for an evening's entertainment.

After they anchored and started ashore in the canoes, Henri pulled Alexander into a long embrace. He kissed Alexander deeply.

"Ah, you make me a happy pirate, my little one." Alexander gripped Henri's large bicep and went limp in his arms. "I got something special planned for you tonight. Come with me."

Alexander accepted over the last few days how Henri's eyes strayed. They'd enjoyed another threesome with a different pirate, but only Alexander slept with Henri and stayed in his quarters. He came to understand sexuality had nothing to do with his special status nor endangered him. He liked the sex, too, though the last one came with such a large penis he was completely intimidated. Henri took him from the back end while he tried to get this other member down his throat.

So Henri and he had some version of a relationship, but the arrangement failed to conform to anything Alexander had ever envisioned. However, their status allowed him to survive, and happily so.

The fact Henri planned something special for him, when everyone else described a free-for-all in the pirate hideout, meant the world to Alexander.

As they navigated the crowded streets, Alexander and Henri shouted greetings to pirates from their own ship, and Henri ran into several people he knew some other way.

"Henri the Twisted! Living up to your name, I hope?" A pirate with an eye patch, bright-red coat, and tanned face greeted Henri.

"But, of course!" Henri growled back. "Sometimes practice for sport."

Henri engaged in a long conversation with the man, who Alexander learned captained another pirate ship and occasionally banded together with Henri for a particularly large heist.

"I best keep moving. I got plans for tonight."

The pirate captain shook his head. "A whore's warm booty would do you a might bit better than these womanly men you bandy about."

Henri laughed heartily, slapped him on the back, and moved Alexander along.

They soon stood outside a dilapidated building. On the second story balcony, several scantily clad women blew kisses to the crowd and called to the men. Henri entered first and shouted a greeting to the stout woman sitting in a chair, talking with another woman and a couple of men.

Unlike the outside that looked about to collapse at any minute, the inside's simple elegance enchanted Alexander, with nice furniture and candles glowing throughout.

"Henri!" She jumped to her feet and ran over to hug him. "Your man came ahead and already paid. We're ready for you."

"You're the best." Henri kissed her hard on the lips.

She pushed him away and punched Henri playfully in the chest. "Get on with you. I only guarantee hot water for so long; then you pay more to heat it up."

"That's the thanks I get for overpaying?"

She laughed and shoved him toward the steps.

Upstairs, Henri led them down a hallway to an open room. He went inside and waited for Alexander to enter before closing and locking the door behind them. Alexander peered at a simple bedroom, with a rather large bed fitted with silk sheets and lots of pillows. A chest of drawers stood against one wall, and in the middle sat a tub full of steaming hot water.

"A special gift for you, love." Henri made a dramatic motion to indicate the room.

"For me?" Alexander glanced at Henri. "I don't understand."

"A thank-you. For saving my ship from the storm, perhaps." Henri removed his hat, sat down, and worked on his boots. When he got both off, he tossed them to the side and jumped to his feet. "Ah, hell.

This here has nothing to do with a reward or payment. I wanted to shower you with something special. We don't get many baths. Come here."

Alexander's heart melted at the gentle caress and the way Henri handled the next several hours. First, he slowly undressed Alexander and then gently guided him into the tub. He left for one moment with their clothes. "We need these laundered before they stand in the corner."

They cleaned each other with soap and a sponge. Henri lingered over every part of Alexander's body. He massaged him, scrubbed until Alexander looked as clean as he did after a brisk swim in the creek by his uncle's mill.

When the water began to cool, Henri lifted Alexander to his feet and carried him to the bed. He licked at every inch of Alexander's body. Unlike the passionate and desperate sex Alexander had grown accustomed to with Henri, this felt tender and loving. Alexander cried out with pleasure when Henri entered him and moved in and out until Alexander begged for him to complete inside his ass.

When they finished, Henri asked Alexander a thousand questions about his past, which Alexander answered with as much detail as possible. Henri especially marveled at the magic Alexander knew and probed for more about his power. Alexander explained as best as possible what he could and could not do, what he easily controlled, and what came as more of a chance.

"Which is why you weren't sure about the storm?"

Alexander nodded. "I had no idea if I could control so much wind.

I succeeded, but sometimes the power refuses to obey. But what about you? You know about me. What's your story?" Alexander tensed, waiting to see if Henri would answer the inquiry, though previously he always deflected the question.

Henri ran his hand through Alexander's hair, kissed his forehead, and sighed. "I suppose you deserve to know. There's not much to tell. I'm French. Learned English quite young because my father was a diplomat. I was the youngest in the family and hated the life of privilege. Always behaving, and expected to act a certain way, I wanted to join the navy but they forbade me. I was slated for a life at court as a politician. I had the responsibility but none of the privileges, which would go to my eldest brother. I ran away once and joined the navy, but my father called me back through his sources and the captain kicked me off the ship.

"So I started spending my free time at various ports and learned the trade of a sailor. I stole aboard a Spanish merchant vessel to the Americas. But getting ordered about for little money got old pretty fast, and I liked the anonymity of the New World. I figured my father could never find me here. So I stayed but joined a pirate ship when they attacked our vessel and threatened death if we challenged them. I suppose my education and former status gave me the means to rise to captain. Not to mention my unorthodox ways of enforcement."

"You mean how you got your name?"

Henri winced. "I don't like talking about my nickname with you. It's not the most charming trait of mine."

"No, but it's an important one. I'm not afraid of you."

"Maybe you should be." The implied threat contrasted sharply with the intimate moment, especially the way Henri continued to pull his fingers through Alexander's hair. Henri let his comment linger before continuing his tale. "When our ship attacked a Portuguese slaver and took control, I went from first mate to captain of the new vessel. Eventually, we parted from our fellows on the other ship and started our own crew. We ditched the ship for a new one and eventually commandeered this one in battle. End of story."

A thousand more questions swam through Alexander's mind, but Henri started playing with his balls. Alexander lifted his legs and relished the feel of Henri's tongue plunging into his anus.

After another passionate bout of lovemaking, they called for more hot water, bathed, and slept the night in each other's arms.

Alexander woke the next morning feeling like a prince. Why had he ever doubted Henri's feelings for him? He could share this man with others as long as he maintained his special status.

As they dressed, Alexander thanked Henri for the extraordinary night.

Henri yanked him into a tight hug before they left the room. "For my special boy. I'll give you this and more."

New Providence had quieted significantly by morning, with no crowds, but a few souls meandering about, and more stray dogs roaming the streets than humans. Alexander swallowed his bile and struggled against vomiting at the wretched stench of puke, feces, and other grotesque smells filling the air. Their ship smelled much better.

Henri guided them back to the spot where his men came ashore, and where they found Spittle commanding the men as they put a large barrel on a canoe to take to the sloop. "Here's the powder, so don't go playing around. One wrong slam against the side of the ship, and you'll be cooked for dinner. I'm not in to cannibalism."

She smiled at Henri and Alexander. "Our bounty yielded quite the profit this time. I hoped for three barrels of gunpowder but got four when the fiend tried to swindle me at first with a barrel half full. Monkey caught him. But we might not want to linger too long."

Monkey smiled as Henri praised him and Spittle. "Well, sounds as if we'd best get a move on. Are all aboard?"

"Everyone but the few here." Spittle motioned to herself, Monkey, and the four others ashore. "Oh, and Lefty. He never showed this morning. I gave him leave, since he did most of the work in Massachusetts. But he promised to be here this morning to help out. He never showed."

"Leave him." Henri motioned for everyone to board the canoes.

"Did we get new sailors?" Alexander asked as he and two others paddled toward the sloop.

Henri shook his head. "I wouldn't add one of the vile snakes from this port unless we became desperate. No need to risk the normal scum residing here."

Alexander rode in silence the rest of the way. He wondered about Lefty. Had he gotten a better offer and joined another ship? Drank too much and slept too long? Or decided to stay in a port for a spell?

They boarded quickly and secured the last of the provisions.

As the sailors responded to Henri's commands and prepared to embark, Alexander's mind drifted away. He disliked the scurry of activity, especially since he still had little to do to help them sail, short of trying to command the wind, which he and Henri decided to limit to emergency situations. He drifted to a realm, part imagined, partially created by his magical mind, in which he and Henri stayed in the bedroom for months on end, being served and catering to each other.

He struggled when the vision threw other men into the mix. No, he could live with multiple partners. It alarmed him more as he fantasized about being taken from behind. In the vision, he turned his head, expecting to see Henri's long, blond hair and muscular arms but was startled to stare into Crispin's earnest brown eyes.

Chapter Twenty

Pirate Trials

30 July 1700

The Caribbean

ONCE AT SEA, Henri called Spittle to his side after Alexander confirmed no bad weather threatened them. "We need to gather for the debate on our next course of action. But I want a controlled conversation, understand?"

"Yeah. Tell me what you want, and we'll make your wishes happen."

"We need a specific mission to focus them. Bring them back together as a force, and not a bunch of separate pirates. Let's get them to agree to find a merchant ship here in the Caribbean to attack."

"Got it." Spittle hurried off and circulated among the men.

"What's he doing?" Alexander asked.

"Planting a couple votes for our side."

"I thought pirates were a democracy? This seems like you manip-ulating them."

Henri frowned and started to say something when he saw Alex-ander's smile. "Well, nothing says you can't be persuaded in how you choose to vote."

Soon, Spittle called the pirates to gather on the deck below Henri.

Henri clapped his hands and glanced at the men below. "Give us a course, mates."

"Let's attack another pirate ship!" one sailor yelled.

"Not my style," Henri said. "But you choose. Other suggestions?"

"Float around drunk!" Everyone laughed.

"What about sailing north to cooler climes this time of year?" The suggestion brought a few ayes to the assembly.

Spittle raised her hand, so Henri pointed to her. "First mate?"

"North may be cooler, but there are merchants aplenty here in the Caribbean, and less competition from other pirates. How about we stay here and get some booty?"

The second mate, as planted by Spittle, seconded the motion.

Soon enough, the pirates voted to sail toward Cuba and Barbados in search of their first treasure hunt in a long time.

They sailed along for a couple of days quietly enough. One morn-ing, Alexander stood alongside Henri at the wheel as he watched his pirates and guided their course with the position of the sun, the stars the night before, and an island they passed.

Alexander used his witchcraft to push the ship toward an airstream to give them better speed. He also gathered a number of the men in Henri's quarters who'd sustained various injuries in New Providence over the last couple days and did his best to heal them.

He pondered the fact being at sea offered him less opportunity to use his magic than he'd anticipated and missed the leisurely days in Massachusetts where he could practice or engage his sorcery in any way he saw fit. He felt good to heal the men, except for the one who yanked out his penis and revealed white growths and puss on the shaft. Alexander refused to administer the medicine by touch, but he attempted to heal the poor guy nonetheless.

Lost in his thoughts, Alexander jumped when two pirates below screamed at each other. One shoved the other across the deck. As he scrambled to his feet, he grabbed an errant rope and whipped it at his adversary. Alexander recognized both but didn't know their nicknames.

The one with the rope lost his footing, and the second pounced on top of him. They punched and kicked and bashed at each other.

A crowd gathered around them, cheering on the fight but refusing to interfere.

"Goddamn it all to hell. The bastard. This better not be about his gambling." Henri stomped his boot on the deck. "Spittle!" he shouted across the ship.

"Aye, captain?" she called from below.

"Aye, captain?" King James squawked.

"Get up here and man the wheel while I take care of this."

She appeared next to Alexander soon thereafter.

"Is this what I think it is?" Henri asked her.

She grinned a crooked smile and nodded.

"Cursed ass." Henri stormed off.

Spittle smiled again at Alexander. "Watch him in action. Actually, I'm not sure you'll want to see this."

"Why?" Alexander had previously told Spittle how much he loved watching Henri take charge of his ship.

"I think you're about to learn how your mate got his nickname."

Alexander turned his attention to the skirmish on the main deck and watched in awe at how the pirates parted when Henri came into their midst. Henri picked up one of the fighting men and threw him effortlessly into the crowd.

"Seize him," Henri spat. "Though I think he may earn a reprieve."

The other man lay on the ground but tried to crawl away when he looked into Henri's eyes. "Not so fast." Henri grabbed him by the collar and yanked him to his feet. Three other pirates grabbed hold of him by the arms and around his waist.

"What was this about?" Henri stared inches from the man's face but continued to shout. "And think twice about any lie."

"Simply a...a...a...um...a duel." The man tried to sound confident but stammered out the answer.

"A duel over what?"

"Private matter."

"This private matter wouldn't have anything to do with your gambling again, no? Because gambling is against the code. The one hard and fast rule I require. You signed the agreement."

The man shook his head, but Henri turned and looked at the other one. The pirate started crying. "We bet last night on a race between two rats below. Big ones, one the size of a cat. We were checking on the water pump, making sure the goods stayed dry. He bet on the cat one, but I thought the smaller, quicker one would win. He lost but won't pay up."

"You'll be whipped for this. Never again gamble on my ship." Henri patted him on the shoulder, almost sympathetically. "Take him behind the others, and administer the punishment." A couple pirates dragged him away as Henri turned around slowly, pure hate dripping from every pore of his face. He walked back to the remaining gambler and spoke loudly for everyone to hear. "The cat-o'nine tails didn't work on this one. Must have liked a good flogging. Bring me a rope." Henri held out his hand. "Time for a woolding."

"No!" The pirate struggled against the men holding him, but they held tight. A buzz of excitement swept through the men. Even Beast cheered his approval at the captain's announcement.

The pirates placed the man above everyone else on a crate as he struggled, cried, and pled for forgiveness. He promised never to defy Henri again. Henri climbed behind him and glared down at the cheering men beneath him.

"I will not have gambling on my ship!"

Henri took the rope and wrapped it around the man's head. He tightened the rope slightly, and then reached for a stick he had slipped

218 -   Damian Serbu

into his waistband. He wrapped the wood around the rope and twisted. The man screamed in agony until all sound left him, Alexander guessed because the pain became too intense. Alexander turned away and concentrated on not throwing up when the force of the rope constricted to the point both eyes flew out of their sockets.

"Send him overboard." Henri casually climbed down and walked away from the men.

"Henri the Twisted. I suppose you see him now," Spittle said with a slight grin. "Pirates aren't easy to control. His use of violence has to be done."

Alexander nodded, then watched as the crew unceremoniously dumped the body into the ocean for the sharks.

"Time to lighten the mood." Spittle stood in front of the wheel and jumped atop the railing. She let out a loud whistle. "What's that? Did I hear His Majesty sent a couple judges to our ship? They claim Tacky there's a pirate?" Spittle pointed at Tacky, who grinned but flipped her off. "Time for a pirate trial!"

Even Alexander laughed and forgot about the earlier episode as the men took to the trial with fervor. They chose a panel of judges, lawyers, and witnesses, and even fashioned makeshift costumes, including wigs, robes for the judges, and a hammer-cum-gavel. Everyone enjoyed the high theater on the seas, especially when the prosecutor, Spittle, put Tacky on the stand.

"You claim you're not a pirate, but how else do you explain your toes?"

Tacky's eyes twinkled. "What toes?"

"Exactly my point, your honor!" Spittle slapped her hands against the makeshift bench serving as the judge's table. "He lost his toes in some mysterious battle he won't tell us a thing about. What other war hero returns with wounds he won't explain, except a pirate?"

The judge gaveled the assembly back to order when they shouted back and forth. "What other evidence, besides his feet, have you?"

"Have you smelled him? He smells of rot and piracy."

Another judge waved his hand in front of his face. "He does reek of rat shit."

Tacky stood and shouted a defense, but Monkey pushed him back into his seat. Spittle sauntered up to him.

"Here's the deal, Tacky. His Majesty, in his infinite mercy, has offered you a reprieve. He hates what circumstances pushed you into the high crime of piracy. Against your will, no doubt. Possibly you lack the foresight to resist because of your skin color." She winked at him.

"Fuck off," Tacky replied.

"If you repent, you may go free. Yes, you heard me. Confess. Tell us where your fellow rapscallions are hiding, and you walk out of here a free man. Otherwise I have the evidence to put you to death by hanging."

"I'd never rat out a friend!" Tacky proclaimed to loud cheers from the men.

"Your honors!" Spittle shouted. "I have no choice but to present the vile pirate, cook, and nastiest hardtack feeder to ever float the high seas. I recommend Tacky for immediate execution!"

The judges conferred with one another before turning back to the men and yelling out at the same time, "Guilty!"

"Guilty!" everyone shouted.

"Put him to death!"

Alexander worried they might execute his friend. However, they carried him around and forced him to take a drink of each person's rum jug as he passed by. Soon enough Tacky sat as the guest of honor while other pirates—including Alexander, taking the lead—prepared dinner for the entire crew.

At some point in the midst of the trial, Henri returned to the deck. He did so without fanfare but gradually took part in the revelry with the men who made up the audience.

And Spittle once again demonstrated her worth as a leader of these men. Where Henri enforced the law, she gauged the climate and alleviated the stress from the execution of one of their own.

A shiver ran down Alexander's spine as he contemplated Henri's actions. What had he expected, after all, from a pirate captain? Love and mercy? He'd heard enough hints to know he acquired the name by some awful deed.

It was also the first time Alexander witnessed death since leaving Massachusetts. He hardly cared about the man and, again, realized how brutality ruled the day on a pirate ship.

His head spun and he took a quiet dinner by himself to reflect on how fast, and with what ease, Henri wielded his deadly authority.

Alexander fell asleep beside the man, in awe of his presence as much as on the day he met him and aroused by his manhood. But he also thanked the stars he was on Henri's good side. He wanted to remain there.

Unable to sleep, he contemplated asking for Henri's assistance against Beast. Spittle recommended against telling Henri because she and Henri steered clear of Beast as much as possible. Beast commanded the respect of a small but powerful contingent of men, and again she indicated his value in battle. Alexander continued to avoid Beast but felt him watching all the time. Eventually, something would have to change, and Alexander hoped Henri would help him when the moment arrived.

Alexander assisted Tacky with cooking breakfast the next morning. The men became excited because the quiet air and calm sea meant Tacky could start a fire to cook up the pig, after it broke a leg the night before and had to be killed. Alexander helped build the fire and then distributed hardtack while the men waited for the day's real feast.

Alexander had long intervals to contemplate while they cooked, and today he reflected back on Henri's comment earlier in the morning.

Henri never addressed the woolding with Alexander but cautioned they were heading for their first battle.

"I've no idea what we face. Every man may need to take up arms to defend himself, including you. The wounded and crippled fall to the back. I expect you to do the same. Stay near Tacky." Henri stared hard at Alexander when he began a protest. "That's an order. You will look better if you heal people as soon as possible, so you're engaged in the battle, but also dispelling their fears about your witchcraft. Use whatever magic you can to help us. But otherwise fall to the rear. Understand?"

Alexander nodded.

Henri placed a hand on Alexander's shoulders and gently rubbed. "You wanted to be a pirate. The life isn't always pretty."

The understatement caused Alexander to burst into laughter. He fell back on the bed and could not stop, which sent Henri into fits as well.

"What's so funny?"

"You are." Alexander pulled Henri on top of him. "Sometimes you scare the shit out of me. You're a cruel pirate, which makes you a good one, I suppose. Then you say sweet things, and it's quite a contrast. I knew pirate life wouldn't always be pretty."

Henri traced Alexander's lips with his finger. "At least my cabin's always pretty with you inside."

After a quick bout of sex, Alexander left the cabin and started right away with assisting Tacky.

Alexander also recalled the death by woolding, which sent shivers through him, followed by the pirate trial, which made him laugh out loud. He loved remembering the strong arms of Henri as they held him tightly through the night.

Pirate life offered the oddest mix Alexander could imagine. Death, yet revelry. An anything-goes atmosphere, followed by strict rules, intense loyalty, and even love. Then there was the stench and disease of unclean men afloat on the beautiful blue seas of poetry.

The more Alexander thought, the more he appreciated at least pirates participated in creating their own climate, signed on willingly, and knew the reality and consequences from the beginning. Unlike the hidden agenda of the Puritans and phantom demons they hunted, pirates looked out for themselves and enjoyed what life threw at them, even death.

Yet Alexander paused to wonder if life could have been different under other circumstances. After daydreaming his entire life about other possibilities and futures, his mind wandered and created imagined kingdoms and realities in which to escape. Could he ever find a less harsh path in life?

When everyone finished eating and Tacky announced they would take a break, Alexander wandered to the captain's quarters and fell onto the bed, needing a moment alone.

He glanced into his crystal. He saw Henri and Spittle bantering with the men as they scrubbed the deck and repaired the sails. Even Henri appeared to be stitching up a tear.

He set an enchantment for his magic to alert him if anyone approached, then asked the vision to show him the mill. In the middle of the day, his uncle struggled with the grindstone, broken once again. The place looked affright, even messier than the day so long ago the authorities had taken Alexander by force to live with his uncle.

He spied upon Caroline in her parents' home. He moved quickly because he disliked her and because she was boring to watch, sitting there sewing some unknown piece of cloth.

Then he tested his skills. He practiced his magic so sparingly that he now wanted to tax himself as much as possible. He needed to sharpen his talents and ready them for the upcoming attack. He asked the crystal to scan the high seas for a ship, and to find a specific individual.

He spied any number of vessels, his head pounding from the effort. He literally felt the veins in his forehead throb with pain. He took several deep breaths and then got a clear picture of Crispin in his mind: his height, his darkened hair and eyes, the firm lips Alexander once kissed.

The crystal whirled into motion. The vision spun across the waters, past several ships, and toward an HMS naval vessel coasting near North Carolina. It zoomed in suddenly, and Alexander gazed upon the deck of a warship protecting the colonies.

Alexander wondered how long he watched Crispin—long enough to learn about his rank and even to understand the conversations he witnessed.

Crispin had risen to a high rank aboard ship. Alexander had no idea how such knowledge came to him by studying the present, but he could tell Crispin and his men had recently survived and won a battle. Perhaps from the charred deck, the wounded men gathered underneath a sail on one end, and the captain leaning against a post as he commanded his ship but held his stomach in apparent pain. The vessel displayed a large hole blown into one side.

While the captain watched the activity in silence, Crispin walked about and shouted commands. Unlike Spittle or even Henri, he did none of the work himself but commanded others.

Crispin walked to the back of the boat and sat amidst the wounded sailors. He conversed with them, and Alexander saw on their faces a lifting of their spirits in his presence. Like Spittle and Henri, Crispin made a good officer.

The revelation hit Alexander. He looked again at the rankings and spotted the signs Crispin now served as first mate, no longer a gunner. He was second in command of the vessel.

Alexander's heart soared with pride. He had always known Crispin would succeed, what with his stubborn determination and rigid, albeit flawed, dedication to duty. He felt good for Crispin.

Alexander also grew excited at seeing Crispin in his tight sailor pants. He longed for the days he waited in some deserted location for the sound of Crispin's footsteps and a romp in the hay. He wished again for the protective way Crispin defended him from his uncle and the Puritans.

Alexander sat stunned. Why had he thrown out his entire past with Crispin? Just because their love failed and he would never see him again did not eliminate their history. Crispin had helped to shape him into the man he had become.

Crispin taught him how to love another man. So much of what Alexander relished about his life came from their chance encounter in the chicken coop. Despite his flaws, Crispin had done much for him. Alexander still loved him — perhaps desperately so.

Instead of a false moving on and pretending their love had died, Alexander determined to allow both his survival and future happiness to coexist with the past. Pain, suffering, and joy made up every day of life. Why hide from reality?

Alexander rubbed the stone, as if he could feel Crispin's cheek against his fingers. He admitted the truth for the first time to himself. "You broke my heart," he said out loud.

The crystal lurched from the scene aboard Crispin's three-mast ship to the captain's deck on this one. Henri climbed the ladder and walked toward his quarters. Alexander shoved the crystal into his pocket and pretended to sleep when Henri walked into the room.

Alexander opened his eyes and saw his new love standing before him. Henri took off his hat, and his long, blond hair fell around his shoulders as he sat on the edge of the bed. He wiped a strand of hair out of Alexander's face and smiled.

"Are you well?"

"I needed a bit of rest from this morning's breakfast."

"You and Tacky cooked up a delicious meal." Henri cupped Alexander's chin in his hand. "You're gorgeous." He patted him on the cheek.

"Did you come to ask me to do something?"

Henri shook his head. "Spittle said you came in here alone, so I wanted to see if you were well. However, since you asked..."

Henri rubbed his hand along Alexander's thigh and pressed a finger into his butt. Alexander spread his legs and smiled. He reached up and pulled Henri toward him until he kissed him so hard their teeth clicked together.

Alexander hurried to undress Henri, loving the look of his large muscles and the light hair covering his chest. Alexander stripped off his clothes and pushed Henri onto his back. Then he stared down at the slight penis bobbing against Henri's chest. Alexander climbed atop Henri and engulfed it with his lips and made sure to moisten every inch.

He licked up to Henri's stomach and toward a nipple he took in his teeth. With his right hand, he reached down and grabbed Henri's penis, shoving the cock into his ass with a satisfied gasp.

He rode Henri like never before, massaging his chest, leaning over and kissing him, and coaxing him into an ecstatic climax. Even then, Alexander shoved down with his butt until all of Henri pushed inside of him, hard, pressing against his insides.

Alexander took Henri's hand and placed it onto his own penis. With Henri firmly implanted in him, the captain stroked him until he shot streams of semen over his chest. He collapsed on top of Henri.

V: Pirate Attacks

Chapter Twenty-One

Preparation

12 August 1700

Windward Passage, Caribbean

DESPITE VOTING TO go on the attack, the pirates sailed without any sign of a suitable target for two weeks. Alexander grew more and more accustomed to the rhythm of pirate life. He enjoyed his function as combination cook and sorcerer, and especially reveled in his growing friendship with Spittle, Tacky, and a few others.

He sat with Spittle, eating hardtack and noticing the increased energy aboard ship as they prepared, at long last, for combat. They tracked a ship for a few hours and prepared to move closer.

"It'll be fine," Spittle told Alexander. Without his saying a word, she detected his nervousness.

"You don't think Beast would take this opportunity to come after me, do you? If there's chaos aboard?" Alexander kept to himself the presence of Portia Nottingham in Beast's body.

"You best keep avoiding him. Only interact within the large group when you have to. Never alone. Listen, I know he likes to humiliate you in those settings, especially with the nickname he gave you. But he can't hurt you with everyone watching because captain would get him."

"But in the midst of a fight?"

Spittle shook her head. "Nah. He's too needed in the battle. Everyone would notice his absence."

"Steady as she goes, and avoid any one-on-one contact with him?"

"Exactly."

Alexander yearned for a final confrontation with Beast-cum-Portia, but being new to the pirate ship and uncertain of Portia's power, he had yet to figure out a strategy and so obeyed Spittle and Henri's instructions to stay away.

Ah, Henri. Alexander lusted after the man and felt safe in his arms, protected aboard the ship of pirates despite his lack of sailing knowledge. He loved sex on the high seas as the captain's lover but without the puritanical notion of monogamy. What at first sent him into an emotional quandary evolved into pleasure. He never went all the way without Henri, but the occasional kiss or mutual masturbation felt good. And having others join Henri and him kept things lively.

Strange in the midst of such liberation his mind often turned to Crispin. He figured he and Crispin would have remained happily exclusive with each other. As with so much about his former relationship, Alexander had learned to accept the contradictions and even embrace them.

Spittle tapped him on the head. "Where'd you go? To your magical realm again?"

"No. I was thinking about life with the captain after you mentioned his name."

"Good. Because he's your best security against Beast. Also, he wanted me to remind you to stay back during the fight. Help the lame, concentrate on healing. Nothing else unless absolutely necessary."

"I know." Alexander saluted her, which made them laugh. "He reminds me a lot. I don't need you dwelling on my cowardice too."

Alexander steeled himself for the first attack and what he might witness. Would warfare make the woolding pale in comparison? He knew he would confront more death and see an even uglier side to the crew of men, his family.

"Captain!" The pirate high in the crow's nest shouted down.

"Aye?" Henri called back.

"Ship to starboard! Possible merchant."

Henri grabbed his telescope and peered starboard, while other men raced to the ship's side to try to see for themselves.

"Prepare for attack. But stay the course. I've got to consult my charts."

Henri turned toward his cabin but grabbed Alexander by the arm as he went by. Once inside with the door closed, Henri smiled.

"Part of your duty as official pirate witch calls. Can you see what's aboard the ship?"

Alexander smiled back, excited despite his nervousness. He took his crystal out and sat down to concentrate. A harsh rap at the door caused him to jump and almost drop his crystal.

"What in Bellary's name do you want?" Henri shouted.

"Captain! We need orders!"

"Your orders are to shut your fucking mouth and leave me alone for a minute!"

Alexander sat staring at Henri, unnerved by the interruption. Henri walked over, scowling, but sat and put his arm around Alexander. "Ignore the fools. Do your job."

Alexander blocked out his surroundings and stared into the crystal, which looked down from above—first upon their ship, and then across the water to the other vessel. He ordered the magic to swoop upon its deck and scrunched his brow. He saw a skeleton crew, as Spittle explained he might see because merchants sailed with far fewer men to save money. But he saw no cargo. Not atop the deck, nor below. He could search almost every nook and cranny of the boat but found nothing they might pillage.

He cleared his throat, unsure how to continue.

"What?" Henri asked.

"There's nothing there."

"Shit. Are you sure?"

Alexander nodded. "I searched the whole ship. There's a smaller crew than you even told me to expect. Maybe they unloaded cargo but have yet to resupply."

Henri stood and paced the room deep in thought. "What should I do?"

Alexander raised his eyebrows at Henri's question. "You're asking me?"

"No one else in here." Henri laughed, then slapped his hand hard against his thigh. "They expect a fight." He pointed toward the door and the pirates outside. "Been gearing up for a scrum for too damn long. If I go out there and call off the attack, there'll be mutiny. Remember, we didn't tell them about your ability. The ship doesn't even have foodstuffs we might want?"

Alexander glanced again in his crystal, but the ship had so little he assumed they planned to dock any day to resupply. While Henri continued pacing and barked out a dismissal when someone else knocked on the door, Alexander extended his search of the Windward Passage because Spittle said countless merchants sailed there, with the swift winds speeding their transport.

He spied a ship loaded with merchandise, headed toward Europe, approximately a few days journey. "There's another boat. Maybe a couple days away, with plenty of goods."

Henri stopped moving, which started to make Alexander nervous. "Like what?"

"Cloth. Spices. A bit of tobacco. Looks like sugar, maybe. And rum."

"Rum?" Henri's eyes lit up.

Alexander nodded.

"We have to figure out how to manage this." Henri thought for a few minutes. "Ah, fuck it."

Henri motioned for Alexander to follow and strode across the room and out the door. He stood at his usual spot for addressing the men.

"Attention!" Henri shouted. "I have something to tell you. I've been keeping a secret from you, at captain's discretion. Some of you don't have right intentions, which worried me. Anyway, I have to explain this, and I want you to listen to the whole thing before ye get upset. We aren't attacking the ship."

The men, as predicted, began cursing. Henri held up his hand to quiet the crew.

"I told you to let me explain. Alexander here can do more than heal your unworthy asses or assist us time and again with the wind. He can sense what's on a boat." Alexander almost laughed aloud at how Henri attempted to avoid the entire truth. "There's nothing on the ship. Literally, almost nothing."

"We should make sure!" one man yelled.

"We can't go listening to Medusa," another shouted.

"But—" Henri ignored them. "—hang in two more days because he found us another ship, loaded with goods."

This time the men went silent until Beast spoke, "Like what?"

"Spice. Some smokes. And rum!"

This sent the boat into a celebration, the tension from moments ago evaporating. Alexander marveled they so quickly accepted his ability without much question. He knew their reaction had everything to do with Henri the Twisted and little to do with him. He prayed the crystal showed him the truth, for in a matter of minutes Henri orchestrated a near unanimous vote from the pirates to head for the other vessel and prepare for attack. Only Beast and his cohorts dissented.

That night, Spittle focused the crew's energies with a task much like the mock trial. Since they had prepared themselves for battle, a volatile force brewed within many of the men. Another night of lounging about risked skirmishes or too much drinking when they needed sobriety for the next day.

She gathered them about her after they ate. "Boys, the last storm before Massachusetts tore the shit out of our Jolly Roger. We can't do a proper job in the morning without the appropriate signal." Spittle held up a tattered black flag to emphasize her point. "We'll have a competition." She pulled over a large trunk and began spreading out a bunch of cloth, mostly black and red fabric. "Pick a partner or get into groups, and design us a new flag. We'll vote to determine the one to fly from *All Hallows Eve*."

Henri went about encouraging the men, but he and Spittle didn't participate. Neither did Alexander, who was more interested in watching them create these images than in sewing anything himself. He stayed with a few other pirates, including Monkey, who viewed the moment as high theater.

The pirates voted on one made by two of the men whom Alexander and Henri took to bed from time to time, especially Rummy. He had the softest lips, a beautiful skinny body, and light brown hair. Rummy did most of the sewing while his partner chipped in here and there. The other flags looked childish in comparison, and even the men who made them tossed them aside in favor of the winner.

Rummy's flag was bright red, with a black skull sewn on the left side and a bleeding black heart on the right. Alexander had goose bumps as they pulled their colors to the top, hoping the fear it inspired when they approached the merchant ship would induce a quick surrender.

Two days later, Alexander woke but stayed in bed as long as possible. They'd spied the vessel the night before and planned their attack. Henri had left quite some time ago, after dressing and placing a multitude of weapons on his person. Alexander pretended to sleep but watched Henri's ritualistic preparation.

Alone, Alexander allowed himself to drift away, like he used to do while working for his uncle at the gristmill. His mind floated out of his body and surrounded itself with a mystical forest of perfection: a comfortable temperature, plenty of food, and no sense of danger. He spotted the old family dog playing in a field, the dog who first alerted him to the approaching Puritans on the worst night of his life. No people appeared in his vision, though he could sense the friendship of Spittle nearby. No feeling of Henri or Crispin complicated his thoughts.

When he had calmed himself in the other realm, he returned to his body and the captain's quarters. He was about to witness a pirate attack in all its glory, gore, and reality. He had known since before he even met these specific pirates what awaited him. The sooner he confronted reality, the sooner he could move to the next phase in his life.

Alexander dressed, remembering to tuck away the two knives Henri gave him for self-defense. Henri told him he doubted Alexander would even participate in the fighting because merchants tended to give up easily. But best to prepare for the worst.

Alexander went outside and saw most of the men meandering about nervously. Realizing he needed to eat, he headed for the food-stuffs. Tacky warned him the night before they would only eat hardtack for breakfast. They had a big fish dinner but could not risk alerting the other ship to their presence with a fire, nor take the time to prepare anything whatsoever. All focus went into the planned attack, even from Tacky. Alexander picked a bit of hardtack and made sure no bugs had taken up residence.

Other men wandered about, all heavily armed, but for the first time a relative quiet fell over a ship typically vibrating with noise and chaos. Henri went from man to man, slapping them on the back and encouraging them as they prepared. When he climbed to stand next to the wheel, Alexander knew the time grew close.

Henri looked at Alexander and jerked his head back toward his rooms, indicating for Alexander to follow. Alexander closed the door behind him and knew before Henri asked he wanted a last look through the crystal at his target.

"The same as yesterday," Alexander said. "Typical merchant crew. Plenty of goods. No indication they suspect us approaching."

"Good." Henri strode across the room, grabbed Alexander by his shoulders, and pulled him to his feet into an embrace. "Listen to me. Stay to the back."

"I *will*."

Henri started to pull away but stopped and turned back to Alexander. He yanked him into a tight hug. "I care about you." He kissed Alexander hard on the lips. "It ain't right for a pirate to make an attachment like this, but you're so different. I want you in the rear because I can't stand the thought of something happening to you. I like having you around. Understand?"

"Understood. The feeling is mutual."

They kissed again, passionately, as if they may never get another chance.

When Henri released Alexander, a transformation took place before his very eyes. The gentle man of seconds ago, who came as close to professing love as Alexander had ever heard, became a hardened pirate. He squinted his eyes, clutched the pistol handle in his belt, and straightened his posture. "Come. This will be fun." He smiled broadly and wiggled his eyebrows. He winked. Alexander spied the darker parts of Henri that lurked below the surface. They had come out to play.

Chapter Twenty-Two

Merchant Attack

13 August 1700

Windward Passage, Caribbean

ON THE MAIN deck, Alexander moved toward Tacky, near the kitchen with its good view. A few others gathered close, each somehow maimed or incapable of fighting, thus prohibiting them from participating in the attack.

Alexander noted the tension in the air, not of fear but of anticipation. The cannons were loaded, everyone prepared their pistols, and Henri ordered the ship aimed at the merchant vessel in the distance.

All Hallows Eve slammed into a wave. The sails billowed with the strain as Henri manipulated what he could to increase speed. As they grew close, the crow's nest reported the ship spotted them and prepared to increase speed.

Henri rubbed the railing affectionately. "They can't outrun this sloop."

True to the captain's words, they fast caught up with the other vessel. Alexander jumped when a cannon roared to life. He scanned to see the pirates fire a second volley toward the side of the ship.

Within minutes, they sailed about fifty feet to the side of the ship. Alexander saw the other crew pointing up at the red flag with its black skull and bleeding heart. Henri moved to the main deck, leaving Spittle at the wheel, where he prepared another warning volley to fire at the merchant ship.

Boom! A flash of fire and a cheer from the pirates sent another warning at the merchant vessel, this time full of glass, metal, and nails. One sailor near the bow of the other ship fell to the deck, screaming in agony.

After the hype and preparation, perhaps more striking to Alexander because he had anticipated intense horror, the swift surrender of the other ship seemed anticlimactic. Without any more threats or further pursuit, the merchant craft lowered its sails and began to slow. Alexander guessed maybe forty men manned it. The pirates used grappling hooks to link the two ships together. They aimed their pistols and even the cannons at the merchant sailors, readying for a defense despite the raised hands and an apparent captain holding up a white shirt.

A few pirates braved the crossing and went aboard the other ship.

Despite his protests and screams of terror, they sent the captain over to the pirate ship and to Henri's waiting gaze.

"So you surrender?" Henri asked the man.

"I do, indeed. I ask for you to spare my crew and the vessel."

Henri nodded. "Rather cowardly to give up easily."

The captain cleared his throat. "We're no match for a pirate ship. We use speed to get away. With your ship you'd win, anyway."

"Weak." Henri punched the captain in the mouth and walked away. He appeard to be thinking about his next move, though Alexander suspected he knew all along exactly what he intended. Henri always planned his next two or three steps in advance.

He walked back to the man and led him to the side of the pirate ship. "I accept your conditions. I'll leave the boat intact and allow them to live, so long as no one resists. I show mercy to you as well with a swift execution."

Alexander's eyes opened wide when Henri pulled out his pistol and shot the captain point-blank in the forehead. Then he shoved him over the side of the boat into the sea.

None of the pirates, nor the sailors on the merchant boat, appeared to react to his death. Perhaps everyone expected the murder from the beginning. Perhaps Alexander should chalk the incident up to the latest pirate lesson. Horror. Death. Violence. He had heard such tales as he'd talked to sailors in Boston. Pirates ruled the seas with ruthless action and by instilling fear in everyone they passed. A surrendering captain expected and deserved death according to rules of the sea.

Alexander was sickened nonetheless. Why kill a man who held

up a white flag and gave his ship to the enemy? Did Henri need such a show of evil to achieve his purposes, both from the other ship and his own men?

Yet Alexander adapted to reality and repressed any misgivings. He was alive because of these pirates and in love with the killer. He even wondered why so little fear of the situation or regret overcame him. Actually, he knew the answer. His early life taught him harsh lessons about the brutalities of the world and importance of survival at any cost.

The next two days surprised Alexander even more. Not because of more violence, thank God, but because of the length of time they took to plunder the other ship. More pirates went across to the merchant vessel, where they imprisoned the crew in the cramped captain's quarters and took turns guarding them. Slowly but surely, the pirates transferred the goods from one ship to the other.

As Alexander had viewed in the crystal beforehand, they found a good amount of cloth, from which they hoped to make new clothes, also tobacco, loads of rum, and a bit of sugar. The pirates who stayed on *All Hallows Eve* got more and more excited at the volume of goods coming over. They accounted, quite meticulously, for everything brought aboard for a fair distribution. They first separated the goods into categories, and then Spittle wrote out an inventory before taking the spoils below deck or to the areas above for storage.

"Medusa?" The pirate called two more times before Alexander registered someone wanted his attention.

Alexander turned to see Monkey on the other ship, motioning toward him. He wondered if this had to do with food, as the cooper went over to inspect their barrels and take only good ones for the pirates. Strangely, Henri said to replace any barrels they stole with a less sturdy one from *All Hallows Eve*, so the other crew would survive. The pirate code of ethics and morality befuddled Alexander.

"Hello, Medusa?" Monkey smirked. "Can you come over here and bring your healing supplies, or whatever the hell you call them?"

Alexander swallowed a lump in his throat, afraid of crossing between the ships while on the swaying ocean. But he nodded at Monkey and went to the side of the ship. First he called forth the wind to carry him to the other ship if he fell. Henri winked an approval, so Alexander retrieved a few of his plants and herbs, though more than anything he needed his magic and nothing else.

Every limb shook during his quick passage over, though he never needed the wind and got there safely, despite keeping his eyes shut most of the way. He stumbled onto the deck and almost lost his footing.

"Who's hurt?" Alexander asked Monkey the second he boarded.

Either Monkey failed to notice or politely ignored Alexander's fear. "The one who got hit with the warning volley."

"One of their crew?"

Monkey nodded.

Again Alexander marveled at the strange rules guiding pirates. They had no qualms about firing the mix of shrapnel at the ship in order to subdue it, with no concern for who might have been killed. Since then, they defeated the boat and proceeded to take all its wealth, not to mention Henri killing the captain, yet somehow Alexander was summoned to heal a sailor.

Monkey led him toward the imprisoned crew. Outside the captain's door, he spotted a makeshift tent, under which sat one of the sailors along with another wounded man lying beside him. Rummy stood guard, while other pirates watched over the rest of the men shoved into the captain's quarters.

Alexander ducked under the tent and held his hands up to calm the one man, who jumped in fear when he entered.

"What's wrong with him?" Alexander asked Rummy.

"Got metal and glass in his thigh and missing calf." Rummy knelt and pointed toward the injured sailor's leg. "We heated the knife before we cut his leg off at the knee. But the bleeding won't stop."

Alexander gasped. They amputated the man's leg, not an uncommon practice to avoid infection, especially out at sea and without a good doctor to assess whether they could save the limb. They made a clean cut, but the bandage was completely soaked crimson.

Thankfully, with no other injuries and no sign of puss, Alexander felt certain he could heal the man. When he started to unwrap the bandage, the injured one cried out in pain. Alexander stopped.

"I have to remove this. Can you help him?" he asked the sailor's friend.

"Yes." The other one spoke soft words of encouragement and held tight to his friend's hand. "Grit your teeth if needed. This is going to hurt."

Alexander spared the man by removing the cloth as quickly as possible, knowing going slower would prolong the agony. He also healed the wound swiftly. He created an ointment with a couple of the plants, uttered his magic under his breath to conceal the power from these sailors, who would think the science of mixing the plants with water alone healed the leg.

The bleeding stopped, leaving a grotesque stump. He placed a hand on the man's shoulder. "Done."

Alexander exited the ship as soon thereafter as possible. Rummy kidded he should take a crate across with him, but Alexander laughed and barely got himself back to *All Hallows Eve.*

"Greetings! Greetings!"

Alexander chuckled. Despite being at this for over a day, King James watched the pirates going back and forth and welcomed them aboard every time a man returned to the ship.

Alexander bowed to the parrot. "Greetings, kind sir."

King James cocked his head, as if puzzled when Alexander returned the salutation. "*Squawk.*" The parrot flew away. Alexander watched until he landed on Spittle's shoulder and pecked at her ear.

The third day after taking the vessel, the pirates disengaged and sailed their own way. True to his word, Henri left the crew unharmed and allowed enough food for them to survive.

Sailing along as the sun set, Alexander marveled at how fast the tension from the impending attack and plundering of the other ship disappeared. With the vast amount of rum and good supply of wine they stole, the drink flowed freely, and their carefree attitude returned.

Spittle led a very fair and orderly disbursement of the treasure. Everyone got an equal share, though they could choose what specifically they desired. If one smoked like a chimney, they got more tobacco, while Rummy took his full allotment in rum. Men asked for cloth if they needed new clothes or wanted a change of pace, and the pirates voted to allow Spittle and the captain extra spoils for leading them.

"Everyone, listen up!" After giving Henri even more rum and a special knife they took from the captain's quarters, Monkey shouted for the pirates' attention. "I got an extra case of wine for one who deserves a bonus. He healed a man over there, so he didn't bleed to death. And he led us by himself to the ship we plundered. A vote, for Medusa to get an extra helping of refreshment."

Beast roared a dissent. "He's nothing but a captain's whore."

Silence engulfed the ship. Their eyes turned not to Alexander but to Henri, who sat stoically admiring his new knife.

"You can vote to reward a fine job by one of your own or listen to the drunkard. Says more about you as a crew than anything."

Henri's words sent the men back to their revelry and a quick vote to award the special plunder to Alexander. He began opening his extra bottles of wine at once and passing them around, though he kept one for himself.

"Well played," Spittle said.

"Well played!" King James flapped a wing at him.

Alexander enjoyed the night's celebration and got pretty sloppy drunk himself. He landed in the lap of the long-haired pirate who'd pinched his butt the first day on the ship. Fittingly, Alexander learned his nickname was Long Hair, though he almost never interacted with him because his good looks intimidated Alexander. He enjoyed the fondling until Henri came over and pulled him off and then helped Long

Hair to his feet. Henri motioned for both of them to follow and led them back to his bed for a special night, where a few minutes later Rummy joined and made a foursome.

Chapter Twenty-Three

Careened

20 August 1700

Coast of Cuba

DESPITE HENRI'S WORRY, the pirates accustomed themselves with relative ease to Alexander's magical abilities, no doubt because of how much they benefited from him. Alexander had saved them from a storm, healed numerous men, and found the perfect merchant vessel to plunder. Any superstitions — and pirates had plenty — became subservient to the benefit of having a witch among them.

Everyone agreed, except for Beast and his lot. They muttered under their breath, and a couple crossed themselves whenever Alexander got too close. No doubt Portia played to this element, without Spittle or Henri overhearing. The other night, as Alexander lay gazing at the stars when they anchored near a small island, one of Beast's minions knelt in front of Alexander and glared at him. "Beast sent me with a message for you. Said you can't ignore him forever. He's watching. We all are."

Alexander laughed. "I'll take your warning under advisement."

"You ought not laugh at him."

"Indeed." Alexander continued to smile. "Tell Beast I've faced much more formidable foes and defeated them without the help I'd have now."

Alexander watched him go. He'd never cowered before in his life, meeting every challenge head-on. He determined to approach Portia-cum-Beast with the same confidence and quit tiptoeing around the boat.

Yet because of Beast's influence over his band of followers, and despite most of the pirates appreciation for Alexander's magic, Henri asked him to peer into the present in privacy, claiming the others would grow nervous if they thought Alexander and the captain could monitor them.

Alexander sat alone on the seat of easement, doing his business and watching the Cuban coast for a suitable place to careen.

Unlike his hesitance with the first attack, Alexander looked forward to the next sailors' maneuver. He hurried to finish and pull up his pants when he spotted in the crystal the exact kind of location Henri described, very near their current position.

He rushed across the deck to Henri. "Here." He held up the crystal and sighed when he realized others might see. He shoved it into his pocket. "Go that way, around a small outcropping of trees, and the cove will be right there." Alexander pointed, hoping Henri could grasp where to go.

"I understand. Stay near and let me know if we get off course." Henri had them sailing toward the spot soon thereafter. Alexander stood near the front of the boat in anticipation. He braced himself when the ship slammed into the shallow water and listed to the port side.

Over the next several days, Alexander spent time on the beach relaxing, even as he helped Tacky make special dinners. The stability of the coast and no need to worry about burning down the ship allowed them to make extravagant meals of fish, plus the game a few pirates hunted on the island.

When not cooking or doing odd tasks, he watched the pirates take care of their ship. They beached in order to burn and scrape off the seaweed and barnacles, which over time would threaten the hull's integrity. Afterward, they repaired other parts of the ship and applied oil to the underside.

By the fourth evening, Alexander understood why pirates got antsy with too much inactivity. He enjoyed their break from the sea but tired of the monotony. He wondered why, because he did much the same thing here as on the sea what with assisting Tacky, healing the fool who stabbed himself in the thigh while hunting, and helping Henri and Spittle. He nonetheless wanted to cast off.

Alexander wandered down the shoreline, enjoying the breeze that cut through the thick heat of the Caribbean during the hot summer months. He paused near a rock and sat. A safe distance from everyone else, he practiced his magic.

He whipped the wind about, transported his mind high above the island and into the sky, then healed the tiniest of scratches on his arm with the power of his mind. He directed a harsh blast of air at one particular palm tree, crashing it to the ground.

His magic seemed in order and at his complete disposal.

To test himself further, he pulled out his crystal and concentrated on extending his reach. First, he located the merchant ship they had attacked, which had arrived in a port and was preparing another load to take across the ocean. Alexander decided not to tell Henri.

Then he spied upon Crispin. Over the seas he flew, gliding along until he sighted two HMS ships sailing in the Atlantic Ocean, continuing to patrol the Colonial coast.

Alexander actually further refined his magical ability. In addition to seeing the present anywhere he wished, he developed a sensory perception to allow him to understand a situation without hearing anyone. He gained a sense for circumstances, a deeper knowledge about activities beyond what the mere glance at the present could tell. He had first done so when he figured out Crispin had risen to the rank of first mate, then again when he searched for a merchant vessel to attack. In addition to seeing the bounty, he could sense the reluctance of the captain to engage in violence. Though he told no one, not even Henri, sensing the quickness to surrender played into what particular boat Alexander recommended they attack.

The two HMS boats in his vision sailed rather close to each other, unusual unless preparing to engage in battle. Alexander concentrated his energy on Crispin, who walked about the deck of the smaller of the two vessels, working to transform it into a warship.

Alexander's power revealed the situation to him. Crispin ordered the repositioning of a cannon. Alexander could see the Spanish papers on a table and the olive complexion of some of the sailors. Either they had seized a Spanish boat, or pirates had captured the ship before the British conquered them. Whichever, the British commandeered a Spanish sloop, which Crispin now commanded, elevating him to captain.

"Looking at your former love again?"

Spittle's soft approach hid her arrival from Alexander, who forgot to have the crystal warn him. He smiled when she scooted him over and sat next to him on the rock, propping her feet up and resting her chin on her knees.

"How'd you know?" Alexander asked.

"Lucky guess."

"Sometimes I like to see what he's up to these days. I told you he loved duty and following rules. I disagree with him but hope he's at least happy."

"And?"

"Seems so. He's a captain now."

"What's with you and captains?" Spittle grinned.

"I need a powerful man to control me."

Spittle laughed. "Well, be careful. Captain suspects you downplayed your old lover. Never say anything to him."

Alexander promised. "Thanks for the warning."

"It's what we do for each other."

"What about you? I know you have to hide on the boat because of your sex. But do you like anyone? I don't even know if you go for men or women."

"Nosy, aren't you?" But she smiled. "I wish I knew the answer. I'm not sure. At home, I resisted expectations from my parents. I never thought about being with a man because I wanted to avoid having one tell me what to do. Once I ran away and became a sailor, the need to constantly hide myself meant I could never figure out sex. In port, I could get a mate for the night, but nothing holds any appeal." Spittle shrugged. "That's that."

"I appreciate your sharing with me. Alexander scanned around and frowned. "Hey, where did King James go?"

"Can't you see him? Right over there." Spittle pointed to another outcropping of rocks, several yards away.

"What's he doing?"

"Guarding. He gets bored without assignments, which makes him talk too much and act out. I give him something to do to shut him up for a while."

Alexander and Spittle talked for a long time underneath the stars and in the warm night. She handed him her jug of alcohol, which they passed back and forth. They gossiped about the crew and by the end made up nonsensical jokes to humor themselves.

King James got bored with his job as a sentry and walked down the beach toward them rather than flying. Once close, he flew to Spittle and landed on her knee.

"Quiet," she instructed. "I don't need him repeating everything we say."

King James perched there in silence. Alexander guessed the bird drifted to sleep when he saw Spittle laying back and asleep on the rock.

Alexander pulled out his crystal, not ready to sleep himself, and unsure whether he wanted to lay down on the hard surface.

He spied Beast, snoring under a palm tree by himself, a sword on one side, a knife clutched in his fingers. His little posse slept nearby. Henri sat awake, chatting with a few men.

Back on Crispin's ship, Alexander saw him in his quarters, his hat and shirt removed for the day. He examined maps spread out before him. A young officer, perhaps his first mate or a lieutenant, sat across the table, captivated by everything Crispin said.

Before jealousy overcome him, Alexander shoved the crystal back in his pocket. He thought of waking Spittle but settled for instructing King James to watch out for her. He left those two on the rock and headed back toward the beach and other pirates.

"There you are." Henri's face lit up when he saw Alexander approach. "Follow me."

Alexander followed him toward the trees and brush behind them. "I found this here spot for us today."

They lay down in a sandy clearing, and Alexander pushed himself into Henri's arms and drifted to sleep with his firm chest as a pillow. He last remembered the soft caress of Henri's fingers moving through his hair.

Chapter Twenty-Four

Heated Existence

25 August 1700

Atlantic Ocean

ALEXANDER TREATED MORE men for sunburn than anything else these days. They had enough supplies and wanted to wait to attack another ship until Alexander spied a big take. They drifted along, enjoying the sea, playing games, drinking, and not worrying about anything but the blasted heat.

July was bad, but August was worse. Despite the danger of sun exposure, many of the pirates walked about practically naked and sweating profusely.

"This is why most pirates move north during the summer," Monkey said over breakfast. He looked up, alarmed. "Don't tell captain I said so."

"I'm not a snitch."

Monkey flipped his long, red hair, tied in a ponytail, behind his back. "See these freckles? Makes the sun worse for me, I tell you. I burn right to a crisp in the sun. At least my job lets me stay below a good bit, even with the smells and rot."

"What do you mean most pirates move north. Who?"

Monkey shrugged as if the answer was obvious. "Pirates in general. We've got no rules. We can go wherever we want. Like the birds, we stay south in the winter and gravitate north in the summer. Keeps us in temperate climates. Shipping is different, too, so provides a variety." Monkey wiped at the sweat on his brow.

Alexander took a bite of the meat and spit it out. "Tastes like shit." One of the hunters, while on Cuba, gathered a bunch of lizards and slaughtered them for food.

Monkey laughed. "Yeah, not my favorite."

"If most move north, why not us? We came south in the middle of summer."

"From another perspective, our plan makes sense, despite my complaining." Monkey pointed his finger at Alexander for emphasis. "We come down here now, because most go up north."

Alexander arched an eyebrow. "Didn't you complain about the backward sailing a second ago?"

Monkey nodded. "The benefit being less competition because the merchants sail down here, and we have less chance of getting into a row with other pirates."

Tacky stormed over as they finished eating. "You've got to go below deck and get something better for dinner," he told Alexander. "There's going to be a mutiny if we serve any more of this poop. Lizard tastes like poop! Literally. I'd waste our precious supply of spices trying to make this edible, and even then would probably fail. I'm dumping the rest overboard."

Tacky turned around and stalked back to the kitchen, leaving Monkey and Alexander to laugh at his tirade.

"I better go pick a better beast for him."

"Speaking of Beast," Monkey motioned over Alexander's shoulder, who turned to see Beast leaning against a stack of trunks and glaring at Alexander.

Alexander winked at him. Beast shoved off and walked away.

"What did you do?" Monkey asked.

"Winked."

Monkey laughed, then after dumping the rest overboard, went to clean out the barrel they used to store the rancid lizard meat.

After seeing Beast, Alexander moved cautiously through the ship toward the opening to go below deck.

"All clear! All clear! Beast on deck! All clear!"

Somehow King James decided to alert Alexander to Beast's whereabouts and knew to tell him he could safely go below.

A few men slept in their hammocks, two played cards, though Alexander watched to see they weren't gambling, and some rodents scampered about. Well away from the others, Rummy leaned against the side wall, sound asleep near the stench of the animalpen.

"Stinky here, yeah?" Alexander poked Rummy.

Rummy smiled when he saw Alexander, after rubbing his eyes. "Yeah. But I can take a nap better because no one comes around."

"Sorry. I had to get something for dinner other than awful lizard. Maybe these chickens. They look half dead already."

"It's not a bother." Rummy reached over as Alexander leaned into the pen and grabbed the younger man by the waist. Alexander landed on his lap, laughing. "Can I ask you a question?"

Those beautiful full lips and pleading eyes intoxicated Alexander. He wrapped his arm around Rummy's neck. "Sure."

"Do you ever want to do something different with the captain?"

"I like how sex goes with him."

"What about with someone else?" Rummy inched his head closer to Alexander.

"What are you getting at?"

Rummy grabbed hold of Alexander's penis. "I only like for someone to do me. Like captain does to us. I wondered if you ever switched."

"I never have."

Alexander allowed Rummy to kiss him. Rummy licked along Alexander's cheek, then stuck his tongue in his ear.

"Would you ever want to try?" Rummy rubbed Alexander.

Alexander reached up and took Rummy by both ears and pulled him into an even more passionate kiss. His animal instinct took over as he rolled Rummy onto his belly and yanked down his pants. He grabbed his bubble of an ass and massaged.

"Take me," Rummy groaned.

With the lube of Rummy's spit on his cock, Alexander mounted the young man and moaned with pleasure as his penis went deep inside his ass. Rummy pushed up, taking all of Alexander and grinding his ass around. Alexander pumped and too soon the tingling shot through his groin, down his legs, and up his body. He lowered his head and almost bit Rummy's tongue off as he came inside him.

"I'd give you all my pieces of eight to do me again sometime." Rummy rolled over and stroked himself as Alexander held him, still recovering from the passion of the moment.

As usual, they said nothing of what happened once they finished. Both put their clothes back on, and Rummy helped Alexander wring the necks of five chickens and carry them up to Tacky.

Atop deck, Alexander was happy to be away from the rats. He swore they'd multiplied since he first came aboard, and their presence, more than anything else, disgusted him. He made sure Henri kept their quarters free of the rodents, and Henri remained diligent ever since the three nights Alexander refused to sleep with him in those rooms after a rat scampered across them in the middle of the night.

With a little time after delivering the chickens before he had to start a fire, which required constant monitoring, Alexander searched for Spittle. He first spied King James, carrying on with a few pirates who needled him to say things. King James seemed to enjoy picking and choosing whom to repeat and whom to ignore. Spittle lay a short way off by herself.

"First mates have to hang alone?" Alexander sat next to her. "Too much responsibility to cavort with the crew?"

Spittle reached over and punched him. "Sometimes I need Spittle time, alone with my thoughts. Can't even take having King James around."

"Yeah, not much privacy on a pirate ship."

Spittle snorted. "None."

"Must be harder for you," Alexander whispered, afraid of anyone overhearing.

"It's not always fun."

"How do you deal with it?"

Spittle shrugged. "I guess I don't think about the circumstances. What are the options? I'd rather deal with this than stay in some damn port and return to womanhood."

Alexander chuckled. "True enough. You really like being a pirate, don't you?"

"Of course. Freedom. The seas. What's not to like? Don't you enjoy pirate life?"

Alexander nodded. "I do. I feel freer than ever before in my life. But someday, maybe something else will call to me."

Spittle shook her head. "Not me. I'm staying with the pirates."

"What would you do if they found out?"

"Figure out a way to make them okay with me. So they'd keep me. And if not, I'd fight 'em off and go down swinging my sword."

Alexander laughed, more at the truth than from the fact Spittle intended a joke.

She had a way of always turning conversations back on him, and this time with a twist to surprise Alexander. "I know what else you'll do. You're going off with Crispin."

Alexander sat dumbfounded. He never even dreamt of such a thing. Why had Spittle brought Crispin up? Was it true? He pushed the idea from his mind, deciding not to bother with the sheer fantasy.

"Well, you would. Wouldn't you?"

"I don't know."

Spittle nodded. "Speaking of which, I got to ask you something as first mate. Be honest. I won't run to captain or punish you."

"What?"

"Beast says something's coming to bring you two to blows. Did you have another row with him?"

"No." Alexander had no contact with him whatsoever after the wink.

"You sure? He says things are just heating up."

"Maybe he's talking about the weather."

"He won't do anything to you." Spittle sent a volley of spit across the deck, as if aiming at Beast. "Not while Henri and I are watching."

Chapter Twenty-Five

Pirate Threat

26 August 1700

Windward Passage, Caribbean

ALEXANDER'S TENSION WITH Beast heated up. Nothing new oc-curred—they had no contact whatsoever. Alexander even steered clear of the pirates who worshiped Beast. But his magical senses tingled, even when away from Beast, alerting him to Portia's presence and growing anger. She had played it cool thus far, much like he did, to conform to life aboard the ship and conceal her real designs. But he knew their feud must come to a head, a moment Alexander feared fast approached.

Alexander sat alone with these thoughts and watched the pirates go about their business as the ship sailed along. The sun beat down mercilessly.

Spittle moved to the rear of the boat with a spyglass. She concentrated behind them, then called the second mate and a couple others to verify what she spotted. Alexander got up and headed toward Henri at the wheel when Spittle headed there too.

"Captain, we may have a problem." Spittle handed him the spyglass. "Ships approaching."

Henri, Spittle, and Alexander walked to the rear. As Henri scanned the distance Spittle and Alexander waited behind him.

"What?" Alexander could barely see the dots on the ocean and wondered how Spittle alerted to them.

"No idea," Spittle answered.

Henri looked at Alexander. "Can you see anything?"

"I'll go look."

Alexander stepped away and went into the captain's quarters. He cleared his mind of distractions and took out his crystal. He often thought of his mother at these moments and wondered when and why she had used her magic. He doubted she kept watch for the same kind of danger, but surely she protected them with her knowledge and ability. Maybe from Indian raids? Why had her ability failed her the night they came to kill her? He stopped these thoughts before they distracted him too much and undermined the magic he called forth.

Staring into the glass ball, the ship around Alexander disappeared, and he floated up and away into the sky and across the sea toward the three ships. He ascertained they stormed toward *All Hallows*

Eve. Alexander saw the drawn pistols and swords, the cannons readied, a captain in a red coat and with a bushy black beard urging them on. Their black jolly roger with a skull flew from the lead boat.

He returned to his present reality when the door opened and Henri entered, rubbing his face with worry. "Well?"

"Three pirate ships, sailing toward us in attack mode."

"Cursed asses." Henri paced back and forth twice before stopping. "Stay by my side, we may need you now, more than ever before."

"Pirates attack each other?" For some reason, this surprised Alexander.

"Why not?" Henri laughed. "No rules in the pirate world. They could be friends, reach us, and let us go. Or they could be on their own. Complete renegades ready to slice us open. You never know. And I don't intend to find out. We're going to need speed. Can you help?"

"I'll try."

Henri nodded and pushed Alexander out the door in front of him.

"Attack! Get ready for attack! We got pirates on our asses!"

Henri's shout sent *All Hallows Eve* into a flurry of activity.

"Get this boat moving! Hurry!" Henri grabbed the wheel and pointed a few of the pirates toward a sail he wanted raised. He also ordered the crew to steer them starboard to get a better backwind.

Spittle stayed at the rear and concentrated on the approaching enemy. "Bearing down fast, captain!" In her alarm and needing to shout, Alexander noticed for the first time Spittle sound more feminine than masculine.

"Damnit, hurry!" Henri screamed at the pirates to prepare for battle while others hurried to speed up the sloop. To Alexander, he lowered his voice. "You got anything for me?"

Alexander closed his eyes and soared his spirit above the boat and into the wind. His essence bumped into another force, a human element floating with him. The other being shoved him higher, above the strongest gale.

Competition for the wind! He concentrated on learning something about his foe. A witch stood at the bow of the head pirate ship with her arms raised in the air, her eyes closed and commanding the elements to their advantage. Not only did those ships move swiftly through the water, they did so at a supernatural speed.

"Alexander!" Henri screamed next to him and thus brought him back down to the ship. "I need more speed."

Alexander glanced over and saw one of the enemy ships already drew alongside them. A powerful blast of cannon fire missed *All Hallows Eve*. Henri commanded them to turn hard to starboard and farther out of range, but the other two ships moved to cut them off.

"All quarter, men! All quarter!"

Alexander knew that command from Spittle and dreaded ever hearing it. Henri instructed them to fight to the death.

Alexander flew above them, positioning his spirit next to the witch's. She manipulated the wind around them to her advantage. Each of the opponents' ships had a force of wind at its back, twisting and turning with the ship. Alexander first attempted a counterwind, blowing a gust with full force against hers.

His attempt worked on the smaller sloop to *All Hallows Eve's*

Witch in the Wind - 271 -

portside. As it lined up to fire its cannons, Alexander shoved a gust of wind at the enemy. Spittle readied the side of the boat to fire off a round of cannon and got a direct hit while the enemy blast landed in the water behind *All Hallows Eve* after the boat stopped dead in the water from Alexander's efforts.

Too late, Alexander understood he could only counter the witch one ship at a time, leaving two to do as they pleased. One circled in front of them. Glass, metal, and debris rained across their bow before the ship sailed out of their path. Alexander heard some of his mates scream in agony.

Alexander changed tactics. "Henri!" he screamed above the noise. "Can you steer the ship?"

Henri shook his head. "I can barely keep her on course. No way I can turn."

Alexander worked to give them a strong back wind. *All Hallows Eve* lurched forward, racing away from the pirate attackers.

Next Alexander brought his mind back to his body but kept his power concentrated on the wind at their back.

Spittle ran past him and Henri, holding her spyglass. "Pursuing as before!" she yelled.

Alexander returned to the air to determine if he could get them going any faster. He called forth more wind, but the witch countered with a similar and perhaps stronger magic to assist their boats. Once again they gained on *All Hallows Eve*.

"Turn your attention to battle!" Henri sounded like he had given up on outrunning them.

272 -   Damian Serbu

The circumstances hit Alexander as he moved back into the witch's realm. They could combat all day with each other as they manipulated the wind to the advantage of their respective ships. And this witch possessed a stronger magic than Alexander ever encountered, perhaps twice as strong as Portia.

Alexander willed his mouth below him to work while his soul floated above. "Keep the speed, captain. We've got one more chance to escape."

Henri frowned but nodded.

Alexander sped high into the sky. He bumped at the witch intentionally, to make her feel his presence. They each commanded the wind to push their ships at greater and greater speeds.

On *All Hallows Eve*, Alexander raised his arms high in the air and motioned them quickly down to the deck. His spirit in the sky mimicked the motion by swooping from high in the air and redirecting the wind and back to the lead enemy ship, right toward its bow.

As Alexander's force exploded toward her, the witch's eyes grew wide with terror.

Onboard *All Hallows Eve*, pirates fell to the deck and slammed into everything as the ship slowed by half with the loss of Alexander's wind power. Even Alexander fell to the ground next to Henri.

But the strength of the redirected air slammed into the witch and pitched her overboard. Alexander kept at his magic, forcing her deep into the ocean and plummeting her farther and farther into its depths. He returned to the surface when he feared losing attachment to his body.

A tornado of water swirled into action and obliterated one of the enemy ships. High in the air, Alexander determined their ships no longer had extra speed. Their pirates, too, fell with the loss of their witch's magic.

With no time to inspect the damage, Alexander forced the wind to push *All Hallows Eve* faster and faster, away from the enemy and toward safety. Men flew about the deck and grappled to steady themselves.

Alexander returned to his body but kept the gale at his command. Some of the pirates regained their footing when they shot forward again. Alexander grabbed his crystal and peered into it. The pursuing pirates lost their magical ability as *All Hallows Eve* sailed into the Atlantic Ocean and well away from the enemy.

Alexander kept them moving swiftly for some time before he collapsed in exhaustion on the deck, spent.

He had no idea how long he lay there passed out. When he came to, *All Hallows Eve* returned to her normal rate of speed, using the natural wind in her sails. The crew reorganized the ship and calmed down.

Spittle leaned down next to Alexander and smiled. "Nice job, Medusa."

Alexander flipped her off but grinned. "Are we safe?"

"As safe as pirates ever are. What happened out there?"

"Yeah, what happened?" Henri joined them. Before Alexander answered, Henri directed them toward the privacy of his quarters.

Inside, Alexander explained.

"Excellent work. Excellent!" Henri listened and his smile got bigger and bigger as Alexander told his story. Now Henri laughed uncontrollably.

Spittle and Alexander joined the revelry, Alexander more because Henri and Spittle laughed so hard than from thinking anything funny.

Before they returned to the main deck, Henri hugged Alexander and kissed him hard on the lips. "My little witch pirate." He gripped him, almost tugging the air out of Alexander's lungs.

By evening, the pirates turned to celebrating their escape from near disaster. Henri made no special announcement about Alexander's service, but by this point most of the pirates knew what had happened. Many men clapped Alexander on the back or insisted he take an extra swig of their personal liquor supply to thank him for the magic. Alexander had also attended to the injuries sustained among the crew during the encounter.

Eventually, word about the enemy witch's defeat spread among the crew, Alexander assumed because of Spittle.

"Enemy witch dead in the ocean!" Almost every pirate burst into hysterics when King James picked up on someone making that announcement and went about the ship repeating the mantra over and over. "Enemy witch dead! *Squawk!*"

The party intensified as the night wore on and pirates became more and more inebriated.

Alexander found a spot off to himself after a bit, when a melancholy took hold of him. At first, he began lamenting his first kill. He never took responsibility for Portia's suicide or even the fools who died the night they sentenced him to death. One was a suicide, the other a residual effect from self-defense. As a pirate, he had killed like a soldier in battle.

The brief feeling of regret stemmed more from the alcohol's effect than any real remorse. Murdering her had as much to do with self-defense as his first kill in life. Pirates killed.

He gulped the last of his bottle of wine and laughed. He made to get up when a pirate shoved him back to the ground and lorded over him.

"You best stop the sorcery before the demons turn on us instead." Alexander recognized one of Beast's minions, one with a particular fear of the spiritual.

Alexander pushed his arm off his shoulder. "I saved your ass today, or you'd be dead."

"We'll all be dead if you keep up with the devil's work."

The pirate put his hand on the handle of his knife. Alexander rolled his eyes when Beast appeared behind him.

"Got a problem?" Beast pushed his buddy aside so he stood above Alexander, holding him to the deck by slamming his foot into Alexander's crotch.

"*Squawk.* Got a problem?" King James landed on the ship's side, above Alexander and eye to eye with Beast. The bird repeated his question over and over, getting louder with each one.

Alexander saw the spit land at Beast's feet before he saw the first mate step into his vision.

"Get the fuck out of here, Beast." Spittle shoved him back and off Alexander, who lurched to his feet and prepared his magic.

Beast looked to the sky and raised his eyebrow. "Feel that?" he asked Spittle.

"I don't feel a damned thing."

"He's doing magic again. Begging me for a fight to try to kill me." Beast jabbed his finger toward Alexander.

"Get." Spittle shot a wad of saliva onto Beast's foot, grabbed a knife, and stepped forward, inches from the man's chest.

Beast sneered but walked away.

"He's more afraid than his bluster lets on."

"I gotta tell you something."

When Alexander finished explaining to Spittle his entire history with Portia and her possession of Beast, she shrugged and thanked him for the information. "I got your back."

Chapter Twenty-Six

Piercing

28 August 1700

Windward Passage, Caribbean

SOME DAYS AT sea, Alexander wondered what to do with himself. Since the attack by the pirate ships, *All Hallows Eve* had drifted along aimlessly. They searched for a suitable merchant vessel to attack but nothing called to them despite Alexander's ability to steer them toward targets. The ship had ample supplies and pirates tended to be a lazy lot, unless desperate, defensive, or with a large enough bounty worth their time and effort. None of those conditions existed, so the crew contented themselves with sailing the seas and drinking themselves into a stupor.

They did stop one night at a pirate cove to cavort with others and engage in trading. Alexander marveled at another dichotomy. Here, a number of ships anchored side by side, no threat to one another even though they could very well turn on each other at sea. Alexander stayed on the ship, uninterested in meeting more pirates and needing a break from the constant interactions with other people. He remained aboard with the skeleton crew and cooked for them so Tacky could trade for better food.

The pirates narrowly voted after one day in the cove to get back to sea. The vote flipped on the fact a few reported growing tension between the two largest pirate crews.

They sailed away and back to cruising along. In many ways, Alexander found himself quite lucky at the moment. No responsibility. No significant worries. A happy crew, and a captain who loved him. Yet he grew restless with no action and nothing to do but cook.

Tacky and he prepared another dinner, so Alexander pried open a barrel. He jumped back when he saw several spiders scurry around. "This one's contaminated," he said.

Tacky limped over and looked inside. He pinched one particularly large spider in half and brushed the others aside. "Not so bad."

"It's disgusting."

"Right. And food we may need. Here." Tacky grabbed the lid, picked up a hammer, and nailed it back into place. "We won't use spider spices tonight. Get another one."

The next barrel proved more secure. Alexander sifted around but found no spiders, worms, maggots, or other invaders to spoil their food.

Monkey assisted them this evening because Tacky built two fires. They pooled resources in the cove to trade for a bunch of birds. Some wanted to hunt for them, but their decision to leave so quickly prohibited an excursion. Alexander had never seen some of the birds, but they smelled delicious as they roasted over the fire.

As each bird cooked to perfection, Tacky called another round of pirates over to enjoy dinner, along with overly salted vegetables and, naturally, as much hard tack as anyone wanted.

After eating, Alexander joined the men on deck as they sang songs, joked, and passed around their bottles.

"Man overboard!" someone yelled.

Alexander and almost everyone scrambled to one side of the boat, where several men already worked to save him. The pirate in the ocean barely grabbed a rope and hung on for dear life. The pirates hoisted him up, twice almost losing him.

He fell to the deck, gasping for breath and shaking. Though some men assisted him, most began laughing while dancing a jig and jumping about too violently.

As quickly as the situation erupted, the crew returned to their drinking and cavorting.

Alexander went in search of Henri, who sat with several men telling stories about how each got the various scars decorating their bodies.

"I got this one from an alligator." A pirate Alexander seldom interacted with pulled up his pant leg to reveal a huge scar.

"You're lying. You probably got wounded from some maiden who didn't take kindly to your small pecker."

Alexander jerked his head to get Henri away from everyone and alone as the jabs continued to much merriment.

"I ain't never even seen a gator," Henri said as he pulled away from the others. He spoke to Alexander when they were alone. "What did you need? Did you see something to tell me about?"

Alexander shook his head. "Sometimes, I need time alone with you."

Henri halted and reached over to grab Alexander into his arms. He pushed his nose into Alexander's hair and breathed deeply. "Sounds good to me."

Alexander stepped toward their quarters but veered to the side. He leaned his elbows against the ship and stared into the blackness beyond with only the stars illuminating the night.

"Do you ever get bored or look for something more than all this?" Alexander asked when Henri put his arm around him.

"Getting philosophical on me? I don't know if I can handle too deep a thinker tonight. What's got you down?"

Alexander leaned his head into Henri's chest. "I'm not down. Just wondering. You've been at piracy a lot longer than me. I wonder about the purpose of life. Sailing along until we plunder, then drinking and carrying on until the next adventure."

"Sounds like a pirate's life to me." Henri played with Alexander's fingers.

"And I've only been at sea a couple months."

"You're not backing out on me, are you? We have a good thing going."

Alexander turned sideways to face Henri. He pushed into him, lifting his chin so their eyes met. He shook his head. "Not in the least. I like thinking. I mean, someday the life ends, right? In death. Or you said once some retire."

Henri held Alexander tightly. "The one who first captained me just went away one day. Took his spoils, and he'd been saving up, and walked off when we came to a port. I learned later he bought himself some land and became a respectable farmer with a family."

"That's what I mean. Don't you envision a different future?"

Henri looked out to sea, away from Alexander. "Not now. I love the sea too much. Love the crew. The smell of the ocean. The thrill of the chase. Besides, where else could two blokes like us take up and not get strung up in a tree?"

Henri had a point. Pirates lived by a much different code. Though few talked about sex, and Alexander could tell some disapproved, for the most part the men could take whatever lover they wanted and engage in whatever sex they so desired.

"Come here. I got a gift. But we'll need Spittle's help. Spittle!" Henri shouted across the boat.

Henri took them into his quarters and sat Alexander on the bed. "I was going to wait for a special occasion, but what the hell would be special on a ship? Sounds like you could use a gift tonight." He rummaged around in a chest, throwing clothes and other things onto the ground. "Ah-ha!" Henri held up a small box, which he handed to Alexander.

"For me?"

Henri nodded. "Open."

Alexander took the carefully crafted wooden box and opened the lid. He gasped. A gold earring lay on a bed of silk. Alexander told Henri once he intended to pierce his ear because he wanted to begin looking more like a pirate. He thought about a tattoo or other adornments but settled on an earring because he thought them sexy.

Henri agreed Alexander would be hot with one, but he and Spittle counseled Alexander to hold off a bit, until he knew for sure he wanted to take the step. Alexander pointed out several pirates with wonderful earrings in the cove, whenever he could, to let Henri and Spittle know he was ready.

"It's perfect." Alexander jumped up and lunged at Henri, kissing him square on the lips.

They both laughed when they heard Spittle cough at the doorway.

"Spittle! Perfect! Come in." Henri ushered her into the room. "We need some help. It's time this one start looking the part."

Alexander held up his earring for Spittle.

She whistled her approval. "Gold?"

"Pure." Henri took the box from Alexander and removed the earring. "I don't know how to put one in."

Spittle took hold of jewelry and twirled it around. "Hurts like hell."

"What if I use my magic first? To numb my ear?"

"You'd know better than me." Spittle sat on the edge of the bed and patted Alexander to join her.

"Get on with the surgery, then." Henri stood above them and

clapped his hands.

Alexander reached over and pulled out his medicinal box. His supply of herbs had grown short, especially after healing the crew who got injured during that attack by enemy pirates. He warned Henri he would need more, and soon, or they risked him performing the healing without the subterfuge of science. And some charms worked better with the herbs.

Tonight he needed a plant to make the potion to isolate the numbing directly on his left ear. He enchanted the spell in his mind and felt the tingling sensation run down his arm, into his fingers, and onto the plant leaf that gradually became a milky white ointment.

Alexander rubbed the concoction on his ear, then nodded to Spittle.

She clutched the earring. Alexander couldn't see — or thankfully feel — anything, but knew she grabbed a nail or something and jammed the item through his ear. He took a little more of the ointment to stop the bleeding, then let Spittle remove the nail and insert his earring.

Alexander drifted to sleep later, his discontent from earlier subsided. He loved his gift and showed Henri how much with a particularly passionate bout of lovemaking. Henri laughingly complained his nuts got sore after Alexander forced him to come twice in a matter of an hour.

Alexander felt his ear again, which burned slightly but otherwise had healed, according to Henri the last time he looked.

Henri snored softly next to him.

The earring became a rite of passage for Alexander. The next level of commitment, so to speak, into the life of piracy. He could hardly return to Massachusetts with an adornment in his ear. Of course, he could take the earring out and heal the spot. But he had no desire to ever reverse course. He wanted the visible sign of piracy, the physical reminder he had escaped the judgment and brutal life among the Puritans.

Whenever he wondered about some different and utopian life, his earring would remind him he chose piracy. And piracy, in turn, chose him.

VI: High Crimes of Piracy

Chapter Twenty-Seven

The King's Act

7 September 1700

New Providence, Bahamas

THE BOREDOM OF floating aimlessly heightened tension among the crew. Henri pleaded with Alexander to find a suitable target—anything—to divert their attention from each other and onto a new enemy.

Alexander and Henri withdrew to their private quarters and sat with his crystal. Alexander played with the gold ring in his ear as he searched for a ship but only found vessels too far away to be of any use to Henri until he spied upon a small merchant vessel sailing about a day away.

Alexander glanced from his crystal to Henri. "I wouldn't recommend this one most of the time because it's not carrying enough for us. The main cargo is slaves."

"You know my policy on slaves. We free them."

"Right. But it's the only ship within a day of us, besides a couple of pirate ships."

Henri scratched his head. "And we don't attack other pirates. It doesn't have anything else besides slaves?"

"Some silk and a good amount of sails."

Henri's eyes lit up. "Sails fetch a good price, and we always can use extras lying about. Let's set course for her."

Thus they attacked an inbound ship carrying silk, extra sails, and slaves. They pillaged the silk and sails, massacred most of the crew, and freed the slaves by turning the boat over to them.

The pirates celebrated for a day before heading toward a pirate port with their new goods.

They docked in New Providence to trade or sell off the excess sails. Spittle led a group who went through the lot of them, picking the best to keep as backup for their own sloop, then setting aside the rest for barter.

Once they anchored and started moving the canoes toward town, Alexander went with Henri to find trading partners.

The stench of the town hit Alexander square in the face as he wandered through the crowded streets full of people purchasing goods, fighting, or searching for sex. He stayed close to Henri, noticing men such as Henri parted the crowds with nothing more than their commanding presence.

They approached a dilapidated building with a crooked sign advertising "likor." Alexander stepped over a pile of vomit near the doorway as Henri entered and shouted a loud greeting across the room.

"Well, look at the rogues over there!" Henri pointed toward two men drinking at a corner table. They looked over and smiled when they spotted him.

Henri motioned for Alexander to follow as he went to the bar and ordered a bottle of rum. "Good friends over there. We can trade with them." With the bottle in hand they joined the other two.

"You two look like pirates up to no good." Henri slammed the rum down on the table. "Let me get you drunk, so I can take advantage of you."

Henri pointed for Alexander to sit next to him but never talked to him and failed to introduce him to the other captains.

"I have sails for you off a slaver coming from Africa. Good quality." Henri put his boots on the table and tilted back on two legs of his chair.

The pirate in a royal blue coat and wearing a silken bandana drank a shot of rum and smiled at Henri. "Always with the pricey stuff with you, yeah? No wonder you so readily bought the first bottle. You're planning to fleece us." He smiled despite the edge in his voice. Not knowing his name, Alexander nicknamed him Royal Blue.

"I've got a good crew." Henri poured them each another shot. "Maybe Scarface wants them, and I don't have to deal with you."

The other man across the table scratched the scar along his right cheek and grinned. "Don't look to me for your riches. I'll probably take some. What are you asking for them?"

Alexander zoned out for several minutes as the three pirates haggled over the combination of barter, pieces of eight, and ducats. He did notice Henri get excited when Royal Blue included a good amount of doubloon in the transaction. Alexander had only seen one such gold coin before in his life.

Royal Blue soon took his leave, agreeing to meet Henri in the morning for the exchange. When he left, Henri smiled at Scarface and winked. "Another bottle for my old friend. By the way, this here's Medusa." Henri pointed to Alexander as he called the chambermaid over and requested more rum.

"Medusa?" Scarface arched a brow. "Don't see no snakes coming out your head."

Alexander smiled, befuddled as to what to say.

Henri waved his hand in the air. "He's got a bit of special senses to help us now and then. Remember Beast? He labeled him Medusa, and the name stuck."

Scarface roared with laughter. "You still sailing around with that foul monster?"

"Some of the men like him." Henri slammed back a drink. "And you know how handy he becomes in a battle. Medusa," Henri turned and looked at Alexander, "Scarface and I go way back. Long before either of us commanded a ship, we sailed together. Saved each other's dumb ass more than once during an attack." This made both men laugh loudly and toast to surviving.

"Indeed. Like the time we attacked another pirate ship, and you ignored the lassie onboard, thinking no woman could do anything to you." Scarface laughed. "She'd have planted her knife right in the middle of your back if I hadn't spotted the attempt and shot her through the head."

Again they found this story uproariously funny.

"Anyway," Henri leaned closer to the table, whispering. "You know I'll give you a better deal. Best I can, without my men getting suspicious or angry they aren't getting their fair share."

This negotiation went much quicker. Alexander marveled at the fact they had completed a fake deal in front of Royal Blue, both in the know. When they finished, Scarface ordered the next bottle.

"What do you know about this new act against pirates?" Scarface asked. "I heard one guy saying his entire crew abandoned ship and went back to the Brits, hanging their captain out to dry."

"Traitors." Henri shook his head. "Why would their threat to kill us at sea and not drag us to London make any difference? You'll be hanging from the rafters soon enough, either way."

"They took to the pardon. Abandon piracy, and they let you go free." Scarface began laughing.

"What's so funny?" Henri asked.

"Them idiots fall for the royal nonsense. A pardon? What the hell does that get you? It won't buy you a legitimate merchant vessel. Or a farm. So you get absolved for being a pirate but have no damned future. They can stick their new act where the sun don't shine."

"And without anything to grease the way!" Henri lifted his glass.

This time their joking made Alexander laugh, too, and they included him in the conversation.

"Speaking of them traitors, I heard something before you arrived. I'm wondering if they didn't mean your ship?" Scarface traced a finger along his scar, his drink held firmly in the other hand.

"What are you talking about? You always did get a little nutty after too much of the demon rum."

Scarface threw his head back and laughed. "Not this time. Listen to this. Some pirate, looked like he just came out of his Mama's womb, got sloppy drunk and told stories about how his ship surrendered to the British Navy a while back to get the pardon. But a bunch of the men, including him, got to the next port and joined a new pirate ship."

Henri laughed. "See? What did I tell you about their fool act?"

"Right you are!" Scarface slumped further in his chair but took another drink. "Here's the kicker. Some of his mates got mad he told. They worried they sounded like cowards. He waited until they left and resumed his story. Come to find out the captain got killed in the bargain, which was why they kept the whole thing quiet. Anyway, I know the story sounds simple enough, except what he said about the British ship."

"Does this story have a point? Or an ending?" Henri grinned and took a swig of rum. "Because you sure as hell sound like you're on a drunken rant to me."

Scarface cackled and wiped his mouth with his sleeve. "Get this. This young one claimed the Brits let their ship go easily because they were in search of one *specific* ship. They didn't care about the pirates because their captain needed to find one particular sloop and didn't want to waste time with any others."

Alexander felt the buzz take over his body. "Must be a bad ship, to single out."

"Perhaps. The sailor said the captain described particular pirates he saw in Boston and needed to find. Weren't you up North a while ago?"

Henri nodded.

"He described you." Scarface pointed at Henri. Then he quoted the description, a dead ringer for Henri. "This is the weirdest part, with you two coming to sit in front of me. He said the captain was looking for someone looking like you." He turned his finger to Alexander and detailed an explanation of Alexander. "He didn't mention an earring, though. But I swear, this pirate relayed who the British captain sought. He's looking for the two of you. Even claimed one knew a spot of magic. I ain't making this up."

By the time Scarface finished his story and included another portrayal of Spittle, Henri grew quiet and frowned down at the floor. "Well, good seeing you. We'll trade in the morning. Then we best be off, lest this British captain saunter into New Providence looking for us."

Henri drank a gulp of rum, stood up, and pulled Alexander to his feet. They stumbled through New Providence until they got back to their own canoes, where a couple men rowed them back to *All Hallows Eve*.

In his typical way, Henri talked with the pirates he passed as he moved across the deck. However, instead of Alexander going his own way as usual, he sensed a subtle worry in the way Henri held his shoulder and forced his laugh, so he stayed close to him. Scarface's comments had troubled Henri.

As Alexander predicted, Henri moved through his men quickly and ushered Alexander back to his quarters, where he closed the door and started pacing.

"What did you think of Scarface's story?" Henri asked.

Alexander shook his head. "Not much. Strange, I suppose. But we're getting a third hand account from a drunk captain, who heard from an even drunker pirate, who allegedly heard from a British captain."

Henri scratched his head. "Scarface gave a description sounding like the two of us. And what of the spot-on picture he gave of Spittle. Scarface hasn't ever met him. You got anything to help us? Any magic we could use?"

Alexander sat for several minutes in contemplation. His power over the wind or to heal would do nothing to give them any information. "My ability to see the present might assist us. I could spot a British warship, maybe try to see if they searched for something specific, but even then I may not understand the details."

"At least try." Henri pointed to Alexander's pocket.

Alexander got out the crystal and rubbed the smooth surface. He drew in a deep breath and felt the firm hand of Henri upon his back, offering support.

His eyes stared at the globe as his mind took flight, away from the boat, away from New Providence, and out over the ocean. He manipulated his thoughts to the British Jack, then further narrowed his vision to official naval vessels.

Predictably, he could not ascertain anything specific. A handful sailed within the confines of the Caribbean, all seemingly wary of pirates and protecting merchant vessels. Nothing extraordinary popped into his head, from what he could see.

However, one military ship sailed by itself. Alexander narrowed his vision and noticed the first mate spying a pirate ship but shaking his head and continuing the vessel on a different route. Perhaps the boat had a specific mission in mind?

Alexander described what he witnessed to Henri.

Henri scratched his forehead. "Keep an eye out, will you? Scarface may like his drink, but he's a damn good captain and fine pirate. I trust him with my life. If he wondered about our being in the crosshairs, so we better too."

Chapter Twenty-Eight

A New Mission

8 September 1700

At Sea, Caribbean

HENRI KEPT ALEXANDER awake much of the following night as he tossed and turned, even shouting in anger during his sleep. Alexander had never seen him so restless.

When they woke that morning, Henri dressed and went about his routine but without his usual whistling or light conversation with Alexander. In fact, he said nothing. Alexander learned over the last couple weeks to leave him alone when one of these moods overcame him. Yet Alexander was troubled that Scarface's comments spiraled Henri into such worry.

Alexander stayed in their quarters a while longer before moving to the deck and finding Tacky already busy cooking up a huge breakfast.

"Where's captain?" Tacky asked. "I didn't see him this morning. He usually eats first."

Alexander shook his head. "Not sure. He wasn't himself this morning. Maybe he went to get those sails traded."

Tacky sang one of his many songs as he went about cooking, giving Alexander various duties and feeding the men. Cooking always provided Alexander plenty of time to think, whether about the danger from Beast, his lot as a pirate, or musings about the past. Today, he focused on Scarface's story and Henri's subsequent demeanor.

He felt stupid to have taken so long to pinpoint the cause. Spittle mentioned Henri felt jealous of Crispin after Alexander told him their story. And Henri knew Crispin had joined the Royal Navy. He must think Crispin's boat was currently searching for them in order to reunite with Alexander. While Alexander thought the notion ludicrous, he wondered if Henri was jealous.

Alexander felt Henri's envy was endearing. Alexander paused, almost burning the fish he seared over the fire when he wondered if Crispin *was* after him. He dismissed the idea. Crispin chose duty and obligation over their love. He never even had the gumption to fight for their relationship when they lived close to each other; he would never search over miles and miles of sea for Alexander once he had freed himself from the distraction.

Besides, Alexander reminded himself, he chose the life of a pirate and Henri. He had friends, a new family — the first one since his mother and father died. Could he leave them behind because Crispin sauntered back into his life?

The flurry of activity when Henri and Spittle returned from their mission to trade the sails diverted Alexander's attention. Pirates scattered about, either putting away supplies or readying the sloop for sail as Henri barked orders and urged everyone to work faster. He was in the same foul mood.

As Alexander worked to secure a barrel of flour, King James flew over and landed on its rim and cocked his head at Alexander. "First mate calls! *Squawk.*"

Alexander followed King James to the lower level, where they found Spittle securing sails. She scrunched her brow at Alexander and motioned him over with a jerk of her head.

"We're sailing after some British ship the captain thinks is hunting for us. Do you know anything about this?"

Alexander started to shake his head but paused. "Maybe."

"Out with whatever you know. I'm trying to protect our ship. When Henri gets this way, he becomes careless and foolhardy. What's going on?"

Alexander explained to her what Scarface said. Even before Alexander could voice his suspicion Henri may be worried about Crispin, Spittle said the same thing. "He thinks they're after you. Shit. He's jealous." Spittle shot a wad of spit across the boat.

As if on cue, the boat groaned into motion and Alexander felt the wind catch in their sails. Even without his assistance, the sloop moved swiftly away from New Providence and out to sea.

Spittle grabbed Alexander's arm. "I've dealt with him before when he gets like this. The men will follow him, if anything because they love an adventure. You and I have to get him back under control as best as possible. Don't irritate him or try to order him to do anything. But whatever sway you have, use it. Most of all, don't say a damn thing about Crispin."

"But he's worried about him. I'm not leaving Henri. I should tell him."

Spittle shook her head. "Trust me. Don't go there."

Spittle turned without another word and went above, followed by Alexander. Henri had not only set sail, he'd prepared the entire crew for battle.

"Spittle! Medusa! Up here, now!" Henri shouted down at them.

When they got to the wheel and Henri, he ordered Spittle to continue preparations for war as he pulled Alexander into his quarters. He sat them down on the bed and patted Alexander's pocket. At least he comforted Alexander by placing his arm around him.

"We're not safe until we find the British ship." Henri stared hard at Alexander. "Find the nearest naval vessel so we can attack."

Alexander thought to protest, to profess his love for Henri, and try to prevent the madness, but he remembered Spittle's warning to stay quiet. He planted a hard kiss on Henri's lips and leaned close to him before getting his crystal out. Soon enough, he spotted a nearby two-mast sloop, with about sixty cannons, patrolling the water. For himself, he searched for Crispin but only viewed a bunch of unknown sailors and officers.

Alexander told the coordinates to Henri and they went back outside. In what felt like a matter of minutes, though probably took over an hour, *All Hallows Eve* came upon the British ship.

The warship, too, spotted its predator. Unlike the flight of a merchant vessel, this one swung around and sailed headlong toward the battle.

Alexander thanked God he already trained himself to help in battle without engaging his mind. He refined his skill to drift mentally away and escape but still hear Henri if he called. Alexander could protect himself if necessary and heal those in need, all while his brain floated away to a cloud high above, peering out across the skies and upon the beautiful blue ocean, as if the battle below had nothing to do with him, as if his body acted of its own accord.

He was frightened far less to operate this way than to focus on the rumble of cannons when these two warships drew alongside each other. He could dodge the shrapnel and duck the chain shot across the deck without worrying about the men, his friends, who failed to get out of the way.

His visit to the alternate realm deadened the emotional angst when a pirate carried Rummy to him and flopped him onto the deck. "He got hit!" the man said as he dashed away and back to battle.

Alexander leaned down and checked Rummy for injuries. Beautiful, sweet Rummy, with his good nature, his love for life, his soft lips and giving body. Alexander allowed his mind to seek solutions to heal him, knowing the futility of his efforts. The metal prong stuck out of Rummy's chest right at his heart. Rummy had died instantly.

Alexander screamed in anguish at the loss and for the other pirate friends he saw lying dead below. But up here the battle seemed more surreal. The cloud sheltered him, as if he were a Greek god peering down on the silly humans as they slaughtered one another over petty differences and inane arguments.

Alexander moved his human form below deck, where he ordered people to begin a triage. "Cast the dead overboard, bring the wounded here, and then get back up to fight!" He shouted his order over and over, even as he moved from man to man with his healing power. Some he cured so fast they jumped back up, grabbed their weapon, and raced above deck to rejoin the fray. Others lay still, coping with the remaining pain as their bodies mended.

Soon enough the combat ceased. Alexander performed what he could for the injured belowdecks before returning above. The British sloop listed to its left side, engulfed in flames. A second later the ship tipped farther on its side and sank to the bottom of the ocean.

Alexander walked, as if a zombie, up to where Henri and Spittle watched over the crew as they repaired their ship, mourned their fallen comrades, and took stock of what remained.

"We won." Spittle spoke softly. Alexander suspected it was to gauge Henri's attitude.

Henri nodded but grabbed the wheel tightly. "We got the wrong ship. They didn't hunt for us. But we needed the practice."

Henri let go and walked away, going down the ladder to the other men and helping them to secure a loose cannon.

"He's going to do this again?" Alexander asked.

"Probably. He's on a mission. But look at the men." Spittle motioned across the ship. "They loved the combat."

Alexander knew the truth of it. He wanted the men to reflect more at the death and destruction they wrought for no apparent gain. No treasure. Nothing had threatened them. They battled for the mere pleasure.

Certainly many of them already missed their friends. But pirates expected such loss and suppressed their sorrow deep within themselves. No one shed a tear. No one said a word about the dearly departed. They simply went about fixing the ship and getting ready to fight again, as if carrying on with a pirate's life honored the fallen more than anything.

Alexander had only before witnessed such behavior in the animal kingdom. Animals lived in the moment and accepted death and the nature of things around them. So, too, did pirates. These men signed up for adventure. They lived as outlaws, throwing caution to the wind for the loot of rum, silk, coinage, or whatever random cargo they could secure. They lived for physical pleasure and high drama, or danger and thrills.

Spittle and Alexander circled around, making sure no one else needed Alexander's assistance. They found King James cowering under some fallen crates of food. He flew to Spittle's shoulder and nestled his head into her hair.

Eventually night came, so Alexander stopped his aimless pacing.

He cured everyone he could and ignored the day's events long enough. As most of the pirates took to drowning their sorrows in wine and booze, Alexander hid inside Henri's cabin for a moment alone. Fighting a British naval vessel proved much harder than attacking an unarmed merchant ship. No quarter meant something entirely different.

Henri remained outside with his men, congratulating them for their good fight and rewarding them with his own alcohol.

Alexander appreciated the time to reflect. Moments like this reminded him about how much he lived his life alone, and how he had lost solitude when he became a pirate. He understood he needed this time away from others.

Though a number of his fellow sailors had died, the tears burst forth when Alexander remembered Rummy's dead eyes staring back at him. He had developed a connection with Rummy. At first through sex, nothing more. Rummy taught him new pleasures, made him comfortable with having a threesome or more. He offered his ass to Alexander freely below deck.

Yet more than the physical gratification, Rummy reminded Alexander over and over to enjoy life. His lust for passion and fun focused Alexander on the moment, even if he worried about people's safety or disliked part of the pirate code. This life and this family meant more than anything Alexander had ever experienced in Massachusetts where they hated him.

Alexander's mother had implored him to survive. She gave no other instruction, offered no other clues as to what to do with her demand. Alexander survived by relishing life. Rummy had reminded him of this fact so often, and now he had joined his colleagues in the ocean's depths.

Despite willing himself forward to survive for his mother and Rummy, Alexander drifted to sleep with tears streaming down his face as he honored Rummy and his other fallen comrades.

Chapter Twenty-Nine

Henri's Rage

10 September 1700

Atlantic Ocean

ALEXANDER SURPRISED HIMSELF at how fast he recovered after the attack on the navy ship and the accompanying death.

By the next morning, his fellow pirates went about their business as if nothing had happened. They worked off their hangovers, sailed the ship, and went back to the drink as if the previous day was a bad dream.

Alexander supposed denial allowed them to endure. To anyone outside the pirate fraternity, their behavior might seem crass and uncivilized. Animalistic. To those inside, their actions constituted survival when the emotion or fear might otherwise consume them. Even Alexander found himself drunk and laughing with Spittle and King James, followed by plenty of laughs and singing with Tacky and Monkey as they prepared the meals.

Yet his relationship with Henri remained strained ever since Scarface warned them a British ship hunted for them. Henri slept with him, and they made love, but without the intimacy or lingering affection.

"You don't think he's mad at me, do you?" Alexander gave way to his insecurity while he and Spittle counted out a pile of pearls Henri kept hidden in a chest. He wanted them evenly distributed among the crew for their success against the British.

"Sweetie, you'll know if he gets mad at you. Because you won't be sleeping in there anymore. He's this way because of you. Trust me, I know the captain better than anyone. Maybe better than you. You're his life now."

Alexander lunged for a pearl before it rolled away into a crack in the floor.

Spittle made him feel much better. She never lied to him or softened a message. They told each other the truth, no matter the circumstances. When they finished distributing the pearls among the grateful men, Henri called for Alexander to join him in private.

Henri pulled Alexander into his arms on the bed, and Alexander fell on top of him and enjoyed the softness of Henri's long hair in his face, the hard muscles beneath his clothes.

Henri's finger trailed through Alexander's long hair, then reached up and felt the earring in his ear. "I shouldn't be so attached to one pirate, you know."

Alexander smiled and leaned up to look at Henri. He kissed him hard on the lips rather than speaking.

They fooled around for a while before Henri sighed. "We got work to do."

"Is this about me?"

Henri frowned and shook his head.

"I'm the captain. I make decisions." Henri got up and began redressing. "I'll be the judge of what we need to do to gain a profit and protect ourselves. You worry about your end of things, and I'll worry about mine."

Henri stalked toward the door but stopped. He turned around and stormed back to Alexander, fiercely enough Alexander braced himself to be hit and prepared his magic to defend himself.

Henri leaned over and pulled Alexander to his feet and into a tight hug. "Don't worry about me. Do your thing. I'll do mine. For them." Henri pointed toward the door and crew beyond. "And for you." He kissed Alexander on the nose.

Henri released Alexander and moved back toward the door. Without turning around, he issued one more order before departing. "I do need you to find the next British ship."

Alexander marveled at Henri's command the second the door slammed shut behind him. He reassured Alexander with his nurturing presence and a moment of intimacy yet communicated his authority aboard the ship before he left.

Alexander wondered for a moment if he had gotten into a situation in which Henri took ownership of him. They entered the relationship of their own free will, and Alexander felt open to do as he pleased, like any other pirate.

But no doubt their connection — love? — deepened and took them to a more profound level. Alexander swooned in Henri's presence. He adored his protective nature and dominion over every situation. So what did this signal in Henri's world, where he ruled as monarch? Alexander detected the possessiveness and jealously lurking under the surface. He had seen Henri's ruthless side toward a pirate who defied him.

Yet Henri demonstrated a care toward Alexander far too profound for him to worry about such retribution being pointed against him.

Instead of more pondering, Alexander pulled out his crystal to see if he could find another ship waiting for a pirate attack. He drifted up and away, hovering above the ship and seeing Spittle as she chastised King James for pecking at Beast's ear when he flew by.

Above the sloop, gazing across the distant horizon, Alexander paused to enjoy the beauty before he spied upon the nearby ships. Another pirate vessel sailed after a merchant boat. Near them, a Spanish frigate sailed blissfully unaware of the drama a few miles away. Nothing else ventured close.

There, on the horizon, Alexander spotted the telltale signs of the British Navy. The two mast sloop, the large number of sailors aboard, the ship designed first and foremost for speed despite the 70 plus cannons on deck. Last he viewed the British flag fluttering proudly in the breeze from the ship's highest mast.

He watched from above for a couple minutes, detecting with his refined powers the will of the men onboard. Their captain ordered more speed and instructed them to search for a particularly dangerous pirate ship. Reading these sailors' minds seemed to confirm Scarface's rumor, a British ship hunted in these waters for one particular pirate vessel, not just any on the seas.

Alexander hesitated before trying to learn more specific information or focus in on particular individuals to see their identity. Did he really want to know? He had his suspicions, but why confirm them?

Would he really tell Henri about this ship and drive them into another battle where more pirates would die?

Before he made any decisions, shouting and screaming yanked him back into his body and to the captain's quarters. He jammed the crystal back into his pocket and got up to see what was causing the commotion.

He got to the main deck and found Spittle watching down where most of the men gathered. Henri stood in the center of them, one pirate on his knees before him, with Beast standing behind him and defending the man.

"Silence!" Henri shouted. Even Beast shut his mouth, though his head tilted in an unnatural direction so he could glare at Alexander. He winked.

"Now, explain again."

One pirate, his face burning red in anger, pointed at the man

312 - Damian Serbu

kneeling at Henri's feet. "He tried to steal my loot! I caught him red-handed. He was stealing my coins! I want him punished. I have witnesses."

Henri glanced around his men. "Who saw this?"

Two other men raised their hands and confirmed what the first said. The man attempted to steal another's treasure. The pirate code forbade pillaging. Despite their lawlessness and stealing, pirates on the same ship had to trust each other.

"Then it's confirmed. I'm to determine your punishment." Henri kicked at the criminal to force him to raise his head and look him in the eyes.

"Go easy on him." Beast touched the man's shoulder. "He didn't get away with anything. We're down men."

Henri slowly turned his attention to Beast. "I won't treat him special because he's one of your minions."

"Not like you do with Medusa, who sends you on hopeless crusades."

"Shut it, Beast!" Spittle shouted next to Alexander. A plume of spit shot out and landed near Beast. "Medusa's no concern to you."

"He's my concern when he sails us all for danger on a fool's crusade. We don't need to risk ourselves in search of some damned British boat and captain."

Henri reached over and grabbed Beast by the throat. To Alexander's surprise, Beast made no move to protest or protect himself, even with Portia possessing him.

"Enough." Henri growled and let go.

Beast stood tall but remained quiet.

Henri turned his attention to the pirate whose goods the other tried to steal. "You determine the punishment. He violated your rights, not mine."

"Much obliged, captain." The pirate smiled. "I know you prefer the woolding, but were I captain, I'd prefer a good keelhaul."

Henri nodded. "You and your friends, get the job done."

Henri walked away as the pirates took the struggling man into their custody and forced him toward the side of the boat. Though Beast and his compatriots included him as a friend, no one moved to intercede.

His foes grabbed a rope and began tying him up. They tied the other end to the side of the boat, checked the knots would hold, and threw him overboard to the cheers of almost everyone aboard.

"What happens now?" Alexander asked Spittle.

"He'll be dragged under the boat. Probably scratched all to hell by the barnacles. Most likely fill his lungs with water and die a rather painful death. They'll pull him up in a few minutes to see, in case he survives for a bit. Living would mean the gods spared his life. Dying means, well, he deserved death." Spittle smirked.

Alexander grinned back. He smiled more than anything for having lost his sensitivity to these occurrences aboard a pirate ship. Nothing in the punishment bothered him in the least. The man earned his lot in life. Too, he hardly mourned the loss of one of Beast's followers.

Alexander had become a full-fledged pirate.

True to Spittle's word, a few minutes later they yanked and pulled until the water-logged body came up over the side. Dead. So the men untied him and dumped him back in the ocean.

Chapter Thirty

Double Cross and Battle

11 September 1700

Atlantic Ocean

ALEXANDER LINGERED IN Henri's quarters, wishing he could get off the boat and avoid what he understood as inevitable. He peeked out the door to make sure Henri was not returning and then glanced again into his crystal. The British warship headed toward them. Yet Alexander found aspects of the boat's approach odd. The sailors had disguised parts of the boat, and they flew no flag. No matter, for the danger would come either way.

He also wondered if he should tell Henri everything he learned in his visions from the previous night. But how could he explain keeping the information a secret this long? Deep inside he knew the feeling pulling at him—the longing for a forbidden love that had haunted him almost his entire life.

The yearning conflicted with his obligation toward this family of pirates. If he said nothing to Henri, perhaps he could again peer into Crispin's eyes. At least he could know for certain what choice Crispin finally made, though Crispin had seemed so certain the last time they were together in Massachusetts. Why did Alexander hope for something different, especially when he had such a connection with Henri?

Alexander took a deep breath and admitted the truth to himself. He may not tell anyone else, but he must wrap his own mind around the mess of contradictions and emotions or he risked killing everyone aboard this ship, the British vessel, and the people he loved therein.

He loved two men and had no idea how to rectify the situation. This dual calling rendered him inactive and ineffective. In the end, however, this very inaction gave him the answer otherwise eluding him. For if he really loved them equally, he could side with Henri and stay in his current life.

Alexander could have pointed them toward someplace else, chosen a different ship to attack and steered them away from the one hunting for them. Henri would never learn the subterfuge, for he trusted Alexander. Alexander had betrayed Henri with this incapacity to decide.

For whatever hopeless and foolhardy reason, Alexander kept longing for another chance with Crispin no matter how remote or impossible, no matter the danger to his pirate family.

Alexander pushed these emotions from his mind and concentrated on the predicament at hand. He had spied this British ship yesterday on three occasions but never said anything to Henri, though Henri requested the information over and over. By last night, Alexander took to claiming he was ill with a headache that blocked his ability to use the crystal.

This avoidance led him to the current problem. Not his emotional state, but the actual danger at hand. At first Alexander hoped to steer clear of the British, no matter who might be on the ship and searching for them. Then he could also avoid all emotion and not see more of his comrades die in battle.

Except Alexander realized the two captains, beyond his control, determined to search the ocean for each other. With no help from Alexander, they steered their vessels on a collision course. Did they know the personal war they engaged?

In the crystal, Alexander sailed above the sloop and toward the enemy ship to better gauge their true intentions. They armed for battle and sailed rapidly toward *All Hallows Eve*.

And there, commanding them, stood Crispin. Erect posture as always, the spy glass held tightly in his hand, his lips pressed hard together, his stare determined and confident.

Alexander dropped his crystal and started when the door swung open. Spittle walked in, frowning.

"What in the hell's going on? We've got a ship bearing down on us, full blast ahead and flying a pirate flag. We signaled but got nothing back. What do you know?"

"I can't see. I—" Alexander stammered and stopped. What could he say? "I couldn't see the ship. I'm not sure what's going on. She looks like a pirate ship, but other aspects seem like British Navy."

Spittle squinted at Alexander, the skepticism written on her creased brow.

"We best prepare for battle." Alexander got up and began his own preparations in an attempt to spur Spittle into action.

"Would have been nice to know this an hour ago." She spun around, stormed toward the door, and slammed it behind her.

Alexander got onto the deck to see the men blazing with action. Henri and Spittle barked orders at the men who scurried about in preparation for battle. When Alexander got by his side, Henri nodded at him and grabbed the spy glass to examine the other ship.

"Another pirate attack. I don't understand." He paused. Henri looked pale when he set the spy glass down and looked at Alexander. "She looks well-armed. Like a war vessel."

"I can see now. I checked. I think it's a British ship, the navy. We aren't prepared. We need to get out of here."

Henri removed his hat and scratched his head. He glanced at Alexander and grunted, then looked around the sloop for answers before he spun around. He reversed his previous orders and had men hauling up the sails and attempting to turn the ship around and speed away as fast as possible. Alexander figured Henri would come back for the fight eventually but wanted more time. The surprise caught him entirely off guard.

"Check again." Henri pointed to Alexander's pocket and the

crystal.

Henri never allowed him to use his magic in front of the others before, signaling either the urgency of the moment or his ire with Alexander. Alexander knew what he would see before glancing into the magic. A British naval ship bore down on them, prepared for battle.

"Definitely a navy ship."

Henri cursed. "But the flag." He pointed toward the highest mast and a black pirate flag with a skull fluttering from the top.

As if on cue, the sailors aboard the other ship hauled down the flag and replaced it with the British Jack.

"Of all the treachery! Playing a pirate trick on us in reverse!" Henri moved into action. "Hurry about! The British are here! Hurry about. Get this baby under sail in all haste! We're not ready for the fight! Go, I say! Go!"

Alexander removed himself to his usual spot during these intense moments, near the wheel but off to the side and out of the way, where Henri could summon him when needed.

Alexander worried but eventually sighed in relief. With the die cast, fate took over, and he no longer had decisions to make about the life and death of the crews around him. He felt small for having been such a coward but saw no other way to handle the situation now.

All Hallows Eve picked up speed just as it appeared the other ship would overtake them and force the battle. Her pirates were too good at sailing to be taken so easily, especially with Henri's and Spittle's leadership.

Lost in the intensity of the moment, Alexander jumped when

someone nudged him from the side. Staring hard toward the British ship's pursuit, he failed to see Beast come upon him. Beast yanked him by the neck and pulled him into the captain's quarters without anyone noticing.

Alexander's heart pounded as he scrambled to call forth his power and could feel the heat of energy coming off Beast.

"You and I have a reckoning to come." Beast shoved Alexander into a chair. "Sooner than I anticipated. You're not the only one who knows who's on the other ship."

Alexander tugged at the wind and created a ball in his fist.

Portia's voice laughed from within Beast. "Going to throw me out a window again?"

"You've got to stop. He makes his own decisions. If he's come back, he's made his own choice."

"A choice you can quell. I expect you to." Beast stalked toward Alexander but stopped a couple feet away. "Relax. I won't do anything. Yet. I thought you should know your options."

"Options?" Despite her assurances, Alexander stayed on the ready for a fight.

Beast nodded. "Get him to leave and send him back to his wife and future in Massachusetts. If you denounce his love and proclaim yours for Henri, he'll leave."

Alexander paused, wondering what leverage might force him into this lie. "Or what? You'll sic your little minions on me?"

Portia laughed. "I'd never allow such an easy and painless remedy. I'll kill them, one by one. First Spittle, after I let the crew take turns raping her." Beast smirked. "You didn't think she could keep her little secret from me, did you? The others you care about will suffer. Even brave Captain Henri controls me because I allow him to, in order to hide my true self. You know the lengths I'll go to if I need to protect my son."

Alexander spat out a laugh. "You never cared about protecting him. Only controlling him to your bidding."

Beast stepped forward and ran a finger along Alexander's cheek. "I never needed your understanding for what I did. You have a decision. Crispin or your friends. Of course, choosing my son doesn't guarantee I won't come after you again and win in the end, with your only other alternative for survival already in taters because of your wrong choice."

Beast turned and casually walked out of the room. Alexander took a moment to compose himself before standing up and following him outside. Once again, his head swirled with confusion and contradictions.

What to do?

He hoped the course of events would make a decision for him. If *All Hallows Eve* could outrun the British warship, then no predicament would remain.

Such fantasies came crashing to a halt when the first cannonball shot across the deck and exploded in front of him.

The explosion hit close enough to Alexander to slam him against a barrel that tumbled to its side and rolled around, narrowly missing his hand. A crate crushed the leg of another pirate, already knocked out by the blast. His head flopped to the side, the dead eyes staring back at

Alexander.

Alexander thought of Monkey's irritation at having another barrel to repair when he watched it slam against the side of the boat and crack open. His mind went there to avoid dealing with the death and he looked around to see what other damage the blast inflicted upon *All Hallows Eve*.

Alexander kept his head to the ground but heard the second blast, farther back on the ship. He spotted Henri's boots walking by him. The captain stopped and turned around, then knelt down and Henri gently ran his fingers through Alexander's hair.

"You hurt?"

Alexander shook his head.

"Good. Help us. We're going to have a lot of wounded."

Alexander watched as Henri marched away, once again standing near the wheel and commanding his ship, which had fallen into chaos after the cannon fire. Alexander stood up to see Crispin's ship draw beside their boat.

"Drop the sail! Prepare for battle! We didn't make it! Fight, men! Fight!" Henri held his sword high in the air as he rallied his troops.

Spittle and the second mate worked frantically below, further organizing the pirates and getting the cannons on the side of the ship ready to fire back at their attackers.

To distract himself, Alexander hurried to an injured comrade and enchanted a healing spell over the gash in his arm. With the urgency of the moment and more battle to come, Alexander stopped the pretense of needing lotions, leaves, and herbs as medicine and directly applied the magic. As he crawled on his knees to another pirate lying nearby, he heard the loud and authoritative voice from the British ship.

"Halt your attack! We mean you no harm, and won't arrest or injure your crew if you surrender. Negotiate a parlay!"

The crew paused in their activities, probably as surprised as Alexander to hear such an odd request from an archenemy. Everyone peered at Henri for a response.

"I'd rather die than give us over to those fiends!"

A roar of approval went up from the throng of pirates who returned to their task and prepared to fire a volley back at the British.

Instead, the British took further control of the situation. Three of their cannons roared to life. One shot directly hit the stern mast, which cracked and crashed down, the top half falling into the sea. The front cannon missed, much to Alexander's relief, for it would have slammed right into Spittle's head if aimed a bit lower. The remaining blast hit on the deck, killing a group of pirates working on one of the cannons.

"Dammit all to hell. The wind. What about the wind?" Henri glanced to Alexander, searching for a way to escape their situation.

Only then did Alexander wonder why he had failed to think of using his power over the wind to their advantage when they'd tried to run away. Too late, again, to use his magic to help them. He was useless. Alexander ran the possibilities through his mind, wondering if the one remaining mast and its sails could give them enough power to move away from the British with the advantage of his wind manipulation.

"We can try." He wished for something more assertive but doubted he could achieve anything. Henri needed to know the truth.

"Try? What the hell does *try* mean?" Henri whipped his head to look at the British, who floated alongside but had halted the assault, despite their clear advantage.

"I can command the air but don't know if we'll get enough power with one mast. They're at full capacity." Alexander pointed toward the other ship.

Henri walked to the side of the boat.

"Ready to fire at your command, captain," Monkey announced from below.

Before Henri said a word, someone from the other ship shouted at Henri and his men. "Don't! We'll not lose this battle. But enter a parlay and spare your ship, men, and self."

Henri stared hard at the other boat. Spittle joined him, along with Alexander, who stayed a step behind. Alexander had never seen Henri so befuddled and unable to make a quick decision.

"He doesn't make a damn bit of sense," Henri said quietly to Spittle. "Pirates parlay with one another, not official naval ships. What the hell is going on? What do you think?"

"Not sure, captain. Strangest thing I've ever seen. I do know we're in no condition to win. We can call full quarter and hope to overtake them in hand-to-hand combat. We look about equally numbered, if they don't blast us into submission first. Seems risky at best."

Henri nodded. "A minute?" he screamed at the British. They answered with a bellowed, "Aye."

"So you think we negotiate?" Henri clutched his sword and glanced around at the men surrounding him.

Spittle pointed at Alexander and cleared her throat. "Maybe he can tell us something more since his headache's gone."

Alexander winced at her bitter tone. She knew his subterfuge, when even Henri continued to trust him.

Henri nodded. "Good idea."

"Here?" Alexander asked.

"We have to act fast. They won't wait long."

Alexander pulled out his crystal, concentrated his mind, and allowed his essence to hover above them. He stayed close this time, a few feet from their bodies, then sailed his vision the short distance across the water and onto the British deck.

To his complete shock, Crispin looked directly at him, as if he could see him spying there. "Tell him to parlay with me," Crispin said to Alexander. "I won't harm them."

Alexander raced back to his body, his mind in utter chaos. What on earth was going on? How had Crispin seen him? Henri, Spittle, and the others stared at him in anticipation.

"It's genuine." Alexander steadied himself, wanting to give the appropriate information without giving away the one-on-one interaction. "A parlay will save us."

Henri scratched his head and threw his hat across the deck. "I've never been surprised before. Never!" He kicked hard at a case of ammunition. "I've never been outmaneuvered! Who captains their boat? Beelzebub? How did he command the ship thus?" He slammed his fist atop the wheel. "And why not kill us? They're behaving as strangely as I've ever seen a ship act. And I've dealt with conniving pirates my whole life! Cursed asses!"

Everyone stayed frozen as Henri ranted, unsure how to react, until he calmed down and returned to Alexander's side. He grabbed Alexander's arm but gently held him as he forced them to stare into each other's eyes. "This parlay isn't a trick?"

Alexander shook his head. "I honestly think they mean it. Actually —" He cleared his throat. "— I know they do."

Henri nodded and turned his attention to Spittle. Alexander did too. She was staring right at Alexander.

"Well?" Henri asked her.

Without looking at the captain, she glared at Alexander. "Are you with us? Tell me."

Alexander took a deep breath and exhaled. "I swear, Spittle. You know me. You'd know if I was lying. This is the only way to save ourselves. It's safe."

Alexander held her gaze, pleading with his eyes for her to believe he spoke the truth.

Spittle nodded and looked at the captain. "Agreed. Enter the parlay."

"Heal as many as you can. Help these men." Henri motioned around the deck, instructing everyone to do as he ordered. In the meantime, he and Spittle headed to the edge of the ship and began shouting back and forth with the other vessel, negotiating a parlay. Alexander had never before witnessed such a thing and concentrated on healing the men who needed him.

He also repressed the pounding of his heart, not in fear of the battle, not in anticipation of the situation, or out of concern for the wounded. No, his heart beat faster at having heard Crispin's voice and raising his hopes something more was afoot than the British Navy hunting for pirates.

Alexander went about his job, helping as many as possible. Surprisingly, he ascertained they lost but a handful of men in the battle and again wondered if the British had avoided injuring them on purpose.

He had just finished binding a broken arm and telling the man to leave the sling on, while secretly mending the bone, when someone grabbed him from behind.

Before Alexander could struggle or cry out, one hand clamped over his mouth while the other arm lifted him easily off the ground. Just mere feet from the steps to below deck, Alexander feared no one saw as Beast kidnapped him.

Beast lugged him two decks below, to a part of the ship Alexander had never seen, down where they kept cargo. This level stank worse than anywhere else. More rats scampered about, not even afraid of the human presence.

As they approached a dark corner, Alexander called forth the wind and blasted it into Beast's face. He faltered a second before Portia's laugh filled the air. Alexander's power sapped out of him, leaving him more human than he'd been since his mother had died that fateful night. He was at the mercy of Portia's bidding.

"You should have been introduced to our jail long ago." Beast threw Alexander into the corner room violently enough he flew through the air and slammed hard against the side of the ship, then dropped

- 328 - Damian Serbu

onto the carcass of a dead rat.

Alexander scrambled to his feet and ran to the door, but Beast locked it shut. He heard Portia on the other side, chanting some spell to further drain Alexander of his witch's power. He felt in his pocket for the crystal with relief, but one glance saw nothing but a gem, no magic to help him.

No healing power either. No command of the wind. No ability to see the present anywhere except here in his cell.

He ran his hand across the wooden walls. A spot of hay here and there lay on the ground, along with one completely rancid blanket. He kicked the rat into the corner and out of his sight, then returned to the iron-reinforced door. No window to the outside there either. Only the dim light of a wall candle flickered to illuminate his surroundings.

Chapter Thirty-One

Reckoning

12 September 1700

Atlantic Ocean

ALEXANDER STIFLED THE rising tide of panic when he lurched awake in complete darkness. He had fallen asleep directly under the candle, hoping the small bit of light might protect him from the rats and other forces lurking below.

He got on his knees and felt along the wall for several minutes before his hand bumped into the sconce. The candle had burned out.

Alexander stood and leaned against the wall, fighting the weight pressing on his lungs and making breathing impossible. The darkness stole his oxygen. He scratched at his throat and broke out in a drenching sweat from the heat of panic.

Gradually, his breathing returned to normal as his logical mind convinced him he had plenty of air to breathe and only lost vision because of the darkness. He took inventory of his body parts and felt nothing amiss, though searching for his magic proved as useless as the night before.

He began to wonder how long he'd stayed below and whether or not anyone knew Beast had jailed him. Would they even notice a missing pirate, or assume he died in battle? But Henri, Spittle, and most of the other men saw him healing people while the captain negotiated the parlay. Surely someone wondered at his whereabouts?

Despite breathing normally, he sweated profusely from the extreme heat. No air circulated here, and the only sound to reach his ears came from the splash of waves against the side of the sloop. Best as he could tell, they remained still in the water.

He drifted toward sleep but reached up and slapped himself on the cheek, afraid of losing consciousness and being attacked by vermin or missing an opportunity to scream for help if he heard someone approach.

He finally heard the jangling of keys and then footsteps, right before the light of a lantern glowed through the crack in the door. Alexander squinted at the brightness when the door flew open, the identity of the person hidden behind the blaze of light.

His eyes adjusted enough to see the silhouette of Henri standing in the doorway. The commanding posture. The beautiful long hair.

"Henri?" Alexander croaked the name, his throat horse from

inactivity.

Henri stepped into the room and set the lantern on the ground. "We need to talk." He sat against the wall and kicked his feet out in front of him.

Alexander hesitated, unsure where to place himself, until Henri motioned for him to come sit next to him. He slipped to the ground and leaned into Henri's chest. Henri reached over and grabbed Alexander around the shoulders, pulling him into a kiss.

Alexander released himself to the moment yet kept some of his passion back, unsure of Henri's intentions.

"I was afraid of that." Henri let him go but grabbed his hand.

"What?"

"Your reluctance."

"I don't understand?" But Alexander did, regardless of his words. He kissed back because of their previous fondness and passion, the continued love he felt for Henri, but not because of any current desire or relief at having the captain come for him.

Henri sighed. "I can't talk to you as a lover. I'm here as your captain to get a full understanding for your imprisonment. Tell me what's going on. We've got the most peculiar situation going on above deck, and I can't have uncertainty on my own boat."

Alexander remained at a loss for words, with no idea how much to tell, or even what exactly Henri hinted at. His silence must have given enough of an answer, anyway, for Henri spoke again without one.

"I know Beast brought you down here. He claimed for treachery against the crew and endangering us. Of course, I thought him full of shit."

Henri reached into his coat pocket and pulled out a flask. He took a long swig of his whiskey, then passed it to Alexander. He drank deeply.

"At least, I did until Spittle spoke up. He didn't necessarily agree with Beast, who claimed you betrayed us and should be sentenced to death. He wanted me to woold you. But Spittle said you had something to tell me, something hidden. Thing is, I might have doubted him too except for this parlay."

Henri paused for another drink, then wiped his mouth with his sleeve.

"A parlay? Involving me? I don't understand."

"Neither do I!"

Alexander allowed a silence between them, unsure where to even begin. Anything he spoke would implicate himself and possibly risk his life. What did Henri want to know? After a painfully long period of time, Henri spoke.

"We should've had this conversation a long time ago. I never wanted to know the rest of the story. You picked a pirate life, after all. But I should have made you tell me more about this Crispin and your history.

"Because Spittle filled me in when I took him aside to get the damn story straight. You were his best friend. If Spittle turned on you in front of everyone, then something was amiss no matter how much I wanted to ignore the truth to save you and our relationship. You love this Crispin. Of course, he's the one hunting us. Scarface told the truth, a British ship hunted special for *All Hallows Eve*. Not because we're pirates or because of me. No, it was you. I'm wondering how long you knew and what this Crispin meant to you. I also understand Beast somehow took your powers away. I won't let him return them to you until I know this crew is safe."

Alexander felt the tear trickle down his cheek. He loved the man sitting next to him, feeling the emotion more at this moment than ever before. Not merely the lust that drew them together in the first place from Henri's confidence and domineering sexuality, his strong muscles contrasting with the silky blond hair. Attraction gave way to a fondness and caring for the man who carried himself with a cavalier attitude to mask deep feelings for his crew and especially his friends. Henri loved Alexander and protected him at every turn.

Yes, Alexander loved him dearly. He wished other circumstances confronted them, because he would have fallen into his arms and forced the captain to make love to him right there amid the rat shit and dank smells below. How he longed for their naked bodies pressed together, the sensation of the captain's small but powerful penis inside his mouth, shooting semen down his throat, and allowing Alexander to swallow the captain's power into his stomach.

He cried and took several minutes before he gathered himself enough to speak. Given all he felt for Henri, how could he ever bring himself to break his heart? For despite the allusions Henri made about his harsh demeanor and flippancy toward death, he loved deeply and cared with a passion.

Alexander wiped at the tears and scooted closer to Henri.

"Why make me say it if you know already?"

Henri looked over and ran his fingers along Alexander's cheek. "Because I only know bits and pieces. I need to learn the harder truth so I can figure out what to do for this boat. Did you betray us?" Henri choked on the last words.

Alexander shook his head. Despite his indecision, even with his concealment of what he knew about the British ship sailing after them, in his heart he never betrayed these men. He loved them. He loved their piracy and respected the life they lived. Others may disagree, but he had no doubt he never betrayed them or his captain.

"Never. I love all of you too much. Especially you. I never betrayed you."

"But you knew?"

"Not really, no."

"Then what? Why do I feel like you're about to drop something on me, forcing me to send you straight for a woolding."

Alexander gulped back his fear. "I still love him. That's all." He shrugged. "The circumstance has nothing to do with piracy or the men above. Not even really anything to do with you. Because I love you too. I never lied or made up how much you mean to me. In any other circumstances—" Alexander stopped himself.

"You mean if I killed him. Or if he simply let you sail away forever."

"I don't even know why he's here."

Henri moved away from Alexander and slammed his fist to the ground. "But until you find out, those other circumstances don't apply.

You're in love with him, not me."

Alexander reached over and put his hand on Henri's calf. "No. I love you both."

Silence filled the room, long enough a rat peeked around the corner of the door but retreated at the sight of people.

Henri whispered. "But you love him more."

Henri got up, not needing anything else from Alexander. He left the lantern burning on the floor but stopped and locked the door behind him before disappearing.

Alone and back in jail, Alexander despaired. Perhaps he should have lied and professed his love for Henri, and Henri alone. He did love him tremendously. He could see their life together, continuing as lovers, a pirate captain and his witch.

Then he remembered Portia and her warnings. Had he doomed them to death? Because she lurked outside somewhere, waiting. If Alexander repressed his love for Crispin, he could be with Henri, appease Portia, and protect them. Had his confused passion doomed everyone aboard *All Hallows Eve*?

Alexander lived most of his life for himself, confident in his identity, sure of his feelings, fighting to survive as his mother commanded. He seldom dealt with doubt and rarely confronted such difficult decisions and contradictions.

Then he realized he had no control. He faced the rare problem of being at the behest of others. Portia's magic. Henri's command. Crispin's authority. Alexander accepted others held the power and would fight without his input.

VII: Finé

Chapter Thirty-Two

Footfall

13 September 1700

Anchored Off Tortuga Island

ALEXANDER SNAPPED BACK to reality. His eyelids shot open, he scanned his surroundings, and remembered he remained locked in the *All Hallows Eve* prison. His senses tingled, almost as if his magical ability had returned.

But nothing happened when he reached for his crystal to see the present. Without testing, he knew he could not heal, either, or control the wind.

Yet he had drifted away mentally because he somehow retained the ability to escape from his predicament by taking his mind to another realm. Had Portia allowed him to keep his escapism as a form of charity? More likely she saw no danger and thus ignored it.

He had gone to an invented reality in which he floated in a cloudy orbit, without concern for humans, his own safety, or the world spiraling out of control somewhere below. He slept. His body rested. Nothing concerned him in his mystic realm.

Growing up after his parents' death, when Alexander used to flee to this place to get away from his uncle, he envisioned conversations with his mother about whether or not he pleased her thus far by surviving despite his circumstances. She always affirmed him and offered her unconditional love.

He didn't need to feel or experience her essence as often in his adulthood, but she had reassured him again during his latest visit. He had gotten himself into quite a conundrum. Though he admitted he probably invented the conversation, she once again comforted him and assured him of her undying love. Survive. No matter the circumstances, survive. And he had.

But would he for long?

His heavy heart felt unburdened after his jail conversation with Henri: painful, yes, emotionally raw, and awful. Destroying his relationship with Henri and telling his pirate lover the truth ripped at Alexander's heart. But the truth liberated him. More than the message to Henri, Alexander appreciated how the truth forced him to confront his deep feelings for Crispin. His longing came to the forefront of his mind.

Yet had this psychological liberation come with a death sentence?

Alexander remembered he drifted away to figure out his feelings, but something had pulled him back to reality.

Not something. Someone.

Alexander's heart stirred at the sound: First, a distant cadence coming down the narrow steps to the lower level. Then, a firm step, pounding across the boards, determined and in command. As the prison door creaked open, Alexander didn't need to see his silhouette to know who approached. The footfall alone told him everything.

He choked back a cry of excitement when the door swung fully open, and there stood Crispin in his officer's uniform, frowning at Alexander and peering around the jail. The vein in his forehead pulsated with...what? Anger? Fear? Consternation?

Alexander grinned despite the situation. He remained standing in the center of the room, not sure what to expect, but elation stirred through his body. He had to fight off the urge to jump into Crispin's arms.

Alexander also glanced around but saw no one else with Crispin.

The silence between them became too much. Unnerved, Alexander searched for something to say and felt foolish with what he asked. "Where are we?"

"Tortuga Isle. We came here to negotiate the remainder of the parlay." Crispin let out a deep breath, as if relieved to answer such a mundane inquiry.

"Ah." Alexander nodded, returned to a loss for words.

An awkward silence descended upon them. Alexander fiddled with his fingers and wiggled around, while Crispin stayed planted in the doorway, taking in his surroundings.

"I'd hoped they were taking better care of you." Crispin stepped into the room. He leaned over and set his lantern next to the one Henri had left for Alexander. The dual power of their fires illuminated the sparse, damp space.

Alexander smiled. "Well, it's jail. I've experienced worse."

Did he detect the hint of a smile at the corner of Crispin's mouth?

Alexander fought the tide of nervous energy threatening to consume him. He had longed for this moment, but with Crispin standing before him, he lost all words and felt hopelessly bewildered. He wished for the ability to read Crispin's mind, to better understand the situation. What would he do if Crispin failed to reciprocate his love?

Perhaps he hoped Crispin would begin or tell him more, but true to form, Alexander realized he needed to initiate their interaction. His heart might pound right out of his chest if he waited any longer.

Alexander cleared his throat. "I never expected to see you again. After, you know. Massachusetts. Unless you came to assassinate me for the high crime of piracy. Are you here to murder me?"

Crispin really did smile. "No." He shook his head and pressed his lips together.

"Then why? What's going on? I don't understand this parlay business. I thought pirates only parlayed with each other, not with the British Navy."

"I'm afraid in many ways my ship has, indeed, become a pirate ship. We need to finish negotiating because I want to return the vessel to its duties, at least for the men who want such a thing."

"Oh." Alexander's heart sank. What did Crispin mean? He doubted Crispin meant to enlist Alexander in the Royal Navy.

"At any rate, I won't be on it, whatever the crew chooses for their future."

"I see." Once again Alexander said something to fill the void because his head spun with each passing second. Why did this have to be so difficult? "Um…so are you taking me prisoner? I'm at a bit of a loss here."

This made both of them laugh. Alexander lifted his hands to the side to emphasize his confusion, then dropped them down with a slap on his hips.

Crispin took two steps and closed the distance between them. He reached out and held Alexander by both shoulders. "I didn't know if I'd ever see you again either." He choked on the last words.

Alexander's eyes welled with tears. "Right. I see you've done well. All the way up to captain." Alexander smiled, somehow proud of Crispin despite how much he hated his call to duty. "This is getting a little strange though. I don't get the parlay. Or why you're here. Or what's going on with me. What have you been doing?"

Crispin clutched tightly, with both hands, to Alexander's shoulders. "Obeying you."

Alexander's heart fluttered, the tears trickled down his cheeks, and yet he clamped down against any hope until he knew more. "What do you mean? Where have you been?"

"I've been working my way up to captain so I could command a ship and go in search of you. Ever since I walked away from you in the abandoned barn, I've lived in complete regret. You've been haunting me. When your memory almost drove me mad, I vowed to live the rest of my life by obeying you, until I either died or found you."

"What were you obeying? I never gave you orders. You'd never take them from me, anyway."

"You're wrong." Crispin shook his head. He took his hand and wiped the tears from Alexander's face. "My heart always obeyed you, even when my mind refused. I took too long for my logic to catch up with the emotion so they could work together to obey you." Alexander glanced at Crispin in confusion. "Yes, I did obey you. You told me to fight. So I've been fighting. I hope I'm not too late. I've been fighting according to your orders. Fighting, Alexander." Crispin leaned over and kissed Alexander hard on the lips. He held the two of them close together for what felt like an eternity into which Alexander wished he could escape forever. "You told me to fight for you with your last plea in the barn."

They kissed again, longer and with more passion.

Before the physical longing took control of them, Alexander sat them down and leaned against the wall, as he had done with Henri not long ago. They sat in silence, holding hands, until Alexander worried someone would interrupt them before they finished their conversation.

"You won a battle against us?"

"Us?" Crispin asked.

"I mean *All Hallows Eve*. The pirates. I'm one of them, you know."

"Of course. Yes, we defeated you."

"And your victory allowed a parlay?"

Crispin nodded. "I could have destroyed this ship. But I didn't think you wanted me to. And I didn't need to go so far to get to you. My first and most important condition was that no one harm you. Also, I demanded to see you before we finished the terms of the agreement."

"You've been hunting for me all this time?" Alexander swooned, recalling the story one of the pirates told him about the Ancient Greeks and Helen of Troy. Had Crispin's love for Alexander moved even just one ship into battle?

"Yes." Crispin pressed his lips together as tears sprang into his eyes. "I couldn't do the charade anymore or live without you. I tried to do everything they expected of me to fulfill my obligation. No matter what I did, all I could think about was you. You in the damned chicken coop the first time you kissed me. Your smile whenever I visited. Your naked body pressed against me in the tavern. Everywhere I turned, you were like a witch haunting me."

Alexander laughed at the reference. "I must have bewitched you, though I'm afraid even my powers aren't so strong."

Crispin leaned over and kissed him again. "You've no idea."

"So what now? I don't think my pirate friends like me very much anymore."

"They seem to have mixed emotions. Especially your captain. But I think we can protect you well enough." Crispin reached over and played with Alexander's earring. "I like this. Nice touch. Very pirate. Though I'm not sure I like calling you Medusa."

"Don't. I hate the name." Alexander decided not to say anything yet about Beast. "But the earring was my idea. I mean, I'm not ever going back to live with the damned Puritans. So why not go all the way?"

Crispin leaned over and licked at Alexander's ear, then used his mouth to play with the earring. Alexander leaned back and closed his eyes as he reached over and took Crispin's hand in his and squeezed.

Crispin rubbed at Alexander's crotch. "I wish we had time for this."

"Yeah. Me too. But we probably don't, huh?"

Crispin shook his head. "No. I needed to see you first to know where we stood before I went any further. I had a number of directions I could have taken with the parlay. I think I know where I want to go. But I must know something from you. I fought for you. I hope I'm not too late. I know I hurt you. I know I drove you away."

Alexander reached over and placed his fingers on Crispin's lips to quiet him. "I'm sorry too. I should have given you more chances. I knew what you felt, but I hurt so much, so I gave up too easily."

"We hurt each other."

"What about Portia? You thought I killed her. Crispin, I swear. I didn't. Never. I'm so sorry about my feud with her."

Crispin patted Alexander's cheek to quiet him. "I know. I told you I figured out the truth, even before we parted, when I found the evidence of her witchcraft. I learned you weren't at fault, she was. I know. In fact, I learned even more since then. God forgive me, I should have seen her machinations from the first. You don't have to apologize."

Alexander almost asked something else but stopped himself. Not yet. Crispin hid something from him, and he would learn what in time but wanted to be patient and not push too hard. He remembered when he drifted to Crispin's ship at Henri's request, and Crispin stared back at him, as if he, too, knew magic.

"But listen. I need to know." Crispin reached over and touched Alexander on the cheek with the back of his hand. "Can we recover? Can you forgive me? Tell me, and the rest will fall into place."

Alexander allowed himself to cry. The tears streamed down his cheeks. "I already did. I'm all yours, Crispin. I always have been. No matter what I did or what happened, I've been all yours since the first day we met. I love you more than anything. I always said I survived because my mother ordered me to. That was true at first but isn't as accurate since. I survived because I never gave up hope we'd be together. I survived because I love you too much to give up."

Crispin leaned over and pressed their lips together.

Alexander pulled away but held tight to Crispin's hand. "Now, what does this parlay mean? What can we do?"

"In time. I promise. But I have to leave you here. Henri wants to see you again. He can't harm you. Don't worry. I'll be back for you soon."

Crispin stood and pulled Alexander to his feet. He kissed him on the cheek and turned to leave.

"Wait!" Alexander grabbed Crispin's shoulder and turned him around. "One more thing. When I floated over to your boat to investigate, you looked at me, didn't you? You knew I was on your ship. Am I right?" His patience had not lasted very long.

Crispin grinned and nodded.

"How?"

"There's so much to tell you. But I promised this visit would be quick. They're waiting. I'll explain later. Trust me."

Crispin kissed Alexander softly on the lips and took his leave. He left one lantern lit with Alexander and closed the door behind him, though Alexander noticed he failed to lock the prison.

Chapter Thirty-Three

Bitter Negotiating

13 September 1700

Anchored Off Tortuga Island

AFTER CRISPIN LEFT, Alexander opened the door to see if any air flowed through his tight space and to alleviate the stifling heat. He stayed in his prison, not wanting to antagonize the situation or lead anyone to think he wanted to escape.

A contradiction of emotions sliced through his body at every thought. He practically floated at his reunion with Crispin. Except he fought a rising tide of panic because somewhere Henri lurked and would not take kindly to this betrayal, no matter what they said to each other at their last parting. Alexander saw firsthand how Henri handled his anger when someone betrayed him—their eyes popped out of their head in a bloody mess. Could Crispin's parlay protect him from such raw rage if Henri determined to punish him for the treachery of their love, or more dangerously, the perceived duplicity against *All Hallows Eve?*

He cursed Crispin for refusing to tell him more. Alexander always hated not knowing the entire story. He tried to come to terms with the fact his fate lay in other people's hands, but no matter how much he could intellectually understand reality, his very being fought against accepting the circumstances.

Crispin's professed loved calmed his nerves.

The moment boiled down to trust. The thought hit Alexander with such force he worried it might knock the very breath out of him. The town elders smashed whatever youthful trust Alexander possessed into the snowy ground when they scared his father to death and sent his mother to suicide. The painful moment taught Alexander not to trust a soul. Not his uncle, certainly. Not any of the people around him.

Alexander even held his pirate friends at arm's length. He trusted Henri so long as their relationship held firm yet was always troubled at the idea of what may happen to him if they ever grew tired of each other. He trusted Spittle more, but she so quickly abandoned him when she decided he'd betrayed the pirates, without ever hearing his side of the story.

Thus his discomfort at being in the dark about what parlay these two men negotiated above him, while he sat in the dank and shit-smelling cell.

Crispin also held responsibility for Alexander's lack of trust because he cast him aside to follow his duty, to pretend he would marry, to enter the navy, and to leave Alexander behind forever. Alexander became a pirate when Crispin left him little other choice.

Except he found out Crispin had defied the odds and searched the oceans for him. Crispin not only forsook his duty but put his very life at risk. Crispin entirely and totally cast his lot with Alexander.

The warmth of the revelation dissipated when every muscle in his body tensed at the sound of footsteps. Not Crispin's. Then the light of another lantern cast a shadow upon the wall.

Henri stood before him.

Alexander took a step back when he saw Henri's face a few feet from him, bright red with rage.

"I thought we understood each other?" Alexander hated the fear in his quivering voice. "I love you, Henri. I never lied to you." Alexander's back rammed against the wall. He had nowhere else to go, and Henri kept pace with him, standing mere inches away.

Henri reached behind Alexander's head and yanked at his long hair until Alexander cried out in pain. Then Henri smashed their lips together until Alexander shoved him away and gasped for breath. Only then did Alexander spot the rope dangling from Henri's pocket, the stick poking out the top.

"You wouldn't do that to me, would you?" Alexander pointed at the deadly weapons.

Henri laughed, the mean-spirited cackle Alexander heard him use when he was blinded with fury. "I should. Maybe I should have long ago. Maybe I will, but the parlay speaks against justice for you."

Henri stood quiet before Alexander, leaving Alexander to try to guess at his presence.

"What do you want? I thought we were at peace."

"We were, until I had time to think at how you played me for a fool. In front of my men, no less. How you used me to escape from the Puritans when I should have left you there to hang from one of their trees instead of leading me to my own demise. You know how I feel when someone disobeys my orders. We can't have such behavior and maintain any kind of stability on a pirate ship. Even when I was here last time—" Henri paused, glanced around the jail, and then walked over and slammed his fist into the wall. "Even last time, I let my emotion get the better of me. I'd lost. Lost your affection to him and couldn't understand. Now you should see how the men look at me, as if my actions with you led to our defeat. Maybe something does need to happen to you so I can regain control of my ship."

Henri stormed back toward Alexander but stopped, again mere inches from his face. "Then I remembered this is greater than the two of us. That was my mistake, thinking about you and me first. I must be a pirate and a captain first. You should have been incidental, sex or a companion, maybe a friend, but not someone special to me. I lost sight of reality and allowed you to dupe me."

Henri balled his hands into fists but, thankfully, kept them at his side.

"You're wrong."

"I'm wrong now, am I?" Henri spat the words, but Alexander made no move to wipe off his face.

"About what I felt for you, I mean. I love you. It's just complicated."

Henri stepped back and punched hard at his chest with both fists. "Does it matter? Because you're his now. I don't mean shit to you. You've destroyed me. I gave myself to you. Regardless of what you may feel for me, you've ruined me in order to run off with a damned officer in His Majesty's Navy."

"I'm sorry," Alexander whispered the lame words, at a complete loss for anything else to say. He deserved to hear Henri's harsh condemnation, whether or not he agreed. Alexander had chosen to dump Henri to go with Crispin. Henri deserved his space for mourning and anger, even if Alexander had to stand and listen to the bitter words.

Alexander's heart nearly broke when he saw the tears streaming down Henri's face; then he screamed in terror when Henri reached for the rope and walked toward him.

The tears on Henri's cheeks seemed to dry before Alexander's eyes as he walked steadily toward him. His eyes, usually bright blue and full of life, became black pits of hatred. Alexander recognized what he saw before him — the captain of *All Hallows Eve* preparing to enforce pirate law upon his ship.

Alexander called for the wind to blow Henri back or rock the ship so he would fall, but he had no magical abilities.

Thankfully, Henri kept the rope firmly in hand but not the stick and instead punched his fist hard into Alexander's stomach. As

Alexander keeled over in pain, he could see out the corner of his eye as Henri made to uppercut his other hand into Alexander's face.

Before the fist smashed into his nose, however, Henri screamed in rage as someone grabbed him from behind and threw him across the room with such force Alexander doubted a mere human was present.

Alexander had never even heard someone else approaching, let alone Crispin.

The two men squared their shoulders and prepared to continue the fight. Only Alexander stepping between them stopped the madness.

"Please." Alexander held up both his arms between them. "Stop."

"We had an agreement." The veins in Crispin's neck pulsated as if they might burst, and he set his jaw so tightly Alexander feared he might crack his teeth in half.

They waited for Henri. His bright-red face softened, his muscles relaxed, and he lowered his head and nodded.

"According to the terms," Crispin continued, "if you harm him in any way, the parlay is negated. Perhaps you forgot who has the upper hand in this deal? I could destroy you, your ship, and execute every last one of you for the crime of piracy. Do you understand?"

Crispin stepped around Alexander's outstretched arm and glared at Henri. Alexander never saw Henri so cowed, defenseless, and at the mercy of someone else. Henri nodded his assent.

"Good. Now, since you violated the terms, I'm giving back his magic."

Alexander tilted his head in confusion.

"I don't know if I can get Beast to comply," Henri spoke softly, utterly defeated.

"I don't need Beast. I'm explaining that in our original deal he was to regain his power once we left the ship. But he'll need magic for his own protection before then. He'll remain with me now. His prison sentence has ended."

Henri stared at the floor.

To his surprise, Alexander felt his witchcraft return to him. First the healing power soothed his aching stomach from Henri's punch. The pain disappeared without Alexander having to concentrate. Then the crystal in his pocket tingled, as if awakened from the dead. He wiggled his fingers and felt the force of air they created, enough so the flame in Crispin's lantern flickered.

Alexander wondered again at how this occurred, but Crispin kept them moving forward.

"Come." Crispin stepped toward the door but reached out with one hand to grab Alexander's arm and pull him along.

As they moved across the cargo hold and toward the stairs, Henri stayed behind.

"I don't understand. What's going on?" Alexander asked. "I'm tired of being in the dark."

Crispin pulled Alexander up the stairs and remained silent. When they got to the next level, he paused and pulled Alexander into a tight hug, kissing the top of his head.

"Not now. This whole thing is rather precarious. In time, I promise." Crispin lifted Alexander's chin so they stared at one another. Alexander shut his eyes to taste Crispin more completely as he leaned over and kissed Alexander on the lips. "Please, trust me."

Alexander opened his eyes and stared at Crispin. "I do." Alexander followed as Crispin led them up again, onto the deck toward the two crews waiting for their captains to return.

Chapter Thirty-Four

Farewell and Reconciliation

13 September 1700

Anchored Off Tortuga Island

ALEXANDER SQUINTED FROM the sun in his eyes after emerging from below deck. He held tightly to Crispin's hand as he walked authoritatively across the ship toward the area where two groups of men assembled, one pirate and one British.

Alexander realized he could not even be sure about how much time had passed in prison. He guessed not more than a day, since the men seemed tired, and he doubted the two crews could coexist for too long.

The British warship was attached to *All Hallows Eve* as before, though Alexander thought half its sailors had come over here. Most of the others remaining on their ship gathered at its side to watch.

Crispin stood before the pirates and glanced over the motley crew. "Your captain will return shortly, so we can continue our negotiations," he said.

Alexander had never seen anyone address the entire pirate crew except Henri or Spittle. It almost unnerved him when he peered into the crew's eyes, his family — or former family — at any rate. The atmosphere and comfort he so often experienced with these men had evaporated. Of course, they glared at Crispin since his command led to their defeat. Alexander could anticipate the hatred boiling within them because he'd witnessed their wrath toward ships they'd conquered, let alone one that had defeated them.

It hurt more when those scowls stared back at him. By appearing with Crispin, Alexander became the enemy. He wished he could explain, to tell them, as he did with Henri, how much he loved them. He also understood any words would fall on deaf ears, and, no matter what, he'd lost them forever.

Only Crispin's firm grip kept Alexander's heart from breaking.

Alexander spied Spittle standing to the side, in command of these defeated pirates. He knew with but a word she could instigate an all quarters battle. Instead, she, too, watched these proceedings in silence. Yet the look in her eyes hit Alexander even more. She alone glanced sympathetically back at him. The frown he last saw upon her face was gone. She appeared to search his eyes for their old connection. He hoped he reflected the same message back to her.

He could swear King James cocked his head and winked at him.

"Lieutenant James, a word?" Crispin addressed one of the officers from his ship. As he stepped aside and moved far away from the men, he pulled Alexander along with him, and this other man followed.

A stab of jealousy shot through Alexander, for this was the man he spied, on more than one occasion, sitting in Crispin's private quarters with him. He was quite handsome. As tall as Crispin, with the same stature and commanding presence, green sparkling eyes, and a muscular body as well.

Before they got too close to the lieutenant, Crispin leaned over and whispered in Alexander's ear. "You've nothing to worry about—from him or anyone else."

Again, Alexander wanted to inquire as to how Crispin read his mind.

"Lieutenant, do we have our story straight?"

The man shuffled his feet but looked right back at Crispin. "Aye, sir. You died in battle against the pirates. I already prepared and dated my report as such. The men understand as well."

"Good." Crispin smiled. "And you, John, congratulations. I believe you're now Captain James."

Jonathan James smiled broadly and turned red.

"You're going to have to get used to the title." Crispin righted his posture and saluted him.

John cast his head down, though the grin remained. "Thank you, sir, for your confidence. I should get back to the men."

When he walked away, Crispin turned his attention to Alexander. "You don't need to be jealous. Nothing happened between us. We're friends, and I admire his service and dedication. As far as I know, he only likes women. Besides, I only ever think about you."

Alexander was at a loss for words. He was embarrassed at how easily Crispin discerned his emotion, and his head whirled at the pieces of Crispin's grand scheme as he learned of them. Crispin and this John had concocted some story about his death, and the lieutenant was taking over their ship. So where did Alexander and Crispin belong? Because Alexander highly doubted they would be welcomed among the pirates. Despite his questions and their moment alone, Alexander smiled at Crispin.

Crispin laughed. "I don't recall your ever being at a loss for words."

"I suppose it's because I have too many questions. I want to know everything. But we'd better return."

When they got back to the main deck, John James stood to the side of the men but organized his sailors in orderly lines where they waited to hear from their captain, or perhaps, former captain. The pirates, on the other hand, milled about and kept their distance from the other crew. Spittle watched over them, Henri conspicuously absent.

Though Crispin gave command to John, he again addressed both parties as if in charge of the scene. "I'd like to explain one bit of the parlay." Crispin looked each of his men in the eye, then glanced at the skeptical pirates as they frowned at him.

Spittle stepped forward. "It's true. Listen up." She slapped a pirate upside the head who slumped over from too much drinking, then glared at another to force his conformity.

Crispin cleared his throat. "Anyone who would like to change sides may do so. Sailors, you're fine men in His Majesty's Navy. Yet wanderlust can strike anyone. You may join the pirates, freely and without retribution from them for having taken part in defeating them earlier. And, you—" Crispin turned and motioned at the pirates. "—current law allows you to come into the navy without punishment for past deeds." A few pirates grunted and some laughed, but everyone stopped when Spittle hocked back and threatened to launch.

When the men calmed down, Crispin continued. "And, finally, I want to inform you I will not be returning as your captain. Lieutenant James, now Captain James, is your commander. I leave with them."

Jonathan stepped forward, to cheers from his men, while the pirates stood absolutely bewildered at the news. If not awkward enough, Henri returned but stayed to the side, nodding at Spittle. Several of the pirates glanced his way, but he jerked his head for them to pay attention to Spittle and Crispin.

Eventually, a handful of men from the navy went over to the pirate side, while two pirates decided to become proper sailors.

Alexander remained beside Crispin, figuring he would follow his love, regardless of the consequences, which he imagined would be quite bad if they stayed with the pirates. What would keep the pirates from assassinating them once the naval ship sailed away?

As a couple pirates said farewell to their comrades who switched sides, and Captain James organized his men and started returning them to their own ship, Alexander looked back at Henri, who hid behind some of his most loyal men. The loss had cowed him, taken away his defiance and commanding presence. Without a formal declaration, Alexander would swear Spittle led *All Hallows Eve*.

As the HMS ship prepared for departure, the pirates milled about, drinking, chatting, and at peace with whatever might happen. Alexander wondered if they knew more than he but then remembered the nature of pirate life. Piracy took all sorts of unexpected twists and turns, one moment a party, the next a bloody battle, from revelry to angry fisticuffs, from camaraderie to keelhauling. Most of these men had lived the life for a few years, much longer than the couple of months Alexander sailed with them, so perhaps nothing surprised them anymore, and they went with whatever circumstances presented themselves at the moment.

As the British vessel shoved off and then lifted its sail, Captain James came to the side of his boat and saluted Crispin. Crispin, no longer a commanding officer, waved in response, a satisfied smile on his face.

Until the military ship disappeared on the horizon, nothing changed on the pirate boat, as if they went about business as usual, which in this case meant drinking.

Alexander was soothed somewhat because Crispin never left his side and seemed unworried. Tacky came to Alexander, handed him a jug of rum, and drank with him by way of showing he maintained affection for their friendship.

Yet every muscle in Alexander's body tensed when he spied Beast standing at the back of the pirates. In the commotion, and with other men in charge of both crews, Alexander almost allowed himself to forget entirely about the real threat to himself. Portia had never forgotten him, and she sat watching her son and staring daggers at his lover.

The hair on Alexander's arm stood straight up, and his knees began to wobble. He checked again to see he possessed his witch powers but then worried, even with them, he could hardly ward her off. He'd deluded himself all along he could combat her. At the moment of their fight, she somehow had stripped him of his magic and carried him off. In death, she'd obtained even more power than in life.

Still, Alexander would never surrender to anyone without a fight. His boldness returned as he reminded himself he had escaped his latest prison sentence and Crispin stood next to him. Perhaps Crispin could reason with the spirit of his mother.

The press of Crispin's hand against his back pulled Alexander away from his concentration on Beast. "Stop worrying."

"There's something you need to know about one of the pirates."

The corner of Crispin's face curled up in a smirk. "I know. And I said not to worry."

"I don't think you do. Yes, he's a hulk of a man. A very dangerous one who can snap a person in half with ease, not to mention one who despises me. But the problem is worse." Alexander hesitated, unsure how to explain to someone their dead mother had taken up residence in a filthy and deadly pirate, and furthermore intended to kill his lover. Despite himself, Alexander began laughing.

Crispin giggled too. "I don't know what you could possibly think is funny. But again, I understand the situation. I have so much to explain to you. I realize Beast poses an unusual problem. I find it most unnerving to stare into the eyes of a particularly vulgar gentleman and see my mother staring back."

The smile disappeared from Alexander's face, and he looked at Crispin with complete shock. "You know?"

"Indeed. I said so already."

Alexander started to respond when King James flew over and perched on his shoulder. "A word with the first mate. *Squawk.* First mate calls. *Squawk.*" King James flew off but landed on a nearby barrel, where he turned to wait for Alexander.

"I have to follow him."

"The bird commands the ship?" Crispin stifled another laugh.

Alexander shook his head. "No! He belongs to the first mate. He's my friend."

"The bird or first mate?"

Alexander laughed loudly. "Both, but I was referring to Spittle, the first mate. He's a right fine pirate, and an even better person." Alexander thought in time he may share Spittle's secret with Crispin, but he needed to know more and would not betray his friend, not even to Crispin. "And friend or not, I have to obey the first mate, yes? You're not in charge anymore."

"Correct. You'd better follow the bird."

Alexander noticed, as he stepped away, how Crispin monitored him, eventually stepping into the path between where Alexander found Spittle and Beast's continued gaze. Beast hardly moved his head even as he his eyes rotated to spy upon them both.

Chapter Thirty-Five

Pirate Decisions

14 September 1700

Tortuga Isle

AFTER KING JAMES summoned Alexander to see Spittle, Alexander grew nervous at what his friend had in store. As he approached, however, Spittle gave him a reassuring smile.

"We don't have much time," she said, "because I got to get these men moving and in action before they explode. There's too much negative energy, what with us losing a battle, a ship about to fall over and missing a mast, and a bit of a leadership problem. I wanted to make sure you stayed right close to Crispin, understand? No one will mess with the parlay, even though his ship left. Pirate honor and all."

"Of course." Alexander wanted to say more but felt awkward.

Spittle reached up and patted his shoulder. "We'll talk. I promise."

Alexander returned to Crispin and felt much better about where
things stood with Spittle.

Soon thereafter, *All Hallows Eve* erupted into activity with a glance
from Henri and at Spittle's command. The pirates moved things about,
threw damaged goods overboard, and limped their severely damaged
ship ashore for repairs.

The pirates reverted to their typical drunken revelry, despite the
day's defeat and strangeness. They drank, had a feast after hunting on
the island, and celebrated without a care in the world. Alexander never
left Crispin's side as they sat by themselves, propped against a rock and
watching.

Alexander noticed only Beast acted out of character. Beast sat un-
naturally atop a high rock and glared at Alexander the entire night,
seeming to soften the stare when she turned her attention to her son
who held Alexander as he sat between his legs.

By late the next morning, Spittle had ordered every pirate to either
work hard on repairing the ship or to run around the island, looking for
food and other items to mend *All Hallows Eve*. Monkey led a contingent
of men who ventured to see if they could locate an acceptable replace-
ment for the missing mast. Henri had regained his commanding posture
and went with them.

Spittle returned to Crispin and Alexander because they were not given an assignment.

"May I have a word with your mate?" Spittle asked Crispin.

"Naturally."

Alexander got up and walked down the shore with Spittle. King James hopped along a short distance behind them.

When they stopped at a growth of trees, Spittle motioned for them to sit, and an awkward silence fell between the two. Alexander wanted to apologize and plead forgiveness but fumbled for the right words.

Before he found them, Spittle spoke, "I was too harsh. I'm sorry."

Alexander looked at Spittle, astonished, and shook his head. "I should be apologizing to you. I never meant to hurt you or put the crew at risk. I was confused about what to do. I wish I could prove to you I never betrayed you, or this ship. I love these pirates. It's just—"

Spittle reached over and placed her hand on Alexander's knee at the same time she interrupted him. "You don't have anything to explain. I should have known anyway. I got carried away with being a pirate and forgot to think like a human. You must have been pulled in a million directions." Spittle grabbed Alexander's hand and squeezed. "I know where your loyalty lies. I always did. And I know how much that one means to you." She pointed toward Crispin with her free hand. "Seems like a good catch, though you're risking a lot. Anyway, I needed time to let you know all is well between us if you can forgive me."

"I'm the one who needs forgiveness for what I did…or didn't do."

"You're always in control of yourself, always doing the right thing. You need to let yourself be vulnerable."

Alexander scrunched his eyebrows together in confusion. "I don't understand."

"Right. When it comes to the boy over there, you're not sure what to do. You told me about yourself. Don't you think I figured you out along the way? You don't like to rely on anyone else, and given what's happened to you, that makes sense. But in order for you to love someone else, you have to let down the defenses." Spittle laughed and shrugged. "I know, how did I become an expert when I hide from everyone myself? Listen, I know a thing or two about people. Like what you and I have always done for each other. We shared our deepest secrets, which is why I need to apologize to you, because I should have seen what was going on. You weren't betraying me or the crew. You were confused and in turmoil. Like you understand the secrecy I need, being a woman among these pirates. You're not alone in the world anymore. Frankly, even with what he did to you, I don't think you ever were once Crispin came into your life. I'm here. He's here. Don't keep trying to go this alone."

Spittle jumped to her feet, cutting off their conversation.

As she pulled Alexander up, he grinned. "You sound like you're very much in command."

"First mate duties."

"It's more."

Spittle shrugged. "We'll see. Henri's got a new plan."

The crew continued to work on their ship and set up camp. Alexander enjoyed returning to the routine of assisting Tacky with food preparation. He learned the pirates planned to remain beached here for some time because of the extensive repairs needed on the ship. Crispin assisted with other things but never ventured more than several yards from Alexander.

With so much to do, the day passed quickly and soon enough evening descended upon the sweating and tired men. Spittle announced a meeting, giving everyone a few minutes to get their drink of choice, grab some food, and then gather around a roaring fire.

Crispin and Alexander sat behind them, slightly removed from the proceedings. Alexander watched as Henri joined the group as a leader. He grabbed Spittle and forced her to stand before them.

"What's going on?" Crispin whispered to Alexander.

"A meeting. This is what we do. They're probably going to decide what to do next. Except I've never seen Spittle in front of them when Henri's here."

As if on cue, Spittle put her fingers in her mouth and whistled loudly at the assembly. Everyone stopped talking and turned their attention to Henri and her.

Henri cleared his throat. "We need to make some decisions," he said.

One of Beast's minions shouted to the men. "Yeah, and first is about our lack of a captain, because I say we vote out the last one for losing his mind over a boy!"

The words stung Alexander. He refused to even glance at Henri as a debate commenced about Henri's fate.

Alexander worried until Spittle blasted a wad at the foot of the offending voice and Henri stalked over to him.

"You got a problem with me?" Henri towered above the man,

who shook his head.

Alexander wondered what might come next when the familiar red hair popped up from the middle of the assembly. "Henri is our leader. Anyone here who never made a mistake, stand your ass up, and I'll cast the first vote for you as captain. Otherwise shut the fuck up, and we got to move on. I think captain and the first mate got a plan I'd like to hear."

Henri stepped away from his confrontation and stood back in front of the men. "I always put this crew first." A few snorted but Henri stared hard at them to shut them up. "I learned from our little mistake. No more single cavorting for me. See, I admit my mistakes, unlike some of you." He shot a glance to Beast and his comrades. "I need variety and spice, not bewitching. Enough personal nonsense. I recognized we have a bigger need. I have a new vision for us, mates. We'll never get surprised again if we got two ships."

"We ain't got one working ship right now," a pirate smirked.

Henri roared a laugh. "Yeah, *All Hallows Eve* needs some work. We'll get her up and running in no time. Followed by our next adventure. Men, our first mission will be to commandeer a second ship. We're creating a pirate force, two vessels in lock step, pillaging and sailing together!"

The men roared approval. Alexander wondered how they got on board so fast with such little detail. But he knew. Henri's authority had returned, and they were desperate for their normal pirate life.

Henri held up a hand to silence them. "The plan presents one problem, however. We've only got one captain. We'll need two."

The pirate who first denounced Henri stood and shouted at the throng. "Time for a captain election, then! I nominate the fiercest pirate among us. One who would never betray the crew and could never be defeated in battle. 'Tis Beast or nothing for me!"

With his broad smile and exuberance, the man obviously intended for everyone to shout an agreement. However, the usual suspects backed his announcement with a *huzzah* while most of the other pirates pressed their lips together and shook their heads.

Tacky pushed himself up with the help of a couple pirate shoulders and addressed the men. "With all due credit to Beast and his mates, he'd split us in half. We know the choice here. The real choice, who kept us together and can get us out of this parlay quickly and on our way. Spittle is my captain, and the only one I'll sail under other than Henri."

The vast majority of the pirates cheered assent. Once several other men spoke in favor of the selection, Tacky orchestrated a vote to put Spittle at the helm of the second, as of yet not possessed, ship. They turned their attention to her and shouted for her to address the crew.

After several minutes of cheering, Spittle held up her hands to quiet them. "I'm not the speech-making type. Henri's the sophisticate among us. Thank you for the honor. We'll be back on our feet in no time. Our repairs are organized. Once she's well enough —" Spittle pointed at *All Hallows Eve*. " — we'll be off to find a ship, to make me a real captain instead of a fake one." Her comment drew laughs from the men. "As for settling the rest of the parlay —" Spittle pointed at Crispin. " — not tonight. We've been through enough. Let's celebrate our new direction, and your captains will bring us together tomorrow for weightier matters."

With their quiet agreement, she grinned broadly. "One more thing. I like to think in advance. If *All Hallows Eve* is to get a partner, let's find a name in advance. I have a recommendation from a good authority, so let's try one for size." Spittle looked behind her, where Alexander spotted King James sitting on a low branch. "Come here," she instructed her parrot.

King James flew over and landed on her shoulder.

"What name do you like, King James?" Spittle asked him.

"*Squawk,* King James's Palace! *Squawk,* King James's Palace!"

The pirates laughed loudly and shouted approval until Spittle led them in a more formal vote to affirm the name. "She's got a name, then! Soon we better go find King James's Palace!"

The evening returned to pirate revelry. Even Henri enjoyed himself, back to sharing his alcohol and making out with a pirate Alexander had never seen with another man before. A stab of jealousy hit Alexander but gave way to a happiness at seeing the captain back to his typical self.

Crispin and Alexander removed themselves to the side. Alone, Alexander asked Crispin what to expect going forward. "Will they kill us?"

Crispin shook his head. "The terms of the parlay protect us. They won't allow us to join one of the crews, but they'll leave us somewhere. Tomorrow they'll determine our fate."

Alexander grew too tired to ask further questions. Even the sudden realization that Crispin had said nothing about the problem with

Beast failed to keep him awake as he drifted to sleep with Crispin's stomach as his pillow.

Chapter Thirty-Six

Final Confrontation

15 September 1700

Tortuga Isle

ALEXANDER WOKE WITH a start and peered at the horizon, where the sun peeked over the ocean's edge. He lay on top of Crispin and felt almost every muscle in his lover's body go tense at the same time the hair on his arms stood straight up.

"Get up," Crispin whispered.

When they stood next to each other, Alexander surveyed the situation. Every pirate within his view slept in peace. He and Crispin had slumbered several yards away from everyone else—where the atmosphere was too quiet and eerily calm. The disturbing force came from another location, strong and angry but not close.

Alexander glanced at Crispin, who scanned the island. He held his hands in the air as if ready for an attack, so Alexander prepared his magic in case something came after them.

Crispin spun around and tilted his head as he stared hard into the woods behind them. He held his fingers to his lips. Alexander turned to look and finally heard it. Portia's soft laughter, which she always used when she felt superior.

"Come on. Stay close to me." Crispin stepped forward cautiously, then grabbed Alexander's hand and pulled him along.

When they got a few feet into the woods, Crispin dropped Alexander's hand and motioned for him to keep up.

The farther they went, the louder the laughter became and the more every magical sense within Alexander tingled an alarm.

"Crispin, I'm not ready to fight her." Alexander halted. "This isn't safe."

Crispin stopped. He glanced with a gentle look at Alexander. "This is inevitable. I need you to get your magic ready and attack her the minute you see her. Understand?"

Alexander shook his head. "I don't think I can beat her. We need a better plan. I don't even know what we're doing."

"We're fine. Blast her with wind the minute you see Beast."

Crispin gave Alexander little choice but to comply as he stalked forward, moving rapidly through the growth toward Beast.

Alexander wanted to obey Crispin's wish and protect them when they got to a small clearing and saw Beast sitting several feet up in a tree, but he froze in disgust. Beast sat naked on a branch, his head tilted at an unnatural angle, his legs bent back behind him in such a way they would have snapped off from a normal human body.

"There you are!" Beast grinned and clapped his hands together, Portia's voice a combination of her natural sound and a demon's.

The clapping snapped Alexander out of his stupor. He blasted the wind at Portia to knock her out of the tree, but she leapt to the ground before the wind hit her and tossed a fire ball at him. Before he could react, the flames hit him in the middle of the chest, but instead of lighting him on fire, a net wrapped around his body, which then flew up and hung from a tree before he could consciously react.

Alexander concentrated the breeze on the limb from which he hung and snapped it off, too late to realize the net controlled him. He landed hard on the ground but on his side, in time to witness what transpired next.

Beast walked strangely toward Alexander, her motions awkward and stilted, as if losing control of her human possession, but laughing and clapping at her triumph. "I told you, you'd never possess my son!"

Too sure of herself, she ignored Crispin. Strange, how she always claimed to act on his behalf and to protect him, but at this important moment she disregarded him. Before she reached Alexander, Crispin sprinted over but halted a few feet from her. As she turned to look at him, Crispin raised his arms high in the air and sent lightning bolts out of his fingers.

Beast burst into flames, his body flopping to the ground, and the man's deep voice screaming in agony as he burned to death. Portia's spirit launched out and headed toward the sky.

Crispin looked at Alexander. "Blow her back to me."

Alexander obeyed, shoving the air downward against her force. He stopped her upward momentum enough so Crispin could raise his arms, this time shooting a purple beam at her. Portia exploded.

Alexander felt the air around him grow still as her essence disappeared. Crispin had obliterated his own mother. Somehow, Alexander knew she was gone, this time for good.

A silly grin spread across Alexander's face as Crispin hurried over and cut away the ropes. He fell into Crispin's arms once freed and hugged him. He smiled stupidly and began laughing when he noticed Crispin started chuckling first.

They both fell to the ground in each other's arms. When they calmed, Alexander climbed into Crispin's lap.

"So you're a witch too? Were you always a witch? The surprises you've had for me since you returned!"

Crispin's hand, holding Alexander's butt, felt wonderful. "I wasn't always a witch. I wanted to explain to you, but there was never time because I had to concentrate on monitoring her. After you left Massachusetts, I cleaned out the house because I had no intention of living there. I discovered her black magic and how she manipulated everyone, especially me. I suppose I never saw because she was my mother. I learned about the darkness within her. I told you I had learned about her magic, which is why, before you left, I knew you hadn't killed her. But afterward, I figured out the evil behind what she did."

"When—" Crispin choked on the word and pressed his forehead against Alexander's before he continued. "When I learned what she could do, I knew you told me the truth. I knew she attacked you, so I determined to learn the magic for myself. I cast a spell to see the past and witnessed her suicide. She never loved me, only the thought of a son to control. She hated you. I thought I could make up for her transgressions if I found you. To fight for you."

"So you taught yourself magic? To figure her out?"

Crispin kissed Alexander. "No. I learned the magic to help me find you. Besides, the magic is in my blood. I have a family legacy, like yours. I was searching for you. She was always too arrogant to learn to harness the full potential of the magic."

Alexander wrapped his arms around Crispin. "Did she know you were a witch?"

"I'm not sure. She must have suspected but got careless. And she never dreamt I could defeat her. I had the element of surprise and more control because rage so blinded her. I think she also trusted I'd never attack my own mother."

Alexander wanted this moment alone with Crispin to last forever, but the nearby "*Squawk*" and parrot announcement brought them back to the world around them.

"*Squawk*. Captains need you! *Squawk*."

Crispin let go of Alexander. They got to their feet and traipsed back through the forest toward the pirate encampment.

They arrived to find the pirates assembled and Henri and Spittle commanding them. "Good," Spittle said when they got there and sat down. "We can begin."

King James flew to Spittle and perched on her shoulder. Tacky tossed a nut to him, and the bird caught it and ate to the delight of the men.

Henri halted the merriment by holding up his hand. "We've got one more decision to make."

"Wait!" One of Beast's minions stood. "We can't start yet. I don't know where Beast went to."

Spittle shrugged. "The fact Beast abandoned us means I hardly care what he thinks. Anyone seen him this morning? He causes a lot of problems by dividing us. I was wondering if we needed to vote about keeping him around. I tell you one thing: he won't sail on my boat."

Henri smirked. "He can on mine. I'm no more afraid of him today than before. He'd have to be here to accept, of course."

Spittle suspected something by the way she kept glancing to Alexander for an answer.

Monkey stood and provided his voice of reason. "His disappearance makes this easy. If he shows up, we'll deal with him then. Otherwise, we need to get moving. I say we vote to maroon Beast on Tortuga Isle."

Even Alexander laughed aloud with the other pirates at how smoothly Monkey solved the matter to everyone's agreement. The vote went fast, Beast's friends either changing sides or remaining silent.

Spittle grinned at Monkey. "Thank you, first mate." With her usual grace, Spittle promoted him and rewarded his assistance.

"Now can we get to the remaining issue?" Henri asked. "Fucking pirates with so much deliberation, it's a wonder we ever get anything done."

The pirates laughed at themselves.

Spittle cast her glance toward Alexander and Crispin. "To finish out the parlay. According to the terms, we decide their fate. Only stipulation is they remain alive."

"We can't punish the traitor?"

Alexander wished he could see his accuser, but the voice came from the middle of the group.

"No." Spittle glared at the pirates and shot a wad of spit to the side. "It's forbidden." Alexander knew her well enough to see she had a lot more to say on the matter but bit her tongue.

Henri shrugged. "We'd risk fate if we defied the parlay. He's not worth the trouble." He pointed at Alexander.

Alexander winced again at the disregard with which Henri referred to him.

"He stays with the captain," Spittle continued, "and we're not fucking around with a parlay and risk the gods' wrath. Not to remind you of bad times, but they already kicked our asses once. The ole captain there deserves a little begrudging respect."

A few pirates mumbled to one another, but no one offered a solution. Alexander got to his feet and looked at Spittle and Henri, a silent request to speak. She nodded assent and motioned toward him. Henri rolled his eyes but stepped aside. The men turned toward Alexander.

Alexander felt his self-confidence come roaring back. He no longer doubted his decisions or any action he ever took. Here was the boy who'd survived his parents' murders, the dark years with his uncle, exile with pirates, and the ups and downs of life. Too, he could own his eternal love of Crispin, as well as his turning toward Henri and their love. Henri had helped to liberate Alexander. They had shared a passion for each other, and part of Alexander would always love him. Except Alexander knew he wanted an exclusive relationship and loved Crispin as much, if not more. Crispin sought Alexander out and reclaimed him. Alexander would take control of their lives this time, and simultaneously honor his pirate family.

"There's a clear choice we both want."

Crispin raised an eyebrow but smiled despite being in the dark about Alexander's decision on their behalf.

"This will honor the parlay and allow you to punish the man who defeated you, and the man who you think betrayed you, though I deny the charge." Alexander smiled when Monkey winked at him, and Tacky laughed aloud, breaking the tension and getting chuckles from a number of the men.

"Well, what do you suggest?" Spittle asked him.

"Maroon us. Pick an island, and drop us off. We'll help get the sloop ready and stay with you until then. Our magic will accomplish the repairs faster. We don't care what island. The solution respects the parlay and punishes me at the same time. Maroon us, and be on your way."

Chapter Thirty-Seven

Marooned

October 1700

The Caribbean

AFTER ALEXANDER PRESENTED the marooning to the pirate throng, he never dreamt how much he would love the isolation and almost certain death facing Crispin and him.

A week into their seclusion, though, Alexander woke each morning feeling safer and more euphoric than ever before in his life.

The pirates had voted unanimously to accept Alexander's proposal, and he resisted afterward when Spittle pled with him to be taken to a port or more populated area with a better chance of survival. He and Crispin stuck to their plans.

And so Crispin and he assisted with repairs to the ship until sea-worthy, though the fixing of the mast left them in a precarious state. Henri decided their first battle had to be against a foe with a boat they could commandeer without too much effort; then they could decide to upgrade the second ship later.

They had sailed for a couple days until they arrived at a deserted island Spittle remembered from a marooning she'd participated in before joining Henri's crew.

"It has fresh water," she said. "Rare for the islands where pirates like to maroon you. You know how to fish, right? Can you two use magic to call for help?"

Alexander placed his hand on Spittle's forearm to quiet her. "This is what we want. Don't worry."

It had felt strange to watch the sloop he'd called home sail away with the only friends he had ever known aboard, leaving him behind for good. But the threat of melancholy dissipated when he felt Crispin press against his back and wrap his strong arms around his waist.

Alexander stopped his remembrances of their recent history and went about getting fresh water with a shell, while wondering what they would eat.

"Seven days and we're not dead yet."

Alexander laughed when he heard Crispin's voice. He turned around to see his naked lover stretching as he woke, and he surveyed the area around them.

"Very much alive." Alexander hurried over and tossed himself on top of Crispin.

"Oomph." Crispin went limp. "You deflated me."

"Not all of you." Alexander reached down and grabbed Crispin's erect penis and started stroking.

They made love, yet again, as they had multiple times a day since arriving on the island.

"We need to slow down or we'll get bored." Crispin ran his fingers along Alexander's back as they lay together after making love.

"Never." Alexander rubbed against Crispin. "Absolutely never. Besides, we don't really have anything else to do. Eat. Drink. Make shelter. But not many ships stop here. I doubt we'll survive for long. And the only other thing to do is to have sex. In the open, over and over and over."

A comfortable silence fell between them until Crispin propped his head up with a hand, his elbow on the ground. "You joke, but we really don't know how long we'll survive. If we can't find enough food or if a storm submerges this entire island, we'll die."

Crispin motioned to indicate the island around them. If they stood, they could see from one end to the other. A few trees grew here, the only exception to total desolation other than the unusual fresh water pond at its very center.

Alexander smiled. "I know."

Crispin squinted at Alexander. "I assume you know, even with the witch power between us, we don't have a damn thing to get us out of this predicament?"

"I do." Alexander tossed his head back and laughed. "I can see the present, which shows me no ships ever come close enough to see a thing here, even if we build a fire. I could blow us deep into the sea, where we'd drown, and I can heal our injuries to keep us alive and alone forever."

Crispin grinned. "You summed up our predicament. I could defend us if attacked. Or mess around with the elements, but as we learned yesterday, we only get so far with the magic."

Alexander laughed even harder at the memory. They had spent the previous afternoon experimenting with their various powers to see if anything offered a solution to their marooning. Nothing worked. Crispin somehow conjured up an imaginary monkey. Another of his spells made their clothes disappear, which led to their best sex yet, until they finished and found their clothes nicely folded in the sand nearby. Alexander used the wind to bring a huge wave to flood part of the island, leaving several delicious options for dinner.

None of these abilities would liberate them from their island prison.

"And you think this is funny, do you?" Crispin laughed despite his words.

"I do."

"And what about our certain doom amuses you?"

"I've always lived with impending doom. You'll adapt." Alexander pecked Crispin on the nose.

"Explain yourself."

"What's to explain? They killed my parents, and with them any hope for the future. I'm surprised my uncle failed to kill me. Or the

Puritans. Or then the pirates when I discovered them. Any time along the way I could have died in battle. I've faced death my entire life. I determined to embrace the danger and live as well as possible. To survive, as my mother instructed. So I'll survive. *We'll* survive as best as possible." Alexander grinned.

"What if I fall ill? What if we run out of food?"

Alexander contemplated. "Worst case scenario, I'm walking right out there and joining the undersea creatures in eternity." He pointed at the ocean.

"You're going to walk into the ocean?"

Alexander nodded. "Ever since I learned about the sea, I've loved it. Sailing away from Massachusetts offered my best chance in life. Then I learned about pirates, and they took me along. The sea's always been my friend. So if the time comes, I'll march into the ocean and let the water take me."

Crispin grabbed Alexander in his arms. "That's morbid."

"Not at all. It's romantic. Even deserted on this island with little chance for escape, we have each other. And no one or nothing can separate us. If worse comes to worse and we have to die, at least we'll be together. It's perfect."

Alexander swore he sensed his mother's presence nearby. Gentle. Caressing. Happy. Whatever happened from here, he had survived and felt confident he obeyed her final plea.

Alexander and Crispin watched the sun rise, sitting quietly in each other's arms. Eventually, Alexander leaned over and nibbled on Crispin's ear.

"Already?" Crispin grinned. "Again?"

Alexander smiled. "Why not?"

"Why not, indeed. How about a nice swim first? Naked in the water?"

Alexander jumped to his feet, getting excited when he spotted Crispin growing hard next to him. He reached over and launched himself into Crispin's arms for a long kiss.

Alexander pulled out of Crispin's embrace and ran toward the water. Crispin closed the distance and grabbed Alexander from behind as their feet got wet. The warm sun on Alexander's back felt wonderful, Crispin's strong arms around him adding an even better sizzle. Crispin pulled them deeper into the water, but Alexander stood his ground and leaned over to bite Crispin's nipple.

"You little devil." Crispin ran a hand down Alexander's back until he grabbed his ass.

"You have no idea."

Alexander screamed in delight and jumped away when Crispin tickled him. He got up to his knees in the ocean when Crispin again snatched him from behind and into a tight embrace.

Alexander tilted his head back and smiled at Crispin. They kissed, lingering together. Alexander turned and stared deeply into Crispin's eyes, thankful yet again Crispin had fought for him. Whether Crispin could understand, life could not have been more perfect, no matter the circumstances. Their tongues intertwined.

Crispin finally pulled his head back and ran a finger down Alexander's cheek. "Let's swim together."

Alexander grinned widely. "I always did fancy the sea." He summoned the wind to carry them into the water.

About the Author

Damian Serbu is an author of gay horror/speculative fiction. After over twenty years of teaching history at the collegiate level, he now writes full time. He lives in the Chicagoland area with his husband and two dogs.

Email

DamianSerbu@aol.com

Facebook

www.facebook.com/Damian-Serbu

X

www.twitter.com/damianserbu

Website

www.damianserbu.com

Instagram

www.instagram/dsettje

Threads

www.threads.net/@dsettje

Bluesky

www.bsky.app/profile/damianserbu.bsky.social

Other NineStar books by this author

The Realm of the Vampire Council

The Vampire's Angel

The Vampire's Quest

The Vampire's Protégé

The Vampire's Witch

The Vampire's War

Simon, the Elf

Santa's Kinky Elf Simon

Santa is a Vampire

The Bachmann Family Secret

www.ninestarpress.com

www.facebook.com/ninestarpress

www.facebook.com/groups/NineStarNiche

www.twitter.com/ninestarpress

www.instagram.com/ninestarpress

bsky.app/profile/ninestarpress.bsky.social

www.threads.net/@ninestarpress